RATON PASS

*Also by Tom W. Blackburn
in Large Print:*

Compañeros
El Segundo
Patron
Ranchero
Short Grass
Yanqui
Sierra Baron

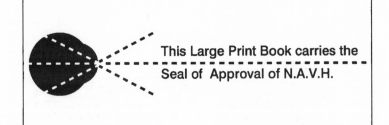

This Large Print Book carries the
Seal of Approval of N.A.V.H.

RATON PASS

Tom W. Blackburn

Published in 2004 by arrangement with
Golden West Literary Agency.

Wheeler Large Print Western.

The text of this Large Print edition is unabridged.
Other aspects of the book may vary from the original edition.

Set in 16 pt. Plantin by Minnie B. Raven.

Printed in the United States on permanent paper.

Library of Congress Cataloging-in-Publication Data

Blackburn, Thomas Wakefield.
    Raton pass / Tom W. Blackburn.
      p. cm.
    ISBN 1-58724-793-3 (lg. print : sc : alk. paper)
    1. Ranch life — Fiction.   2. Large type books.
I. Title.
PS3552.L3422R37 2004
  813′.54—dc22   2004053591

FOR HOWARD AND EDITH

AND FOR ANTIME AND ETHOL

Parents and godparents, through whom
has come what measure and appreciation of
the traditions of the Southwest
is herein contained.

As the Founder/CEO of NAVH, the only national health agency solely devoted to those who, although not totally blind, have an eye disease which could lead to serious visual impairment, I am pleased to recognize Thorndike Press★ as one of the leading publishers in the large print field.

Founded in 1954 in San Francisco to prepare large print textbooks for partially seeing children, NAVH became the pioneer and standard setting agency in the preparation of large type.

Today, those publishers who meet our standards carry the prestigious "Seal of Approval" indicating high quality large print. We are delighted that Thorndike Press is one of the publishers whose titles meet these standards. We are also pleased to recognize the significant contribution Thorndike Press is making in this important and growing field.

Lorraine H. Marchi, L.H.D.
Founder/CEO
NAVH

★ Thorndike Press encompasses the following imprints: Thorndike, Wheeler, Walker and Large Print Press.

PROLOGUE

Dr. Fogarty came out of the other room, callously leaving the door open behind him. He stopped two yards short of the tiny fire wavering in the beehive fireplace in the corner, against which Marcy had unconsciously backed for warmth. He extended his large reddened hands and chafed them, as though the fire was much closer. His eyes were on Marcy. Unpleasant eyes, penetrating. Here was a surety of defense a woman could not overcome. This weary and untidy man had no curiosity and no appetite. Women, as a kind, had lain before him a thousand times in agony and complete revelation. He knew them. Marcy realized he knew her. His head rocked a little, indicating the room he had just left.

"Two weeks," he said. "I'll give him two weeks. Maybe less, with the treatment he's getting. Where'd you take training?"

Marcy met his eyes defensively. Two weeks was too long. In two weeks the place in Trinidad might not be open. She had to be in Trinidad for the winter. Marc Challon would be crossing Raton Pass to Trinidad from his empire on the grass of New Mexico after whisky — maybe after a woman. She had to be in Trinidad, and two weeks was too long.

"You expect to find a nurse with a certificate out here?" she asked acidly. "I trained in a wagon, nursing my father and mother till they died in a Kansas blizzard. Before that, a boardinghouse in Indiana. Where I had to. This isn't my business. Maybe Ed Bennett would do better without anybody to watch him."

"No worse," Dr. Fogarty said. "He's your husband?"

"Would I marry a man who was already dying when I first saw him?"

The doctor's eyes ran shrewdly over Marcy's figure. He shook his head.

"No. Keep this shack warmer, then. Hot liquid food when he wants it. Milk, if he'll drink it. But no whisky. It's touch and go, now, which will get him first — his belly or his lungs. Send for me again if you think I can do anything."

"Yes, Doctor," Marcy said. "Thank you." Reaching into the pocket of her apron; she produced a gold half eagle. Dr. Fogarty tossed it in his hand.

"You can afford it?" he asked.

"Mr. Bennett has a little money."

"Leave enough to bury him with," Dr. Fogarty said. "Save a lot of questions being asked about what happened to the rest of it."

He pulled the door open and went out.

Marcy went into the other room. Ed Bennett's eyes were glazed with fever. His breathing was harsh, fast, and shallow. His body was tense with its struggle. But there was vitality in it still. Too much. Marcy pulled open a drawer in the stand under the broken, burlap-wadded window and lifted out a sweat-stained money belt. It was not as heavy as it had been three months ago when Ed Bennett had sold his wagon and moved into this shack with a woman to die or get well, but it was heavy enough still. Marcy counted the coins in it again for reassurance. When she closed the drawer and turned, Bennett was watching her, his eyes cleared in one of the periods of lucidity to which she could not accustom herself. He had been a handsome man, perhaps even a good one. It showed when he smiled.

"Angel —" he said.

It had a coarse sound in Marcy's ears, its sincerity was so marked.

"Not like we planned it when we buried your folks on the Republican," Bennett went on. "No kingdom of grass out here some-place for us; no throne for you, Marcy. Not like we wanted it."

"No," Marcy said. Not at all as she had planned it. It had taken too long. Ed Bennett had been slow in dying and time had been lost. Time was important. Time was youth, and without youth a woman in this country was helpless. "No," she said again.

"My feet are cold, Marcy. You got to stay away from me. I know that. Had to ever since you climbed into my wagon. This damned cough. But my feet are cold."

"A hot toddy, maybe," Marcy said.

"The sawbones said no whisky. I heard him."

"Yes. A drink, Ed?"

"I don't want to die. I want you, Marcy. I don't want to die."

"Yes. A drink?"

Ed Bennett smiled slowly again.

"A man has got to have something. Load it, angel."

Marcy went back into the other room. She brought a tin cup and the sugar can and a bottle of unlabeled whisky. Forty cents' worth of whisky. A brew so potent that the man at the La Junta saloon had said no one had yet been able to think up a name sufficiently virulent to match it. Unlabeled for that reason. She poured the cup full and sugared it a little. Bennett raised himself on a thin arm, coughed, and drank swiftly. He eased back down and coughed with every fiber of his body. Marcy refilled the cup. Bennett clung to consciousness and slowed his breathing after a little.

"The XO," he said. "You get to the XO, angel. I rode for the Challons once. They'll know me. Let Marc Challon or the old man, Pierre, know you did for me when I was down. They'll remember. They'll do for you. It's like that in the Territory. That's a ranch, angel — those are men —"

"Sure, Ed," Marcy agreed quietly. "I'll hunt up Marc Challon. I'll get to the XO all right. But I won't go begging."

Bennett smiled.

"No," he said. "You won't beg, angel. Not ever. You won't have to. Not from a man. Not the way you're put together. And there's a little money left in the kick."

"Yes," Marcy said. "A little. Another drink, Ed?"

She put the cup into his hand.

Light from a squat, broad-shaded lamp flooded the huge table in the XO office. Marc Challon sat hunched before it, tracing out contour lines on a large plat unfolded before him. An enamel heater against the wall behind his chair clicked with dying heat. A tray containing a coffee service in Mexican silver was pushed unused out of his way. Books on the shelving were in shadow. Wind was astir on the slopes outside. The house was silent. A ghost walked through it.

It was a small ghost, soft-footed. The ghost of the woman who had built the house, coming quietly down the hall to the office she had never occupied but which echoed still to her counsel, although she had been dead for nearly ten years. A woman who had known in her life four loves — her husband, her son, New Mexico, and the XO.

Marc Challon pushed a little back in his chair, smiling, waiting for his mother. Her son, better than any other, had understood Belle Challon's dreaming. Perhaps the XO had been her greatest love. It was his.

Belle Challon's ghost came on into the room, unafraid of the lamplight as the woman in life had been unafraid. It sat on the edge of the big table, running somber, understanding eyes over the crude plat and its laboriously traced lines. It looked at the woman's son with pride. It nodded approval. And this, in itself, was courage. It took towering courage for even the ghost of a small woman to approve or disapprove the work of a Challon hand or a Challon mind, for Challon men were big and their opposition stentorian.

Marc Challon looked at his mother's ghost, remembering her beauty and her strength. Recollections which dwarfed any other woman he had ever known. To have been the mistress of the XO was to have been more than a woman, for the ranch had not been built of sage and sod and luck alone. There had been flint, and loyalty deep as blood and marrow. There had been tempered metal. Pierre Challon had been an old man when he mated and he had wanted love from his wife. He had found it in a measure to satisfy even his occasionally thundering lust. There had been a gusty happiness to match living at the pace to which Pierre's great body had once driven him.

He had wanted a son. Belle Challon had borne him one. And conceived as surely from her husband, nurtured within her, and brought forth in time as Marc had been, she had borne Pierre also the dream of what a few scattered sections of the arid grassland in northern New Mexico Territory could be if Challon wills were turned to it.

The lamp flickered in the XO office and the enamel heater clicked. The ghost was gone, back into the shadows of the house. Marc Challon lifted from his chair, hooked up a sheaf of figure-littered notes from the table, and strode back along the hall to the two steps at the end which led down into the wide living room. He found Pierre there, deep in a huge chair before the fireplace, his small and neatly booted feet propped up toward the flames. His great head swung around at the sound of his son's footfalls.

"Well, you damned farmer?" he asked lazily.

"It'll work. In the rough, it'll work. I'm convinced. A dam across Torrentado and a canal along the west ridge will put water onto better than three thousand acres of bottom land east of the house here."

"It'll cost, too. And you're keeping our heads under water as it is, buying up every whiteface breeder you can lay hands on. Irrigating good grass and breeding up blue ribbons — a hell of a beef ranch this is!"

"Isn't it, though?" Marc agreed with a grin. "The breeders come first. The nucleus of a new herd. Then a railroad to ship whiteface beef on. Then water for irrigation, so we can grow our own topping-off feed. One at a time, Pierre, but all three before long. We break down if we stand still. Look, it'll be sunup in a couple hours. You better turn in."

"And leave you still working?" the old man protested. "Think I want the help talking — claiming old Pierre's lost his grip? Damn it, Marc, I wish you'd get you a woman. Maybe you'd sleep some, nights, then!"

"You mind your own business," Marc said with a widening of his grin.

The semaphore was down at the Carrera place on the Picketwire ford. Hayden set his lines between his fingers and touched his brake. The stage dropped back under the drag of the shoes, taking up harness slack. As it dropped back it tightened Hayden's set reins. Wheelers first, then swings, finally leaders, feeling the check. A smooth, swift stop. Hayden braced himself on his box with a philosophy of patience. He didn't like a Carrera stop. Thank God the flag was seldom down. Ma Carrera hated *yanquis,* and there was corrosive acid on her tongue. It galled Hayden to hear in Spanish things no man or woman could say to him in English, and Ma Carrera knew it. He glared at the door of the station.

It opened. Ma Carrera came out, following a girl, fussing with the hang of the girl's coat, talking with her usual frenzy, but the acid was missing. Concern in her voice, maybe, although Hayden wasn't sure since he hadn't heard this soft kind of talk from her before. Concern for the girl. *Pobrecita! Pobrecita!* Ma Carrera fussing like a hen. *Pobrecita!* Poor little trail tramp, bound down to the shacks of Uppertown, in Trinidad, where a white skin could make a killing among the cattlemen and cattle hands who made constant pilgrimages over the rift of Raton Pass to see what kind of hell the devil kept stoked up on the Colorado side of the mesas.

Then Hayden was leaning down to lift up a single piece of baggage and the girl was there beside the coach, looking up at him, and he saw he was wrong as hell about her. There were no lines of callousness or desperation in this face. It was in repose, at ease, faintly rounded, strong and independent, wide-eyed with the freshness of new experience, beautiful.

"No passengers?" she asked. "Then maybe you wouldn't mind if I rode up there with

15

you in the open. It's a beautiful morning. It must be a big country from up there."

"Tolerable," Hayden agreed. Bending lower, he offered the girl a lift with his hand.

"You keep your gloves on your dirty fingers, *cabrón*," Ma Carrera said sharply in Spanish. "This one is not for you!"

The girl dropped onto the seat beside Hayden, clinging excitedly to the low handrail beside her. Hayden spat carefully at Ma Carrera's feet and rolled the stage. When they had splashed through the ford and up the other bank, Hayden tipped his head at the stream now behind them.

"Rio de las Animas Perdidas," he said. "The Purgatoire. The Picketwire. The Old Trail from the Arkansas to the pass followed it. Trinidad's toward the headwaters."

"Isn't one name enough?"

"Party got lost on it once. Never showed up, I hear. Spanish named it River of Souls Lost in Hell. French made it Purgatoire. Or vice versa. I forget. Yankee figured the French sounded like Picketwire. Makes sense."

The girl nodded. Hayden subsided. He figured his sixty a month covered handling his spans on this run and nothing else. Try passing on some little thing about the country, and passengers right away tried making a guide out of a driver. There were times when a man on a box didn't want to talk — or didn't have time. He was ahead to keep his mouth shut in the first place.

But the girl said nothing, and after a while Hayden pointed out the loom of Raton and Johnson mesas up ahead. Later he turned back to the first thing she had said to him.

"Fancy a big country, do you?"

"Enough to want a piece of it."

"There's a passable amount hereabouts," Hayden said. "Country, that is. How big a slice you want?"

"The biggest on the plate," the girl said.

She smiled. She was looking ahead at the blue lift of the mesas. Her lips were parted a little. Her eyes were bright. Hayden warmed. The fact was that he wasn't driving this stage for sixty dollars a month alone. He had a taste for the country too. And he liked a woman who bit hugely when she was hungry. Most women minced with a thing, even when they wanted it. This one didn't.

They talked occasionally again. Fifteen minutes behind schedule, Hayden set his one passenger down in front of the Las Animas Hotel in Trinidad and rolled on down behind the livery, whistling for a stableboy to step his team out of harness and put the spans up. He was suddenly aware that he had talked much on the road, answering questions rather than asking. He had learned little of his passenger while she had learned much of him. The importance of certain men in

17

Trinidad. The identity of the school board and the location of the best boardinghouse. The legendary history of the XO ranch over in the Territory, beyond the pass.

Still, he could not remember a better run down from the Picketwire ford, and the feeling that in recent weeks he had seen a slattern at the back door of a La Junta saloon who looked much like his passenger was dead.

A little later, washed up, Hayden turned into the Boundary Saloon for his evening's drink. Lou Patterson was at the end of the bar in his usual place. Hayden pushed up beside him.

"The board hired a new teacher yet, Lou?" he asked.

"No. We're meeting tomorrow afternoon to vote. Probably go to the Lopez girl. There's hardly anybody else."

"Brought a better one in on the stage today, Lou," Hayden said. "Waiting at Ma Carrera's for me. From Indiana, I think. Dropped from some wagon party to come on up here because she'd heard there was an opening. Name's Marcy Bennett. She'll see you in the morning. Be a favor to me, Lou. And she's qualified. Very qualified."

Pierre Challon was asleep in his chair before a red-eyed fire in the living room of the XO house. His body was asleep but his mind

18

was awake. Young or old, a body needed rest. But a mind filled with the accumulation of the years worked endlessly. Pierre's mind was working with his ranch, modeling again in the fluidity of his half dreaming the building through the long years. Belle and her part; Marc and his. Pierre's own. The creation of something greater than any of them. A piece of country enclosed by a fence and turned inward until it became self-sufficient, containing the springs of its existence within its own boundaries.

An iron respected across a wide, grassed quarter of the nation. An outfit which had paid bonus wages for a generation. The first sections and the hardest days, which had belonged to Pierre alone. Then Belle, her dream of unity, her way with people — friends to a distance of a hundred miles, so that her husband and her son became barons instead of brigands in their building. Marc's blooded stock and his grasp of Belle's dream. His talk of water on a part of the land and farmed crops where there were no farmers. An immensity which had been only a homestead under the lip of a gaunt mesa in the beginning. No man knew beforehand the mold into which he might be poured.

Pierre remembered once before, long ago, when he had felt this stir of power within him. A time in the almost forgotten days of his youth when blood was strong in his thighs and his arms, and he could break the bones of any man he knew with his hands. Now the power was not in weary flesh but in the thing he had seen grown from the grass. But the exultation was the same. For a thing like this a man could live forever.

The sound of hoofbeats on the hardpan of the kitchen yard roused Pierre and he straightened in his chair. False dawn was silver against windows deeply recessed in the dobe wall on either side of the fireplace. The hoofbeats came in at a slow tempo, the weary lope with which even a good range horse winds up a long night ride. Marc and the young blood of the crew coming home.

Pierre had prodded flame to life among the embers of his fire and was standing with his back to it when Marc came into the room, rolling gloves from his long, square-tipped fingers. Pierre saw his son was sober.

"The hell with this, boy," he said. "You can't expect a saddle crew to sit leather in daylight if you ride it down to its third breeches button by night! There ain't a house in Trinidad with women that can take care of XO boys three nights in the same week. I know."

Marc laughed in a way that made them two men, as Pierre had always wanted it. Two big men, with the world turning between them where they could stop it any time the notion hit.

"There ain't a house in Trinidad would even try," Marc said. "You scared them off thirty years ago."

Pierre grunted.

"You find you a surveyor to run those test bench marks you want up on Torrentado? One that knows for sure which way water runs, up or down?"

"One that'll do. Plenty to pick from, of a sudden. All claiming to be working on their own hook, scuttling up and down Raton Creek, getting in each other's way. None of them improving much on the grade old Uncle Dick Wootton established for his toll road. Uncle Dick says he's got a notion we're fixing to have us a railroad. He thinks the Rio Grande, up Colorado way, and the Atchison and Topeka, coming out of Kansas, both might take a climb at the pass one of these days. Unless they make a deal between themselves.

"I hired us a Colorado man, Pierre. If he backs up the sighting I've done, we'll start getting working plans drawn. And I'll start looking for a place where I can drop a loop on about sixty thousand dollars of outside money. We'll need that, any way I figure. But when we're finished, we'll have something. Not only the biggest whiteface herd in the country, but we'll have water and be finishing off our increase on farmed forage in our own corral lot before we've got rails to ship the beef on!"

Pierre nodded.

"Now we got that out of the way," he said dryly, "supposing you tell me with the skin off exactly what's worth riding eighty miles to Trinidad and back between supper and breakfast. And don't start talking that survey again!"

Marc dropped into the deep chair and pushed his small Challon feet out in front of him. He was still grinning.

"There's a girl over the mesa," he said. "Teaching school in Trinidad. Newcomer this year. Gentled off like a show horse most of the time, but with an outlaw's look in her eye. All woman, Pierre, and then some — even by the measure I was brought up with!"

Pierre nodded again, a deep relief in him he would not show. He remembered he had so described his own wife once. All woman.

"She claims she's going to marry me," Marc went on. He looked thoughtful about it, then stood up suddenly, slapping his peeled gloves down hard against his thigh. "By hell, Pierre, I believe she will, too!"

"Well, let's not be a damned fool, then, boy," Pierre said. "Take a lead horse over the pass in the morning. Fetch her back here. I've got my bellyful of sitting up all night for a chance to talk to you and I'm almighty hungry for the smell of cologne water at the breakfast table again!"

1

The office looked harsh, harshly lighted by the slanting sun. There was grit in the air — the fabric of something whole and perfect now fallen to shards. Marc Challon's eyes swept the walls of the room, seeking refuge from the explosive tightness behind their lids.

A rack of ancient pottery, dug from the mounds of a prehistoric Indian encampment on the upper limits of the XO. Navajo hangings of a kind no longer made and so now priceless. An Apache saddlebow and quiver of war arrows. A green bronze Spanish bit and chain and spurs. A long, heavy flintlock rifle inexplicably uncovered by a flash flood in Dry Wash. The patina of familiarity with which the room had long been glossed.

There had once before been this disbelief, this numbness, this anger — the day his mother died. A man could be stunned beyond conscious thought. He could be hurt beyond bitterness. He could strike back when striking back was instinctive. Then the blow was past and a man closed his wound as best he could, staying on his feet if it was possible, thinking of retaliation.

Challon thrust his long legs out slowly, as though the lengthening of their thick muscles might ease the compression in him.

"All right," he said quietly, knowing with every fiber of his being that none of it was right, that this was a beginning and not an end. "All right, Marcy, what do you want?"

"A divorce, primarily, of course. The rest isn't too complicated, Marc."

Her voice was steady. Her head was a little uptilted, too assured for defiance. She was beautiful. As young and beautiful and sure as the night Lou Patterson had introduced him to her in Trinidad. Beautiful as the morning they were married in the living room at the other end of the hall, with every soul on the XO crowded into the big house to see a new mistress take over Belle Challon's keys. Five years here on the grass had left no mark on the smoothness of her cheeks; in the strong curve of her full, resolute lips; in the deep and sultry somberness of her eyes; in her figure and her imperious, feline carriage.

Five years had not softened the quality of her determination. A determination and self-devotion he had humored, even encouraged, because it had made her something more than a woman. An adversary, constant and challenging. She was not afraid now. Of the three of them facing him, she was the only one who wasn't afraid. He looked at her and waited with a patience which was no part of him.

"Really very simple," she went on quietly. "We want the ranch."

Challon had expected this since the moment an hour ago when he had first learned about Marcy and Anson Prentice. He had expected this, and a remote and frigid corner of his mind had framed an answer. A corner of his mind apart from shock and hurt and the devouring anger which must follow. A part of him which understood fully that he now had left only that with which he had begun — the XO — that he would have to be shrewd and iron-hard, trading with the devil and with Marcy herself in the end to keep the ranch intact.

He had loved this woman. He had lived with her. It was hard, even now, to understand how little of her he had known. Within herself she was not wrong. In her mind she was right. It was not Anson Prentice she wanted, just as it had never been Marc Challon. As she had said, it was really very simple; she wanted the XO. She wanted the vastness and the strength and the power which were rooted in this soil with the grass.

She didn't know the land or the people of which the XO and the Challons were a part. She didn't even know the Challons, actually. There was no need for her to know them. She was inflexible, and in her desire she was invincible. Nothing could destroy Marcy but Marcy, herself.

25

Marc looked at them all again. Pierre's stricken eyes were the worst. Pierre believed in a woman. He had believed in this woman. There had been no ghost afoot in the house since her arrival. Pierre did not fully understand what was here before his eyes, and Marc could not explain to him.

Old Pierre Challon, now well into the home stretch of a century of living. A hundred and eighty pounds of man in boots and broadcloth, even now ducking unconsciously under the high lintels of XO doorways as he passed through them. If the ranch had a personality, Pierre was its incarnation. Rheumy and a little forgetful, but still the Pierre Challon who had homesteaded the first square mile of the XO when the nearest town was Trinidad and the nearest house the mud palace of the Maxwells at the mouth of Cimarron Canyon, a county away.

Marcy wanted only the ranch. Only the fruit of two generations of labor. Only the excuse for a man's existence. Only the dreams of the living and the dead alike.

"It would be simpler to kill Anse," Challon said.

"You're joking!"

"No, Marce; I'm not joking."

Anson Prentice's thin face flushed. A peculiar physical reaction to an apparent enough fear, but there were few things about Prentice which went by the rules most men know.

Challon had never liked the face, impersonal as a packet of new, unwrinkled bills. Patrician, Marcy had once called the high, oval head, the long prehensile nose, the too narrow cheekbones. Challon had a better word for it, from the stock pens, with more meaning. Overbred. The inevitable fault of a good strain. And Prentice trying to correct it for the next generation, at Challon expense!

"It would be a hell of a lot simpler to kill Anse," Challon said again.

The sick look in Pierre's eyes receded. They brightened. He hoisted himself from his chair and bent over Marc's desk, pulling a drawer open. He lifted out a heavy old silver-mounted revolver and handed it to his son. Matter-of-factly. Almost without malice.

"Take the bastard outside, boy," he said gravely. "Blood raises hell with the rugs."

Challon sat motionless in his chair, spinning the cylinder of the weapon his father had handed him. It would be easy, this way. Marcy had deliberately done this to him, waiting for exactly the right time. Prentice had done it deliberately, scheming with her. There was justification for the man's death here, and maybe he owed it to himself, to Pierre. But there was also the XO, bigger than any of them and more important.

Marcy was watching him narrowly, perhaps even following the line of his thought.

"You'd hang, Marc," she said dispassion-

27

ately. "I promise you that. You owe Anson money. Even in New Mexico a man can't kill his creditors."

Marc nodded. He had been thinking of money and what it would build. Marcy was talking of debts while he thought of how much the two of them facing him here owed him.

"I owe Anse sixty thousand dollars, Marcy," he said slowly. "Borrowed it to put in that dam on Torrentado and gave him an assignment of thirty per cent of the ranch for security. If I didn't pay off my note to him, he'd own that much of the XO. Suppose I concede you a right to half of what's left, seeing as Pierre deeded it all to me last year. I had five years with you, Marce. I suppose they were worth something. I thought so while I was living them, anyhow — and that's something you can't take away. That'd give you thirty-five per cent, with a like share for me."

His father was staring incredulously at Challon. Marcy and Prentice were following his figures with cautious concentration.

"What's it stand up to — say two dollars an acre for the hundred thousand acres inside XO fencing? Lock, stock, and barrel. It's worth three times that on the market if a buyer big enough to handle it came along."

Prentice was leaning forward. Challon's lips tightened. A man from north of the pass couldn't know how coyotes were baited in this country.

"Since I haven't let the contracts on the dam yet, Anse's money is still in the operating account," he went on carefully. "All right. I want two dollars an acre for the share of the ranch I hold, the way I just split it up. I want the cash in the ranch accounts. A total of a hundred thirty thousand dollars. My pick of the breeding stock too. A hundred head. My personal horses. And life tenancy on the ranch for Pierre, if he wants it. I can climb the fence; maybe he can't."

Pierre sank back in his chair, without color and without voice. Relief in Prentice was obviously a jolt which left him breathless. Marcy weighed what she had heard carefully.

"I thought we'd have to fight, Marc," she said slowly. "I thought we'd have to make a fool out of you before you'd let go. I didn't think you'd listen to money. So the old order changes, even in New Mexico!"

"There's nothing new in this, Marce," Challon said bluntly. "Rich men have been buying women since we all put on pants. When my money's on deposit in Stuart's bank in Range, have Treadwell send word or bring the agreements over to the hotel. I'll be there. And, Pierre, nobody ever won a pot on the first draw in a poker game. Have Pepe drive you into town tomorrow. I want to talk to you."

Pierre nodded silently, woodenly. Challon stepped into the doorway. He turned there.

"A couple of things to remember, Marce. A quarter of a million dollars doesn't make a man. You've been used to a couple of samples of the real thing around you since you came to the XO. Don't expect too much of Anse or of his money. I know this country, which neither one of you does. I'd be careful how I lived out here till Treadwell's got you legally cut loose from me. Talk can raise hell with friends, and you're going to need more friends than you've got Prentice dollars!"

He stepped on through the door. Marcy followed him out onto the wide ramada.

"Marc, what are you going to do?"

Challon let a surprised note creep into his voice, as though conjecture was unnecessary.

"Me?" he echoed. "What I've always done, of course. Not even you can change that, Marce. Pierre filed in here on the high grass to build a ranch. I've been working for the biggest and best whiteface herd in the country. My wife and a man from whom I mistakenly borrowed some money, thinking he was a friend, have set me back a little today. But that's still what I intend to work for."

Marcy eyed him carefully. There was, as far as he could see, no regret, no self-condemnation, in her. Only wariness. Perhaps she knew a little about him, after all.

"Marc, that talk of friends — do we have to be enemies?"

This, blandly, after the hour from which he had just escaped! Challon smiled unpleasantly.

"Us, enemies — you and me? No, honey, never —"

He bent unexpectedly, his hands clamping her shoulders, and he kissed her in a way which could leave her no doubt of his insolent, mocking intent. Grinning unhurriedly at Anson Prentice, who had appeared in the doorway, he turned down the steps and swung across the yard toward the corrals at an easy, deliberate pace.

Challon reached Range, seat of Red River County and XO supply point at the New Mexico base of Boundary Mesa, in late afternoon. He asked for a room at the Palace Hotel. The clerk fumbled a key from his rack of pigeonholes.

"Thought you just got in from Kansas City this morning, Mr. Challon," he said as he rang a key down on the counter. "What's the matter, beds all full at the ranch?"

The clerk's face blanched under Challon's look. He turned hastily back to his desk. Challon lifted the key and took the stairs to the second floor. The remark could have been innocent. Misguided affability. It could have been something else. There was no gossip on the streets of Range. Things moved

31

always in a straight line. There was only complete ignorance on a subject or equally complete public knowledge. What was worth talking about was worth knowing about in full beforehand. And most folks kept themselves well informed. Challon had this time been gone three weeks from the XO. He hadn't thought about talk.

He put the old revolver Pierre had handed him on the marble top of the bureau in his room and slopped water into a porcelain basin from a thick porcelain pitcher. Having rinsed the dust of his ride from his hands and face, he shoved the revolver into the pocket of his box-tailed coat and went back into the hall. He hadn't thought about this matter of talk at all. It might hinder him. It might help.

On the street Challon saw Hugh Perigord tipped back in a wire-braced chair under the wooden awning fronting his office. One of his Mexican deputies was sprawled on the steps, somnolent in the late sun. Challon crossed the street.

"Evening, Marc," Perigord offered.

"I thought maybe you ought to know, Hugh," Challon said without preface. "I sold out of the XO this afternoon."

Perigord had seen men die in front of him. He had killed them, in line of duty and out. Fatalism was his fetish, stoniness half his stock in trade, imperturbability his tradition.

But it cost him an effort to remain motion-less now, idly slanted back in his chair. He could not keep incredulity from his eyes.

"To Prentice?" he asked needlessly after a long moment. Challon nodded. Perigord slowly lowered the front legs of his chair to the planking of the walk. "Moving your family to town?"

"I said I sold out, Hugh; wagon, tongue, and traces."

It was blunt. It answered all questions. Perigord understood.

"Somebody could have told me weeks ago, Hugh," Challon went on steadily. "I've been gone a lot this spring."

"Nobody could have told you. Trying would have been next to suicide. You wouldn't have believed it. If you had, it wouldn't have changed anything."

Challon thought of Marcy.

"No," he agreed, "it wouldn't. Look, Hugh, I want no talk."

Perigord smiled dryly. His eyes traveled over Challon's frame, lingering on the big, loosely hung, long-fingered hands. He shook his head.

"Don't worry," he said. "There won't be any. Not while you're around."

"Hugh, remember the Casamajors — the ones that used to own everything north of Maxwell's place? I think one of them was governor under Spain. Isn't there a couple of

33

the girls still around town?"

A wicked little light came up in Perigord's eyes.

"Well, let's see," he said thoughtfully. "Seems to me one of them married a homesteader out in the lava."

"Jim Pozner," Challon said impatiently. "Hell, I knew that. Isn't there another one?"

Perigord grinned.

"If you hadn't stayed married so hard while you were at it, you'd know damned well there's another one. Elena. Probably would have been in here mooning around after her yourself. Prettiest thing in Range, I reckon. But unfriendly as hell. You won't do yourself any good with her, Marc. It's been tried by experts. But she'd rather live in a back room in the Uncle Dick Bar up on Goat Hill and sing a couple songs in the restaurant on Saturday nights than take up with the best man in town. Funny how long it takes pride to run down in one of those old Spanish families."

"Didn't figure on doing myself any good," Challon grunted. "I had about all the woman I want for a while. I just wanted to see her. Thanks, Hugh."

Perigord frowned a little.

"Look, Marc, now you're off of the XO, what you going to do?"

"Get some grass. Raise some stock. That's my business."

34

Perigord leaned farther forward, a shadow of concern in is eyes.

"Sure. But where? That's mine."

Challon shrugged.

"Depends on where I can make the best deal. See you later, Hugh."

He swung on up the walk in the direction of Goat Hill, aware that he had shattered the evening's tranquillity for the sheriff of Red River County.

Range was a typical grasslands trading center, fused of convenience, turning wheels, and alkaline dust — but assembled in reverse. The low end of the street contained the business establishments and half a dozen clapboard pretensions to circumstance which housed the families of the leading citizens. Above these, on the talus of the slope footing Boundary Mesa, were the shacks of Chihuahua-town and such divertissements as Range could offer. The highest point was the rocky summit of Goat Hill.

Breathing deeply from the stiff climb, Challon turned into the Uncle Dick Bar, using the dining-room entrance. The place was unique among grass-country establishments. It was clean. Scrupulously so. A frequently whitewashed interior. Caustic-bleached table tops covered with cotton cloths of fine Mexican drawn work, laundered and faded to delicate pastels. The packed clay floor had been so often and so vigorously swept that the inevitable soft spots in the dobe were now hollows and the legs of some of the tables sat on little wooden spacers to level their tops against the unevenness of the floor. The Spanish affection for lacy white curtains was evident. Even the pane in the door was neatly paneled.

Challon took a table near the small fire winking in a beehive fireplace in one corner. There was no other trade in the place. An old woman came from the kitchen at the back, smiling friendliness, bringing with her the smells which made a real Mexican kitchen about as close to heaven as a hungry man could get. Speaking the easy Spanish of the grass, Challon ordered the day's meal, knowing he would have no other choice. The old woman started to turn away. Challon checked her.

"*Momentito, mamasita,*" he said. "I want to see 'Lena too. 'Lena Casamajor."

The old woman's friendliness vanished immediately.

"Dinner is forty cents," she said stiffly. "I serve it; you eat it. Then you go away. Down to Chihuahua-town, maybe, eh? We have only food here. You leave the little one be!"

"You know me?" Challon asked sharply. "Yes? And you heard me? Good. Tell 'Lena I want to see her. And bring me a bottle of Roanoke whisky from next door."

There was anger in the old woman's eyes, but the Challon name sat with Marc at his table and the shadow of the XO still moved with him. She paused uncertainly for a moment, entreaty in her eyes. He thought she was going to voice it, but she seemed to change her mind and vanished through the kitchen doorway. Challon built, smoked, and snuffed out a cigarette. The old woman returned wordlessly with a bottle of whisky and a glass. Challon broke the seal, poured a drink, then hardly more than tasted it, leaving the balance unheeded in the glass.

His dinner came and he ate slowly. Challon was breathing the strong chicory fumes of his second cup of coffee when the girl came into the room. He realized that while he had eaten she had dressed. Her thick jet hair was coiled in a low, tight knot against the base of her neck, its severe, tautly pulled side lines accentuating the slender ovality of her face. Contrary to custom among her sisters, her blouse was primly high at the throat and collared. Her skirt was tight-waisted and full at the hem. She was not tall, but there was a liquid grace to her walk. Challon remembered Perigord's remark about the long-lived pride of the old Spanish families. It did not live so long among some, but it certainly was alive in this girl.

An unfamiliar compulsion brought Challon to his feet. He slid out a chair for her and she slipped gracefully into it. When Challon had reseated himself her glance touched the forgotten whisky bottle on the table.

"Not champagne, Señor Challon?" she asked.

Challon was startled.

"Champagne? Order it," he invited her defensively. "Why champagne?"

"To have Marc Challon come here, asking for me —" The girl laughed softly.

"We'd better get that straight," Challon said hastily. "Why I came here."

"I've been thinking since Louisa told me you wanted me," Elena Casamajor said. "Maybe I almost know the answer. I pay you the compliment of thinking you don't have the reason most of the others have. Otherwise you would have waited a long time. You would have waited until you were too drunk or sleepy to stay longer. But it isn't that, so there must be something I can do for you."

Challon felt relieved.

"There is," he said. "I want to have a talk with your uncle and some of his friends. A more peaceable kind of a talk than I'd be apt to have if I went out to see him alone."

"Jim Pozner?" she asked. "Tia, his wife, is my aunt. She is all the family I have now. We are close. But Jim is not my uncle; just the man she married. It's important to remember that. Why should the XO ranch want to talk to him now? Before it's always been easy.

There were always enough guns along to make Jim stand still if he could be found."

"This time it isn't the XO," Challon said. "This time it's just Marc Challon — with some business that should interest Pozner and his friends."

"Jim might come to your funeral, Marc Challon. Nothing else involving you would interest him."

"Would it interest him to know that I sold the XO to Anson Prentice; that my wife is going to divorce me and marry him?"

The girl's color faded.

"That woman will have the ranch now — without a Challon on it?"

Challon was astonished at the distress in her tone. She started to say something else but broke off as a hard-riding man flung down at the door and banged the door open. Marc had been half expecting this arrival and he grinned at the grim, dusty man who strode across the floor toward his table.

2

Hank Bayard was the most obvious man alive. He stopped beside the table to shoot a glance at Elena Casamajor and a sharper one at Challon. A glance which touched the whisky bottle in passing. His quick estimate of Challon's condition and mood was so open that the girl smiled. Hank ignored her. He dragged out a chair at Challon's knee and dropped onto it.

"Marc, what the hell is this?" he demanded. "Perigord told me I'd find you up here. Look, Prentice came down to the bunk shack tonight and told us he'd taken over the ranch."

"You heard it about right, Hank."

"But Marcy — Mrs. Challon is still out there!"

"Makes it plain enough, doesn't it?"

Bayard swore expressively, without apology to the girl. Tossing his hat onto the table, he ran his fingers nervously through his thin hair. The hat-shaded whiteness of his foreskull was startling in contrast to the deep, ruddy tan of his face. A rangeman looked naked, bareheaded.

"You know this is damned foolishness, Marc," he charged. He glanced again at Elena Casamajor. "Beat a woman, but don't give her satisfaction. Not any. Marcy doesn't have any claim to a single fence post on the XO — not really. And Prentice has damned little if he'll leave you alone long enough to pay back that loan of his. You picked a hell of a place to lie down!"

"You handle your women, Hank," Challon said mildly. "I'll handle mine."

"Sure, Marc." Bayard shrugged. "No offense. None of my business. But nothing in a skirt could ever be worth the XO!"

"You're sure of that?" Elena murmured in Spanish.

Hank fastened an angry eye on her.

"Damned sure!" he snapped.

Elena laughed softly again. Challon touched his foreman's arm.

"Prentice making any changes in the crew?"

"He'll have to! Every jack rode into town with me tonight. The boys are ringy over this, Marc."

Challon nodded. This was a part of what he had meant when he told Marcy she didn't know this country or its people. A ranch without a crew would be a hard thing to manage. He smiled faintly.

"Nothing thirstier than ringy saddle hands — or jumpier. You saddled Perigord with a chore, Hank, bringing the boys in with that

41

kind of a mood chewing them."

"It ain't worrying Hugh as much as the chore he's afraid you're fixing to toss in his lap. He's afraid you're going to move out onto the lava. Now wouldn't that raise the devil!"

"Wouldn't it, though!" Challon agreed. "Look, Hank, I've come out of this with about a hundred and thirty thousand dollars in cash. Prentice has maybe got a million, if we count his old man and a hunk of the Atchison, Topeka, and Santa Fe as behind him. And he's got the XO, for now. But I don't think he's going to keep it. I don't think the Challons will be off of their land too long. You and the boys want to stick around and see?"

"What about Marcy?" Thought of one woman seemed to link all others in Bayard's mind. He glanced again at Elena Casamajor.

"I don't take my women secondhand, Hank — any of them," Challon said.

Bayard stood up.

"I took orders from Pierre Challon before I could set a saddle. When you got big enough to whip me I started taking them from you, Marc. This would be a hell of a poor time to stop."

"I've got a hundred head of blood stock coming off of the ranch. You know the ones I want."

Bayard grinned and reached for his hat.

"I won't leave a stock-show ribbon on the place."

"And my saddle string. Move the works out to the sorings at Tinaja."

Bayard's lips set tightly.

"So Perigord was right! Look, Marc, Jim Pozner and the Hyatts and a dozen others out there have been waiting a long time to get a good bite at Challon beef. Pierre's run 'em and you've run 'em and they haven't forgot. They've been itching for a chance to swing on you!"

"They'll never have a better," Challon said quietly. "Art Treadwell is drawing some agreements. I've got to stay in town till they're signed. It'll be two or three days until I get out to Tinaja. Keep the boys corked till then."

" 'Don't let it rain till I give the word, Hank,' " Bayard mocked protestingly. "Hell, Marc —"

"It sure is," Challon agreed. "Go away, Hank. I'm busy."

He leaned across the table toward Elena. Bayard left the room with a disgruntled stride. Challon was not concerned. They didn't grow buckos on the lava big enough to spook Hank Bayard into a piece of trouble contrary to orders. It wouldn't rain at Tinaja Springs for three days.

When the door closed behind the former XO foreman, 'Lena leaned across the table toward Challon.

"You've given your orders," she said. "If I don't go with you to talk to Jim, you'll go alone then?"

"I can make Pozner listen to me," Challon told her. "I have before. This is different now, and I don't want to do it that way. But I can."

The girl nodded.

"Yes, I suppose so. At least you can try. But it would mean trouble for my aunt — for Jim too." She paused thoughtfully. "If I talked to them first, maybe it would be different. Look, Marc Challon, you told Hank Bayard about a lot of money. Did you think I would be interested in that?"

"Why not? It interested me or I probably would have shot a man this afternoon."

"There are other things more important than money. And something else; you spoke to Bayard about secondhand women. He looked at me. He was making a mistake about that. I don't want you to make the same one."

"I'm not. I trusted the wrong kind of woman once. I wouldn't do it again, even to get to talk to the devil himself."

Elena rose from the table.

"It's late. I want to save Tia all the trouble I can. When you're ready to leave for Tinaja, send me a horse. I'll go with you. *Buenas noches.*"

Pierre showed up in Range at ten the next morning. He was in a shiny XO top buggy, with his own trotter between the shafts. Riding unobtrusively on the little platform over the rear axle, as though borrowing a ride, was Pepe Sheep Man. Thus Pierre and the San Juan Indian who had been his constant companion for half a century met the letter of Challon's instructions that his father have Pepe drive him to town.

Pierre was in his best suit, a heavy dust-green broadcloth older than Marc's recollections. It had a sheen modern fabrics entirely lacked — the depth of quality. It hung flawlessly on Pierre's great frame, hiding the sagging stoop of his shoulders and thirty years of his age at the same time. The biggest full-crown Stetson broadbrim in New Mexico sat at a careless angle across Pierre's rusty white mane. Belted under the long tail of his coat was a magnificently tooled and embroidered Mexican holster containing the gun which for the last ten years Pierre had worn only on local election days.

As the buggy halted, Pepe trotted from around in back. Pierre handed him the reins and disdained the fragile iron bracket of the step as he swung down to the walk. Challon met him at the foot of the steps in front of the hotel. He gestured behind him.

"Suppose we go up to my room."

Pierre Challon fixed watery eyes on his son.

"I never hit town a day in my life that I

45

didn't buy a drink before I knocked the dust from my hat. There ain't a better place to talk than a saloon."

Challon grinned. The old man waved at Pepe Sheep Man. As the buggy rolled past, Challon saw luggage lashed to the rear deck. He said nothing. Pierre pushed across the street toward the dilapidated front of the Red River Saloon. A metropolis might eventually surround Range, but to Pierre Challon there would always be only one place in town where a man could buy an honest drink. The Red River had been the first bar. It had to be the best.

As they entered the place Challon remembered for a moment an almost forgotten time on the XO. A time when his mother was still alive, small and soft of voice. A woman with enormous eyes whose love for Pierre Challon was a worship of a thundering and occasionally unkind god. A time when the thick-walled house at the ranch was so new that the interior wash on the dobe of the walls cracked with each change of season. A time when Challon himself was still a boy, nearly as tall as his father, but not quite a man. Belle Challon had forbidden him to enter the Red River.

With its cracked mirrors, unsilvered and cracked by time, its faded paintings and patched chairs and scarred bar, it seemed only untidy and innocuous enough now. But legend lived in its dark interior. With the Lambert Hotel at Cimarron and the Clifton House on the Canadian, the Red River had had its share in the Territory's history in the days when talk was not of rails but of wagon wheels rolling down out of Kansas for Santa Fe.

Marc rang a coin down on the bar when their drinks were served. Pierre hastily matched it with one of his own.

"I'm drinking none of your whisky!" he said sharply.

"You pull in your horns," Challon counseled gently.

"I ain't got any to pull in any more!" Pierre said savagely. "That's the hell of being old. Otherwise, right this minute you'd be stiffer'n a board from a damned good fist mauling and locked in the spud cellar till you learned better, and I'd be hazing a couple no-good critters off our land!"

"Without doing the XO any real good. We never have tackled a problem exactly the same way, Pierre."

"No, by hell! One of us has got whiskers on his chest!"

"You take it easy, Pierre. You let me handle this. Your no-good critters will be running soon enough. Wait till I've gone to work on them. And they're going to leave something behind that the XO can use."

"What?" the old man asked derisively.

"Tracks in the sand?"

"A railroad, maybe. The iron men to finish Torrentado dam and the irrigation system. Maybe, with luck, some profit over that."

"You say!" Pierre growled. "Trying to take the bite out of it for me. Hell, I'll never be so old I have to be coddled. You're whipped clean out of the herd, and I know it as well as you do. You wouldn't have layed down and let that bitch walk the length of what used to be your backbone, like you did yesterday, if there was fight in you. I want to tell you something, Marc. I'd have given the XO to your mother, lock, stock, and barrel, any day she asked for it. But I wouldn't sell it to her sainted soul for another man's money! The biggest mistake I ever made was deeding the ranch to you last year. I should have made you wait and then left it to my cook's cousin! At least it would have been in better hands than it is now."

"I'm trying to tell you what I've got in mind," Challon protested.

Pierre waved him to silence.

"What mind?" he snapped. "Next you'll be trying to tell me you got guts! Marc, I'm done — with you, the ranch, the whole damned country. You been fool enough; you'll be a bigger one if you try to do anything now. I'm not sticking around to watch that. I haven't been so damned mad since you were born. I'm getting out. Pepe and me

48

are catching the noon stage to Denver."

"Marce make it tough for you out at the ranch last night?" Challon asked with a sharp suspicion. Pierre missed the ominous note in his voice and ignored the question.

"I'm going to hire me the biggest suite in the Brown Palace when I hit Denver, and I'm going to start ripping up the walks. When I've got this mad cut down to a size I can handle, maybe I'll come back down here and finish raising you, though I doubt you're worth it. Maybe I'll come back down and learn you how to handle a woman. Till I do, you leave me alone, boy. I want no part of you now!"

Pierre banged his glass down on the bar, pivoted, and strode out of the saloon. Challon glanced at the glass. It was still full. There was no use following Pierre. The old man was in a monumental uproar when he'd walk away from untouched whisky. Besides, Challon thought the Denver trip a good solution. It would keep Pierre out of the way here in the beginning, where he wouldn't fit. Later the fight might become the kind on which Pierre had cut his teeth. The old man would lose his mad then.

The summons to Treadwell's office came the second day, sooner than Challon had expected it. He had not seen Marcy and Anson Prentice arrive in town. They were sitting in uncomfortable chairs in the dusty litter of Treadwell's inner office when he came in. Marcy did not speak. Prentice uncertainly followed Treadwell's lead, rising and offering his hand. Challon ignored it. Treadwell stumbled inarticulately.

"It maybe doesn't make sense to you, Art, but it does to us," Challon told the attorney. "Let's get on with it."

Treadwell nodded. "Got to have a statement of relevant facts to draw the divorce — you knew there's going to be a divorce, Marc?"

"Just how much security you think I'd put up for a loan, Art? Thirty per cent of my ranch, and my wife to boot? You're damned right there's going to be a divorce!"

Treadwell hurriedly burrowed into the papers on his desk.

"One — identity of the parties; we can pass that. Two — partnership, established *de facto* by a loan from Anson Prentice to Marc and Marcelline Challon, secured by an assignment of title to a thirty-per-cent interest in the land, improvements, and stock known as the XO ranch."

"Cut it short, man," Prentice urged thinly.

"Cut it all, Art," Challon said. "Let them write their own ticket after I get out of here. They've got to go to court; I don't. Just hand across what you want me to sign."

Treadwell squared the heap of papers. He was perspiring.

"As your attorney, Marc — and your friend — I advise you to sign nothing."

"As my attorney and my friend, you handle this the way Mrs. Challon wants it."

"You're being a fool, Marc!"

"I don't think so," Challon said. Lifting a pen, he scratched his signature across the top paper on the heap. Treadwell stiffened resignedly.

"The Bank of Range has transferred the XO balance to your personal account and has accepted Mr. Prentice's draft on his Chicago bank for the balance due you under these agreements. Stuart says he'd appreciate it if you didn't draw too heavily against this second item until the exchange on it clears."

Challon nodded. He turned to Prentice.

"The railroad and your old man's stock in it seemed pretty important to me when I invited you down to spend this spring with us on the ranch, Anse. I wanted you to see why I thought the Santa Fe line ought to touch Range when it came through the pass. The loan seemed important, too, when you showed interest in my plans and offered to let me have the money I needed for my irrigation system. But none of it amounts to much now, does it?"

He paused thoughtfully.

"I'm just wondering about one thing now. I've got about a hundred and thirty thousand dollars of Prentice money in my pocket as of today. Suppose I could raise much hell with the Santa Fe's building program in this part of the country if I spent your money in the right places and the right way?"

Prentice paled uneasily, but he forced confidence into his voice.

"It takes railroad men to cause a railroad trouble, Marc. We might worry about General Palmer's Denver and Rio Grande beating us over Raton Pass, but I don't think the road or my father or me will any of us lose much sleep over what you might be able to do to the rails."

Challon grinned.

"You get my point. I'm no railroad man; you are. I'm a cattleman; you aren't. But you've got a ranch on your hands now. A big one. And I don't like you, Anse. Not any!"

Still smiling, Challon stepped out into the hall and closed the door of Treadwell's office behind him. It reopened almost immediately and Marcy followed him out. She stopped him at the head of the stairs.

"That didn't become you, Marc — shaking a stick like that at Anson after we'd all reached agreement!"

"Scared, Marce?"

"Of you? No. I've lived with you and Pierre too long to be afraid of even the Challons. But you're not fooling me. You're being too agreeable. You're no martyr. Maybe your pride is barked, but you're after something

52

now which doesn't have too much to do with pride, I think. Something you can put in your pocket, Marc."

"I suppose there's dew in your eyes!" Challon mocked. "You love Anse just about as much as you loved me. Where you going, Marce?"

"I'm there. The climb's done. 'Mrs. Anson Prentice, of Chicago and Santa Fe, who divides her time between the palatial Prentice mansion on Chicago's exclusive Prairie Avenue and her baronial cattle ranch in New Mexico Territory.' It's been a long way to come, Marc."

"You're sure you're there?" Challon asked softly.

Marcy's eyes narrowed.

"Don't make it a challenge, Marc. Be careful. Be very careful. I don't think a Challon has ever had to fight a woman before."

She smiled. Challon turned wordlessly and trotted briskly down the stairs.

3

The lava was for a generation the eastern boundary of the grass enclosed in XO fencing. A thirty-mile wilderness lying against the Panhandle. Like the barranca-scored no man's land of the old Indian Territory Strip to the north, a haven for swift travelers and the lawless. The volcano was the landmark of the lava. A geometrically perfect cone from which had been flung not so much ash and molten stuff as great solidified chunks of igneous brown rock which littered a quarter of the country. In the explosion which had broadcast this giant rubble, the level sweep of the grasslands had buckled into sharp ridge folds and upthrusts. Among these was the pyramidal spire of Tinaja.

There was grass in the lava. Scattered patches. Occasional water. Beyond was the roll of the prairies again. It had been Marc Challon who had stretched an XO link through the lava to connect with more acreage on the other side. An inevitable expansion. What had been sufficient empire in the days of wagons along the Old Trail was smallbore with rails already surveying up Raton Creek.

There were homesteaders on the patchy grass in the lava. There were squatters, with no claim beyond their own presence. Sullen men, apart and unfriendly. Deliberately so, for reasons not always too obscure. And all of them remembered the flinty trading by which Challon and Hank Bayard had finally forged a string of leases from the old XO to the flatlands beyond the lava.

Challon spent another day at the Palace Hotel in Range, ordering the immediate details of his plan, the first of which now being the new use he had for the leases in the lava. Stuart, at the bank, sent word Prentice's draft had been honored, from Chicago to Trinidad by wire and over the pass by messenger. Art Treadwell had left with his statements of fact to file the fourth divorce proceedings to be heard before the territorial courts in Santa Fe. Marcy and Anson Prentice returned to the XO. Word came back to the interested town that Prentice had moved into the old homestead house, a mile from the main buildings at the XO, and that Hank Bayard had raided the ranch breeding pens for the stock Challon had expected.

Challon sent a horse to the Uncle Dick on top of Goat Hill early in the morning. 'Lena Casamajor met him at the willows bordering the dry slough on the edge of town. With the sun in their faces they rode toward the lava. The volcano and Tinaja were two blue silhouettes a dozen miles apart on the eastern horizon.

Challon was still puzzled by the girl beside him. He knew her usefulness and didn't minimize it. Her aunt's husband, Jim Pozner, was the leader of the settlers in the lava. A thin, quiet man with the most dispassionate eyes Challon had ever seen. Hard and arrogant, with a strange streak of righteousness. Unpredictable and personally dangerous. Probably the bitterest enemy the XO had made in a good many years of trading friendliness and enmity alike for more land.

If Elena could make this man listen to Challon — if she could make Pozner even partially understand the change afoot with the passing of the XO from Challon hands — Marc knew she would have done something he could not have readily done alone. But he could not easily explain Elena's willingness to help him. She had said she wasn't interested in money. In spite of this contrast to Marcy's open, bald acquisitiveness and the wariness which was his reaction to it, he believed 'Lena in this. He had enough respect for her intelligence to know she realized the risk Jim Pozner and the others took in even talking to a Challon. The old days were not forgotten that easily, and men did not change that much. 'Lena would know this also.

There remained only one explanation. Personal vanity was a Challon heritage, and the strong awareness of the physical which this country bred into its people was as marked in this girl as in Challon himself. She had not married. Perigord had said she had kept apart from the town and the errors of *paisano* women on the grass. Maybe she had found the kind of man for which she had long looked. Uneasy but not particularly displeased, Challon wondered if when she claimed repayment for this service she was doing him he possibly wouldn't find it more disturbing than even an unreasonable demand for cash. It would be interesting to see.

Two hours out of town they topped the long rise of the watershed and stopped to breathe their horses. The sun was strong. The country lay in prismatic brilliance before them. Northward, in the lee of the big mesas, the home buildings of the XO stood out clearly. Not the big house. Belle Challon had planned it, and only Pierre had claimed more of her attention. The dobe walls and mission-tile roof of the house were a part of the mesas and the sandstone ledges and the silver green of the grass. It was there, sprawling and comfortable, but it blended with the country and was invisible at this distance.

The big red barn with its white trim and gambrel roof was plain enough. The corrals, with their white posts and rails. The long, low red equipment sheds. The bunkhouse.

The six little bungalows for married employees and overflow guests the big house couldn't accommodate. The ranch store. The cottonwoods up the slope, shading a little log-and-dobe cabin where Pierre Challon, at fifty, had brought a bride from the river . . . the homestead, where Anson Prentice was now camping. And the lines of white posts, supporting gleaming, tight five-strand wire fencing which parceled the sixteen-section square of the home place.

Elena Casamajor looked northward across the grass for several moments, then turned suddenly on Challon.

"Why did you let her have it?" she asked. "You love her that much still? That woman?"

Under the prodding of this sharp woman's question Challon wondered just how much he had ever really loved Marcy Bennett. There was much which could be forgotten in five years, so many things which could change. Had it been the spark of conflict, the challenge, the winning and losing, even in small things? Had it ever been love?

"You've watched poker played," he said slowly. "You've seen a shrewd dealer throw away a good pot at the beginning to draw bigger stakes in the end, when the game was for blood."

The girl considered this. She looked northward again.

"It's worth fighting for," she said. "And not

because it'll make the man who owns it rich. Not even because it belongs to you, really. Really, it belongs to the country."

Challon could not follow this. He said so.

"How many tables in Red River County are fed with what grows on the XO?" 'Lena asked. "Not the beef. There's more to it than that. The stores in Range and those who work in them. The stage line and its drivers. The saloons that live on Saturday XO trade. Even down to the extra hands hired at roundup. It's the biggest thing in the county, and whatever you do, Marc, the county will watch."

Challon was amused. He had always known ownership of the XO and, with it, swelling pride. It startled him to find an ember of the same ownership and pride in this girl, a hint that there were hundreds like her. She saw his smile.

"You think I joke. If you manage to do what you're trying to do, you'll have to see it. And you'll have to see something else. You know the Clifton House?"

Challon nodded. It wasn't far from the west boundary of the XO. A roofless, windowless stand of mud walls and an askew array of breached corrals and rotting sheds on the banks of the Canadian.

"I heard of it often when I was very small," the girl said. "A busy hotel then. Wagons and coaches traveling the Old Trail stopped there. And great men. Part of New Mexico. Now the roof is caved. I cried last fall when I saw that. Soon it'll be forgotten — gone. And the Maxwell house at Cimarron. A palace when the Old Señor built it — when he owned how much land — three million, five million acres?" She shrugged. "Vanished. The timbers and dobe bricks pulled down, stolen to make little houses, shacks. . . ."

Her eyes swung westward toward the snow on the distant Sangre de Cristos.

"And Carson, the little *yanqui* who really showed the way to Santa Fe? Forgotten already in a sunken grave on a slope behind Taos!"

A sudden fierceness gripped her. Her hands clenched across the horn of her saddle.

"You want to know why I came with you — why I ride into the lava when I know inside it means trouble for my aunt's husband and his neighbors. Then this is part of it! Something has to be left under the mesas to mark the big things that have been here. There's been so much more than just empty grass in New Mexico. Springer's — Chico — the Challon ranch — something has to be saved!"

Challon said nothing. He found himself stirred by 'Lena's fervor, but Marcy had left him a little distrustful of motives in women.

Besides, there seemed to him to be a good deal of common sense in the practice of robbing old and useless structures for the materials out of which to raise new ones. All things dead on the grass were carrion.

"You meant what you said about that poker game?" Elena asked after a moment. "You're risking the XO to break that woman? There's an old teaching that the devil's in a man who wants revenge."

"Then the devil's in me," Challon said, and he gigged his mount forward.

They halted two or three miles from Tinaja Springs, where weeded ruts led up a barranca toward the Pozner place.

"Jim will be down to your camp tonight," 'Lena said. "I'll see to Tia, and Tia will see he comes. The Hyatts and some of the others may be with him. They won't trust you. You've got to expect that. You've got to know exactly what you expect from them and what you'll pay for it. They won't listen to dickering."

"You get them down; I'll make them listen."

Elena nodded and reined away. Challon followed the trail on into the springs. A rider spotted him half a mile out and signaled the camp with his hat. Challon smiled. Bayard was being cautious, beforehand. Bayard was a good man, here as well as within a fence.

A makeshift brush corral was up. The horses were bunched in it. There was a pole-and-brush cooking shelter, a fire circle, and beds on the ground. Challon's hundred-head exception from the XO herds was on grass in an angle between the base of Tinaja Butte and a radial scarp of lava, so that the whitefaces had to be held only on two sides. Challon reined up, satisfaction pulsing through him as it always did at the sight of a bunch of blooded cattle wearing his iron.

To stockmen in the tradition of Charlie Goodnight and John Chisum, to the south, Challon knew he was an experimenter and maybe even a fool. This was longhorn country. But the whitefaces were Marc Challon's real contribution to the XO; his vision the heavy animals on New Mexico grass, his gamble that they would thrive, his belief that when there were commercial herds there would also be an available market. The railroad was part of it. Whitefaces could not stand the punishing drives by which Texans moved their longhorns to shipping pens along the Kansas rails. But chutes and cattle pens on the Santa Fe line at Range would be in the XO's back yard.

Hank Bayard hailed Challon from the duffel pile of the camp. He rode on across and dismounted.

"You stop by the ranch?" Bayard asked. Challon shook his head. "You should have,"

Hank said wryly. "This sure as hell isn't turning out to be the best idea you ever had!"

"Why?"

"Prentice is really scared — or he's coppering his bets on general principles. He's got him a new crew already. Pete Maxwell must have hired a few for him down around Fort Sumner. Some of the bunch that's supposed to run with Bill Bonney down there, I think. Culled the rest around Las Vegas and Mora. Cy Van Cleave's got my old job."

Challon whistled softly. This wasn't Prentice. It was too aggressive, too bold. This was Marcy. She had heard talk of Bonney, the stocky kid who was emptying the boots of some good men down in Lincoln County. Kid Antrim — Kid Bonney — Billy the Kid. And Van Cleave, the rattlesnake of Mora.

Marcy had said she was not afraid of the Challons. These men would not be, either. Wary, maybe even a little respectful, so far as their natures went, but not afraid. This was the kind of thing Pierre had relished in the old days. A pyramiding of odds. The higher they came, the harder they fell. But Pierre was impractical in his enthusiasms occasionally. Challon wasn't pleased. This wasn't good.

"I don't like it, Hank."

"No? The hell! Me, I'm singing hallelujahs, Marc! Very simply, so's I can get it, just what

63

do you aim to do from this pile of black rock?"

"Break Prentice."

"And his old man and maybe twenty per cent of the Santa Fe on a side bet, eh?"

"The old man won't pour too much into a sack with no bottom," Challon said. "And he's a long ways from being the whole railroad. Even if he was, he'd have to quit someplace. The road builds track by building the country as it goes along, not by tearing it down. Anse is all we've got to handle, Hank."

"And Pozner and the Hyatts and some Fort Sumner specials and Cy Van Cleave — you sure you ain't forgot somebody else you could stir into this, Marc? Talk about the hard way! You could have hung onto the XO in the first place, without handing it over to Prentice and then squaring off to take it away from him again."

"Maybe," Challon agreed slowly. "But it would have been a tight squeeze with that demand note Anse held against me. And Marcy would have poured mud into everybody's pockets before she was through. You don't know her, Hank. Besides, you've forgotten something. There's a dam I want to build up on Torrentado. A dam that'll cost a lot of money. Money I'd just as soon came out of somebody else's pockets as my own. I've got Stuart's bank wadded with Anse's money right now. If I was to get the ranch back, too —"

Hank Bayard grinned slowly.

"Marc Challon, you're a son of a bitch!" he said. "Fair enough. Prentice has asked for it. And then there's Marcy."

Challon nodded. "Yes, and then there's Marcy."

There was something distinctive and familiar in the way the men from the lava rode into the camp under Tinaja two hours after dark. Challon did not immediately recognize it. Then he knew. Distrust and caution. Wariness and the sullenness of injured pride. Twenty years ago there had still been Utes on the mesas. Pariahs. An offshoot of the main tribe. To keep a truce with them the XO had held its own Beef Ration Day once a quarter, killing all the meat the Utes could carry away with them. The Indians had ridden into the ranch yard the night before the kill much as Jim Pozner and his friends came into Tinaja.

Dark, silent figures, riding almost to the fire before they halted. Tall men, sitting motionless on their horses, without eagerness or apparent interest in their errand. Challon recognized Pozner, Simi Hyatt, Ed Hyatt, Frank Germaine. There were others, lost in the anonymity of the shadows. More than a dozen, all told.

Among the Indians it was the squaws who dismounted first. Among these was Elena Casamajor. She dropped to the ground and crossed at a little half run to Challon. Her arm slid around him and she turned, pressed in under his arm, to face her uncle and his companions. A woman secure under the touch of her man. Bayard's eyes widened and fastened accusingly on Challon. This was something of which he hadn't been told. Challon stiffened with his own surprise. The girl spoke swiftly to him, her lips barely moving.

"I had to lie before Tia would lie for me, and I had to have her help. I told her you'd taken me and I'd wanted you to. That gave me the right to come to her for help for you. Don't talk here about your poker game for the XO. Talk about hate, Marc. These people understand hate."

"Evening, Jim," Challon said to Pozner. "Light down."

The man dismounted. His companions followed. They moved toward the fire in a compact group.

"There's some bottles in my saddlebags, Hank," Challon said. "Break 'em out."

Bayard moved off. Pozner passed the fire and stopped, facing Challon across a yard of space. The dispassionate eyes were dead. They touched Elena.

"Going to marry her, Challon?"

"I've got one wife too many now, Jim," Challon told him easily. "Not till that's settled."

Pozner shrugged. "Doesn't mean a damned thing to me. Her aunt wanted to know. Some things is important to a woman. I said I'd find out."

Simi Hyatt moved up.

"The hell with the girl, Jim," he said harshly. "We want to hear what Challon sings about why he's of a sudden camped here at Tinaja. We don't give a damn who he sleeps with, but we don't like the XO out here. He better have a reason."

Challon shot a hard glance at the oldest Hyatt.

"Maybe the same reason you and Ed had for holing up out here, Simi. I've got a chore the law won't let me handle my own way if I stay inside a fence."

"The hell!" Hyatt growled derisively. "The Challons can do anything in this country. They always have. They're the XO!"

"Not any more, Simi."

"You going to play it sad and expect us to cry with you?" Jim Pozner asked.

"No. I'm going after a little top hair. You boys have been holding scalp dances out here for years. I thought maybe you'd like to string along with me."

"Against Van Cleave and a bunch from Lincoln County — on your mad?" Simi

Hyatt protested. "Our teeth ain't long enough."

"Wasn't it Ed, there, who took a pair of guns off Bill Antrim and then broke his nose with his fist in Mesilla last winter?"

Ed Hyatt grinned. His brother subsided. Frank Germaine spat and spoke carefully.

"You're right in one thing, Challon. All the hell in the Territory don't necessarily grow in Lincoln County."

Challon felt Elena stir in the circle of his arm. A little movement, encouraging. He looked at Pozner.

"I'm off the XO, Jim. There's nothing on it belongs to me any more. Nothing. Understand? I helped build it. Now it suits me to pull it down some."

"Where's the old man?"

"Pierre left for Denver the day I moved into town."

"Then I reckon you're not lying all the way around, at least. I never thought I'd ever see Pierre Challon whipped enough to pull off his ranch. What kind of hand you aim to deal us?"

Elena stirred again. Challon's confidence increased.

"We never put the XO leases through here in writing, Jim. I want them switched to me, personally, now. That'll cut the home ranch off from the grass out east. I'll keep XO hands — Van Cleave or anybody else — off the leased sections. I want you boys to keep them out of the rest of the lava. Working together, we can do it."

"Those leases will cost you twice what you paid for them when you were the XO."

"I'll pay."

"You've made a deal then, Challon. What about XO beef? Our increases are tolerably scant out here."

"That's Van Cleave's worry."

Pozner grinned. "And the whiteface bunch you've got here?"

"That's my guarantee we're on the same side of the fence now, Jim. It stays here or on the leased sections, where you boys can keep an eye on it, till I've plowed the furrow I want across the XO. It's my show stock, my only chance of getting started again when this is done. It ought to be enough to convince you."

"It is," Pozner agreed. "Draw your cards off the top of the deck and we'll leave this herd be."

"One other thing, Jim," Challon said quietly. "Hugh Perigord is apt to come prowling out this way if it gets so they can see smoke from town."

"He ought to know better!" Pozner growled. "He's never had any business he could prove on the lava beyond the XO boundary. He better not try figuring up any now."

Pozner stopped and studied Challon for a long moment.

"I've got a notion Tia's going to feel a sight better about 'Lena when I tell her about this, Challon. It takes a lot of hate for a man to tear down what he's built, and for a woman. A man's got to love to hate. Maybe you got it in you to keep 'Lena happy. You better try like hell."

Challon said nothing. Pozner spat.

"I'll send Simi and Ed over to see Van Cleave in the morning with notice we're canceling the XO leases out here. There's going to be fat on the fire after that. You better do your part, Challon, you and your boys. The middle is a poor place to be caught!"

Pozner nodded abruptly to his companions. They returned to their horses, mounted, and rode off together, carrying with them two bottles of Challon's whisky, which they had been passing among themselves. Challon dropped his arm from 'Lena's shoulder and turned her to face him.

"That must have been some lie you told Tia Pozner," he said with a grin. "Jim swallowed it whole."

"About your taking me?" she asked calmly. "It wasn't too hard to convince Tia and Jim, Marc. They know that since the first time I saw you on the streets of Range years ago I've wanted you."

70

Challon stared. She laughed softly and swung her eyes over the camp.

"Where will I sleep tonight?"

"Sleep?" the word was jolted from Challon.

"You want them to know I was lying?" the girl asked with rounded eyes. "You want them to think you can't even keep a woman through the first night? Things are different on the lava than they are in town, Marc. And different than they were on the XO. Much different."

She turned away with an oblique backward glance, and with a ridiculous relief Challon watched her pull a roll of bedding from the cantle of her saddle and disappear into the dark shadows of the cooking shelter. Hank Bayard appeared at his elbow.

"Man!" Hank said. "Man!" He was laughing silently.

The girl's voice drifted out of the shelter. Challon thought she was laughing too.

"*Que duerma bien,* Marc."

Challon crossed to his saddle, jerked his own bedroll free, and threw it down at Bayard's feet. Hank was still chuckling. Challon kicked the bedroll flat.

"Hell!" he said.

4

The Hyatt brothers stopped at Tinaja at noon on their way back from the XO. Hank Bayard saw them coming and called across to 'Lena to pour more water in the stew she had on the fire. Challon had been out among the whitefaces all morning, physically removing himself as much as possible from the camp and from the girl, vainly combing his mind for sureness of her motives in the relationship she had thrust on him the night before. Hearing Bayard's shout and seeing the Hyatts, he came in afoot, arriving as the Hyatts were dismounting.

This scene, also, had a disturbingly reminiscent air. The stock, without a fence to hold it. The open camp. The two unshaven men, armed and swinging their thighs high as they came down from leather to clear the butts of the rifles sheathed under the skirts of their saddles. The expectancy in Bayard and his own boys. The expectancy in himself. It was like something out of his father's book, Challon thought — not his own.

"Prentice take the cancellations all right?" he asked.

"Don't know," Simi Hyatt said laconically. "Didn't see him. Van Cleave did the talking, with Mrs. Challon right there to see he said what she wanted. First time I ever saw your wife, Challon. Last night, when you were talking about how you'd walked off of the XO, I thought you were crazy. Now I've seen what you walked off from, I'm damned sure of it!" Hyatt grinned and glanced at Elena bent over the noon fire. "Maybe thunder and lightning when they're young, but they run to fat and lip whiskers in a few years. I like mine with a white skin."

"Stick to business, Simi!" Challon snapped. "Marcy — Mrs. Challon — and Van Cleave got it straight about the leases belonging to me, personally, now? They understand the XO has got to stay off of them?"

"You want too much for nothing, Challon. Jim never told me and Ed to tell them that. They know the leases are canceled. They're both smart enough to know why. We let it go there. Ed and me wasn't hunting a fight, exactly. You post your own trespass."

Challon frowned. Simi could have gone farther. Elena beat on the stew kettle. The three of them crossed to the fire. They found mugs and spoons. The stew was hot. They withdrew together and stood a little apart, waiting for their mugs to cool. Ed Hyatt watched 'Lena ladling out full mugs for Hank Bayard and Buddy Eastman and the rest of Challon's

73

crew. Ed's mouth came open a little and the lids pulled down partially over his small eyes. He watched 'Lena until Challon stirred impatiently. He started then, almost with guilt, and swung his attention back to Challon.

"You do all right," he said. He took a mouthful of stew. His brother scratched the toe of his boot in the dust.

"Van Cleave allowed he was due some notice on those cancellations. Leastways enough for him to bunch the XO stuff out east and move it back across the lava to the home place."

"You didn't tell him he could?"

Amusement came up in Simi Hyatt's eyes.

"No. I said he could try. That's all."

"I hope he doesn't. You should have warned him, Simi. I don't want that stuff out east moved this way at all. I'm cutting the XO in two. The sooner they know it at the home ranch and know I'm going to make it stick, the easier it's going to be for us all."

Simi Hyatt tipped his mug up and drained it as though its contents were coffee. He handed Challon the mug.

"Good luck," he said. "Thanks for the chow, Challon. Come on, Ed."

Turning, he crossed to his horse. The younger brother followed. With tight lips Challon watched them go. Simi was only a little less obvious than Hank Bayard. Challon knew he had gotten a carefully screened report on the talk this morning at the XO. He called to Bayard. His foreman approached curiously.

"Get the boys up as soon as chow's finished, Hank. Move the whitefaces out onto the old leases. We can't hold them indefinitely here, anyhow. Spread them thin so they're strung clean across. And spread the boys with them. If anybody from the XO starts across, I want them warned. Warned, that's all. Don't try to stop them. Warn them and let it go at that. Then let me know, fast. I'll stay here, where I can be found."

Bayard nodded, understanding.

"Another thing, Hank. I want to know what's going on out east. Tell the boys to keep an eye peeled that way too. Hyatt wasn't very talkative."

"Remember what Jim Pozner said last night, Marc — something about being caught in the middle? You sure that ain't exactly where we are now?"

"Get the boys moving, Hank," Challon told him.

Bayard moved among the riders hunkered down with their cigarettes in the shadow of the cooking shelter. They rose unhurriedly and drifted down toward the horses. Bayard lingered in talk with 'Lena for a moment, then followed them. Hank's back was ramrod-straight in the saddle as they presently rode out of camp

A man hired more than another's sweat on the grass. For wages and a roof overhead and an iron for which to ride, a saddle hand turned out his skills and his loyalty and his judgment. Opinion was his right, along with the expression of it. Bayard would not have played this hand quite this way. As a result, he was angry. This wasn't new. Hank was bullheaded. Within an ace of being too bullheaded to work for a Challon. And the springs of his anger were as quick and engulfing as the springs of his loyalty. His hostility troubled Challon a little now. There was, he supposed, enough uncertainty in him already. Under the circumstances, Hank's disapproval had a weight out of all proportion to its actual importance.

'Lena finished up at the fire and came across the camp. Challon was sitting on a grounded saddle. He pulled another around for her. She sank wearily onto it. Working over the fire in the noonday heat had left her flushed, her face streaked a little with dust and smoke.

"Good chow," Challon said. "Makes a difference with the boys. I better put you on the pay roll."

'Lena was watching the riders starting to move the cattle. She shook her head without answering.

"That's all I'm going to do," Challon said. "All I can do. I thought you understood that."

"Last night?" the girl asked without looking at him.

"Last night," Challon agreed.

'Lena swung her gaze suddenly toward him.

"Marc, how many men were killed building the XO?"

Challon frowned, but he accepted the change of subject. 'Lena's question was unanswerable. Hugh Perigord knew part of the answer. Marc, himself, knew part. Pierre knew all of it, perhaps. But none of them would ever put their knowledge together. The spotty violence out of which the ranch had emerged was forgotten and as well left so. Men had died along the base of the mesas in the last half century. Challon still remembered the location of the graves of two of the most recent, if not their names and the details of their deaths. Circumstances and motives were forgotten. Viewpoint changed. There was no longer chance of assessing the justice involved. Recollection was pointless.

"A few," he told the girl carefully.

She glanced at him with faint accusation.

"Are you as cautious in everything as you are with me? Like a child who's burned his hands on a stove? Can't you tell which ones have fire in them yet?"

Marcy, Challon thought, was troubling 'Lena a great deal. He looked at her, forgetting Marcy. Fire, she said. He shook his head slowly.

"No."

She smiled. The smile pulled into a troubled puckering of the lips which matched the faint frown on her forehead.

"The dead men — a few, I know that. I suppose it really doesn't make any difference how many, Marc. Just why they were killed. They stood in the way of the ranch in one way or another, and the ranch was bigger than they were, more important. I don't suppose your father ever really hated a man. Men big enough to earn Pierre Challon's hatred must have been pretty scarce, even in the old days. I don't think you ever really hated a man, Marc. Maybe Hank Bayard hasn't, either. Somebody was in the way. They wouldn't move. That made them wrong. They were removed. It doesn't seem so terrible —"

"You reaching for something, 'Lena?"

"Yes. That the ranch is built. It's finished, complete. Nothing is in the way now but a woman. Why must she be handled differently?"

"Maybe a Challon has a hate now."

"Men are going to die because of that woman, Marc. Maybe a lot of them. Maybe your father. Maybe Marc Challon himself. Have you thought of that?"

"You're trying to telling me to be careful?"

"Yes, Marc."

'Lena stood up. Challon rose with her. The sun was hot. Dust was in the air. The faint sweetening of sage and crushed grass. The whitefaces were gone from under the face of the butte, but the smell of the cattle and their droppings remained. Sweat dampened Challon's shirt and sweat had made tiny ringlets of the stray strands along the girl's hairline. The smells and the sweat and the heat were good. This was the grass country. This was New Mexico. Challon's hands reached out. They gripped 'Lena's shoulders. They pulled her toward him. He watched for an eager, laughing light to come up in her eyes, but it didn't. The frown remained on her forehead, and she slid out of his grasp with a roll of her shoulders and a twist of her body as old and instinctive as provocation itself.

"Jim and the Hyatts aren't watching, Marc," she said a little unsteadily. "And you already have one woman too many. You said so. You're playing poker, remember? All the cards have to come off of the top of the deck — and I'm not on the table."

Challon flushed in the sun. 'Lena returned to the cooking shelter. Challon built a cigarette. She came out and started down to the brush corral. He picked up her saddle and followed her. He watched her walk out among the horses in the enclosure with brisk assurance and slip a hackamore onto the startled pinto she had ridden down from Pozner's. She led the horse back to the brush fence, and Challon swung the saddle up. She

79

cinched it to her satisfaction and mounted, her skirt riding at her knees. He dropped his hand to one of these. She reined the pony away.

"You won't need me the rest of the day. I'm going up to see Tia."

"You're afraid."

"Yes, but not of you."

"Pozner, then — or the Hyatts?" It was an echo of Challon's own thoughts.

'Lena's face darkened with a quick half anger. "You're a fool!"

She wheeled away and was gone beyond earshot before Challon fully understood. It was herself of whom she was afraid. He restrained an impulse to saddle and ride after her. He had ridden after Marcy. Once was enough.

With the crew and the stock and 'Lena gone, the camp under Tinaja was empty and quiet. Challon struggled against restlessness. He felt the corrosion of doubt working. He recognized its roots. Motionlessness had always been as dangerous to him as it had been to his father. They were a moving kind. Their confidence flamed highest when there was wind in their faces. Quietude was stifling and peculiarly unnerving. It was with swift relief that Challon saw a rider beating in from the north, although the recklessness with which the man rode was forewarning he carried unpleasant news.

The rider came on, killing his horse. Challon recognized the Eastman kid. He moved into the center of the camp area and waited impatiently. The kid pulled his heaving horse into a clumsily rearing halt and slid to the ground. Challon saw the animal had a bullet burn across its rump. He saw the chalky white of the kid's face. The boy trotted unsteadily across to him and seized his arms.

"Van Cleave!" he choked. "He —" The boy's eyes rolled a little. Challon saw the pallor of nausea deepen in the faintly stubbled cheeks.

"What about Van Cleave?" he asked sharply. The Eastman boy's mouth worked. Challon saw he was going to be sick and he tried to step aside, but the kid clung to him and began to retch miserably. Fouled by the product of the boy's fear, Challon's patience snapped. He caught the boy by the collar of his jacket and jerked him upright.

"Damn you, if you've got something to say, spit it out!"

His free hand wiped smartly across the white face in an attempt to jar the youngster into coherence. Livid finger marks jumped up into contrast with the pallor of the cheeks. The Eastman boy's eyes steadied. A startled, hurt half anger showed in them briefly and faded. His slack lips stiffened.

"Van Cleave went through," he said in a dull, fixed effort at steadiness. "Didn't give us a chance to warn him. Didn't give me any warning —" His throat choked up. His body stiffened and he came up on his toes, tilting forward against Challon for an instant. Then he collapsed, buckling so suddenly that Challon's grip on his jacket was broken and he hit the ground hard.

Challon dropped beside the boy. The jacket slid up, exposing the boy's white belly and a great tear two inches to one side of his navel. Challon had knocked down a grizzly bear on the mesa with a smaller belly wound than this. And he had thought fear had choked the boy's speech!

Challon didn't go for whisky. He sat on his heels in the dust, his lips compressed wickedly, chewing on harsh self-condemnation. The boy's body fought a little longer, but he didn't open his eyes again. After a long time Challon turned the body over to verify what he already knew. The bullet which had killed Buddy Eastman had ranged through him. He had been riding away, not fighting, when he was shot.

Challon remembered 'Lena's fear that men would die soon. He hadn't thought it would be today. He hadn't believed the wire was yet tightly enough drawn. He had hoped he could trade a bluff and dickering for violence here in the beginning. He had not thought

82

the first to die would be the youngest member of his crew.

Pulling a blanket from his own bed, Challon rolled the body into it and carried it to the shade of the cooking shelter. Cy Van Cleave had done this. It was Van Cleave's way — to hit first and hardest. Marcy had done this because she had hired the man from Mora — because it was essentially her way also. Maybe even Marc Challon had done it, since there was directness in him too. The cost of loyalty was high. Loyalty which made the message Buddy Eastman carried to Challon more important to him than the life pouring from him. This, also, was the grass country. This, also, was New Mexico.

Challon wondered about Hank Bayard and the rest of the boys out on the leases, but when he was into his saddle he rode quarteringly northward, bearing east of the cone of the volcano and away from them. If Hank and the others were all right, they were with the whiteface herd. If they weren't, he probably couldn't help them. Van Cleave had gone through. The XO was deep into the lava already, then. Challon's business was with Van Cleave.

With the familiar motion of the saddle under him, Challon's mind swung automatically to rationalization. With the lava leases cut from under it and become a barrier, the

83

primary problem of the XO crew was to pull in its stock on the grass east of the lava. A consolidation. A step Challon anticipated. One he had deliberately tried to force. Bayard and his boys, stringing out the white-faces across the leased sections, had implemented the barrier the Hyatts had raised with the cancellation delivered to Van Cleave and Marcy this morning. Van Cleave was practical. He had assessed the line for its weakest link. This explained why it was Buddy Eastman, rather than Hank Bayard or one of the crusty and more dangerous veterans of the crew, who had hammered back to Tinaja with a hole in him.

As in most things, initiative here was of tremendous value. In moving his stock Challon had tried to seize it, hoping to wind it constantly tighter until Marcy and Anson Prentice broke under the pressure. Van Cleave had checked him. Van Cleave had the initiative now. If he could hold it, snow-balling his show of strength and inflexibility swiftly beyond the point of resistance, the XO would be secure. There was a limit to loyalty. There was a limit to the hatred and the bitterness of the lava people. There was a limit to what a man could buy.

Challon knew better than most how little a man could accomplish in this country alone. In spite of the ruggedness of individuality the grass stamped on most of those who rode across it, the history of the country had been one of co-operation. Van Cleave had to be choked down before he was too far out in front.

A quarter of an hour out of Tinaja, Challon saw dust ahead. He pulled a little to the right and cut in among great blocks of lava littering a shock ridge thrown up by the ancient explosion of the volcano. He quartered along this, gradually working toward its summit. Dismounting short of the crest, he pulled his rifle from its boot and climbed the last fifty yards afoot.

A lava-littered slope similar to that he had just climbed fell away to a narrow gray carpeting of grass which reached in among the ridge folds from the monotony of the llanos on eastward. A natural bunching ground, part of the eastern sections of the XO, and one the ranch used often for off-season gathers on this side of the lava. A well-defined driving trail snaked around the dying end of the ridge on which he stood and curved through the detritus footing the cone of the volcano to line out along the lava leases toward the XO home sections.

At the northernmost point on the arc of this broad track a much fainter tangent angled off toward the shallower canyons which broke up the eastern end of Boundary Mesa. One of the few dim highroads leading into the haven of the unclaimed and ungoverned Strip.

Cattle were moving in a long, protesting line out of the bunching ground and up this tangent. Challon didn't need glasses to know the identity of the distant riders moving the cattle any more than he needed to follow them to learn where they were going or to question them to understand why the cattle were being moved. The drovers were too far away for identification with glasses, anyway. Challon remembered Simi Hyatt's slow grin when he had said he had told Van Cleave the XO could try to move the stock on the eastern sections back to the home ranch.

Jim Pozner and his neighbors were fulfilling a long-frustrated ambition. The Challons were out of the way. Marc's present stand insured that. And the lava had a long score against the XO itself. Once into the Strip, this herd would be as effectively out of the XO's reach as if it had been driven the length of the Territory and across the international boundary into Mexico. There was grass in the Strip and there were buyers. The herd could be held or sold.

Challon scowled and studied the flanks of the drive. It took him minutes to locate what he was looking for. Van Cleave was still playing cautious and sure, bidding here, also, for a suitable point of impact and the explosiveness of surprise. Marcy's new crew was working along the distant base of Boundary Mesa, raising little dust. They were obviously hidden from the drovers with the cattle, and it was plain they were heading for a notch among the canyons where they could set an ambush across the trail into the Strip.

5

Returning to his horse Challon continued along the side of the ridge he had climbed until its point led him back down onto the flats. He cut over to a dry barranca, the wind-packed, sandy bottom of which afforded good riding, letting him increase his pace as well as giving him cover. He rode for thirty minutes with his attention wholly on the reaching animal under him. At the end of this time the cone of the volcano had swung around to the west of him and the tumbled shards of the eastern end of Boundary Mesa lay dead ahead. He took a small blind canyon, climbed a ridge into a higher one when it petered out, and at the end of an hour he was under the broken crown of the mesa, a hundred yards above the trail leading into the Strip. He swung down, found a vantage point to his liking, and hunkered down with his rifle across the ledge in front of him.

His timing was instinctive, bred of his knowledge of the country and a shrewd estimation of the course and purposes of both of the parties below him. He was barely into a position he wanted when a tiny telltale slide spilled down the opposite wall of the cut through which the trail into the Strip ran. He was momentarily uneasy. He had judged Van Cleave would pick this spot and that he would choose the other wall, but he could have miscalculated time a little. Van Cleave could have come in first. His own approach would have been spotted. However, there were several small signs of movement on the opposite rim in the next few moments, and before they subsided, Challon eased. The XO party had arrived after him. He was secure.

Dust was already sifting upward from the trail below, carried against the mesa by the faint upslope drift of air common in the last hour of the afternoon. Presently the point of the moving herd of cattle threaded a bend and moved past under Challon's position. He grinned dryly. Jim Pozner or Simi Hyatt or whoever from the lava was handling this drive was cautious. Knowing the stock could not stray in this defile, he had pulled in his flank and point riders, bunching all of his men in the dust behind the cattle, where cover was best. If there was trouble, retreat was open behind them; and if the cards came their way, the stolen stock was already past the point of danger before they could be forced into a stand. Challon levered a shell into the chamber of his rifle and watched the head of a grassed slide which stood at a practicable angle for downward-riding horsemen.

The tail of the drive came into view. The lava men were bunched well back in the dust. Challon sifted out both of the Hyatts and Frank Germaine. There was also a man from farther south generally called Brown and three others who had drifted into the lava from Texas or the Strip, avoiding Range and the main trails and so remaining nameless. He could not locate Pozner. He was looking for Jim when the XO outfit broke cover. None had unbooted their rifles. They were counting, then, on close work. They started down the steep slide, knees high and bodies slanted back against the pitching of their bunch-footed ponies. Rocks and turf came with them. Cy Van Cleave and Tom Halliard were in the lead. The others, like Halliard, were Lincoln County men, Challon supposed. He knew none of them.

Raising his rifle, Challon studied Van Cleave's vest in the notch of his sights, but a vanity made him shift his target to Halliard after a moment. Van Cleave had stature on the grass. The grass would expect more of a Challon than a careful rifleshot from cover for the rattlesnake of Mora. Something more personal, if the quarrel was personal. Something spectacular. Legend lived on the grass and was dear to it. Tradition made the enmities of certain men a public property and set the patterns by which they must reach solution. Challon held his sights against

Tom Halliard's shoulder, thinking of the hole in Buddy Eastman's body. The pressure of his finger on the trigger of the rifle increased slowly.

Simi Hyatt was the first among those from the lava to see the XO bunch. His thin, sharp yell carried clearly to Challon. The others with Hyatt reined abruptly toward him, the lot of them milling for a moment in indecision. As Van Cleave hit the flattening talus at the foot of the slope, he shouted something authoritatively. His companions spread obediently, driving through the straggling cattle tailing the drive. Van Cleave's belt gun banged. The sound of this shot was an abrupt additional impact against the tenseness in Challon. It shattered the balance between the trigger pull of his rifle and the pressure of his finger against it, so that the weapon seemed to fire in automatic response to Van Cleave's shot.

Tom Halliard swung both hands high over his head as though reaching for his hat and unable to control the movement, and he went out of his saddle in a flat spill to one side. He rolled heavily for a dozen feet and lay motionless in the droppings-stained dust left behind by the cattle. Van Cleave hauled up short, his eyes leaping from Halliard's empty saddle to the drift of black powder smoke above Challon's position on the rim. The others pulled up momentarily with him.

Thinking of inflexibility and the value of initiative and a personal principle of repayment of injury by multiples, Challon moved his rifle sights to a chunky man in a white shirt beside Van Cleave. He saw the mark of his second shot on the breast of the shirt before the man spilled from the saddle. Van Cleave shouted again, and the XO crew swung frantically down the cut, lying low across leather.

Challon lowered his rifle. This was enough. The Hyatts and the others from the lava, obviously startled by assistance from the rim, had broken gratefully for a side canyon stretching off toward the thickest of the lava malpais near the base of the volcano cone. Challon watched Van Cleave and his men pick a wider angle of retreat, holding more into open grass.

Practical compulsion lifted Challon to his feet. He trotted up the rim a few yards and knelt at a place from which he could cover the head of the still desultorily moving cattle. This was, in the last analysis, Challon beef. He would have let the Hyatts drive it into the Strip to harry Marcy and Anson Prentice. But since the Hyatts had hit the brush and there were other matters to harry Prentice and Marcy now, there was no point in letting the cattle cross the mesa. He dropped three steers in the lead before there was enough blood on the sand to spook the others, mill them uncertainly, and turn them back.

He glanced down at the two fallen men on the trail. He saw that Halliard's horse had fouled its reins in some brush. He shrugged. The horse and the fallen men were Van Cleave's problem. Let Van Cleave care for them. Maybe this would delay the return of the XO crew to the ranch. He wanted that. He had dealt with Van Cleave for Buddy Eastman. But there was still Marcy. He returned to his horse and mounted.

Anson Prentice was sprawled in one of the deep seats on the ramada fronting the XO house. Challon dismounted at the head of the footpath leading across the small, thick lawn to the house. He thought Prentice was asleep. An indication of the man's real interest in the country and the ranch. He had once tried to tell Prentice of the freedom of spirit the grass afforded those who could grasp it. An effort to explain his own position, his desire to keep building on the XO in spite of the bulk the ranch had already achieved. It had been useless.

Anse had been cast in too narrow a mold, and his metal had cooled to a brittleness beyond change. Bulk he understood. Wealth on the hoof. Power. Nothing else. The grass was novelty. Maybe even Marcy was novelty, a bright and wicked current to ruffle the placidity of Anse's life. Exciting, as the taking of another man's wife was exciting. A hollow and somehow ridiculous echo of a daring Anse did not actually possess.

When Challon came in under the ramada, Prentice started violently, so he had not been asleep. He eyed Challon apprehensively for a moment, then stiffened and stood up. He opened his mouth to speak, but Challon spoke first.

"Where's Marcy?"

"She can wait, Marc. What the hell you doing here?"

"Since when has Marcy learned to wait? Where is she?"

"Marc, I want to talk to you."

"What good would it do?"

Prentice flushed. "I was afraid you'd gotten the wrong slant on this from the beginning, Marc. Marcy didn't run you — or the XO — when you were on it. She isn't running me. If you've got business here, I'll hear it."

"I'll buy you out when you've had enough of what you asked for when you started this, Anse. But that's all the business we're ever going to do!"

Prentice lost color, but he smiled a little, unpleasantly.

"You're awfully damned sure, Marc. Let me tell you something. My father and some of the other Santa Fe directors are at Trinidad on an inspection tour. A rider brought a message over to me this afternoon. I'm supposed to build a fire under Perigord in town. The pay train for the grading crews at the foot of the pass was held up last night. They almost caught the bunch that pulled it. They had come a long way. They were on blown horses. And they made off down this side of the mesas."

Challon considered this. The lava bunch had been in his camp at Tinaja early in the evening. Only their battered gods knew where they had gone when they left. This was something they would like. The railroad meant an end to the solitude of the grass and of the malpais and was the work of the rich and the powerful, to whom they were opposed. A hurt to the railroad would give them satisfaction, and pay-train money spent easily. Still, he didn't think it was lava work.

"Did you look in your own corral to see if any of those Lincoln County horses had been on a hard ride last night? Or could you tell if you looked, Anse? Those new boys of yours would feel more comfortable behind masks than they do in their own whiskers!"

"You forced those men onto us, Marc. You took our crew and cut the XO in two. Van Cleave and the others seemed the only answer we could give you."

"And Marcy set it up for you," Challon said flatly.

Prentice set his jaw stubbornly.

"We won't bluff and we won't scare, Marc. Don't try to drag the railroad into this. You'll have your hands full with the XO. Marcy wants it and, like I told you, I'm going to see she has it. I'll be honest with you; I would rather have Hank Bayard bossing the boys in the bunkhouse than Cy Van Cleave. I don't want this to go any farther. Maybe you were trimmed too close for what you had here. How about that breeding stock you've got left? Van Cleave says the strain here won't amount to much in the long run without it. I'll try to make it fair. Suppose I pay you fifteen hundred dollars an animal for the hundred of them you kept? That's about showstock price, I think. And those you kept weren't all show stuff. I could raise enough more cash to about do that. Would you quit New Mexico for another hundred and fifty thousand dollars, Marc?"

"Let's understand each other right down to the ground, Anse," Challon said quietly, "I wouldn't quit now for your father's share of the Santa Fe. I told you, we're not ready to talk business yet. You're going to be on your belly. You're not going to be able to raise a nickel. Maybe there won't be any rails across the pass. You'll hate Marcy as much as I hate her, and maybe she'll know what a sheet of tin you are. When we're to that place, all of us, we'll talk about quitting New Mexico. But it won't be me who's leaving!"

"It's going to get nasty, I'm afraid, Marc," Prentice said stiffly.

"You guessing? I hope you're on a horse you can ride!"

Challon moved down the ramada toward the sunken main door of the house. Prentice followed him and touched his arm at the doorway.

"All right, Marc," he said. "We understand each other. This is something else. I don't meet many people down here. Hard for me to talk to those I do. And I want to keep this between ourselves. That's why I'm asking you. That and the fact I know I'll get an honest answer. Marcy doesn't talk much. But some of the riders do — the new ones. Look, Marc, did you meet Marcy in Kansas City at a — at a —"

Prentice broke off uneasily. Challon stared at him. He felt a surge of scorn. A man might be forgiven the pressures put on him by his desire for a woman. He might be forgiven a lack of understanding of values on the grass. But not narrowness of soul.

"At a pleasure house?" he asked grimly. "No, Anse. Your rider's got the story wrong. Not Marcy. She came from Indiana. I found her in Trinidad, teaching school and waiting for a chance to marry the XO. The woman from Kansas City was something Marcy could never be. She was honest. She married an old man and gave him love and a home

97

and happiness. She gave him faith. She gave him a son. She was my mother."

Prentice swallowed hard. His hand dropped to Challon's sleeve.

"Oh! I didn't know. Marc, I'm sorry —"

"Sorry!" Challon snapped, very close to flooding anger. "You damned fool, that's one of the things I'm proud of! Get out of my way. I'll find Marcy myself."

There were no lights aflame in the fore part of the house. Challon strode rapidly through the cool, dark rooms, holding off their familiarity with a strong physical effort. Marcy's door was a little ajar, and a slanting shaft of light from beyond it played on a crudely carved wooden madonna in a tiny Mexican shrine set in the opposite wall of the hallway. Belle Challon had found the shrine and the figure in Santa Fe. It had meant something when the opposite room belonged to her. Now it was a travesty. Challon pulled the door open without knocking.

Marcy was in a wrapper and lying on the huge bed with her knees bent and her bare feet in the air. The wrapper was not tied and she had twisted about. The hem of the garment was bunched about her thighs, exposing the trim white length of her legs. An inkwell was on the stand beside the bed. A pen was clamped thoughtfully between Marcy's even white teeth. A writing pad and several loose sheets of paper littered the pillow in front of her. She glanced unhurriedly around as the door creaked, and Challon felt a momentary flash of his first anger that she might be expecting Anson Prentice, but not himself.

Her eyes clouded for a moment with instinctive alarm, then cleared. She removed the pen from her mouth and stuck its point into the pillow. She smiled, rolled carelessly over, and sat up, pulling the wrapper closed.

"You might have knocked, Marc," she murmured without reproach. Ruffling the papers on the pillow, she selected one and handed it to Challon. He saw it was a legal filing in the territorial court at Santa Fe, Challon versus Challon. He tossed it back down on the bed.

"Art Treadwell can move fast when he's got real money to work with," Marcy said.

Challon nodded. "Art's a good man."

"You disappoint me, Marc. I thought you'd bleed a little when you saw that. Just a little. You here; me like this —" She laughed softly. "Your iron-man legend is all right out on the range, Marc, but it won't hold together in this house — this room — with me!"

Memories stirred in the shadows beyond the bedside lamp. Memories which began before this woman, but enough of them which embraced her. The first weeks. The plans. The exultation in Marc and later in Pierre that she understood the Challons and the forging of their dreams. The goodness of perfection. And now this.

Challon shook off the recollections with a physical gesture. Marcy, shrewdly watching, laughed again.

"You can't win, Marc. You can't do it. You think the rules are off since I've climbed this step from you to Anse. Maybe they are. I wouldn't know anything about rules. You think that since I lived with you five years and didn't mean one minute of any of it that anything goes now. You think you'll get your ranch back and money for your irrigation system from Anse before you're through; that I'll be taught a lesson I won't forget. That's hatred, Marc. That's revenge. Big hatred, your size. But it isn't enough. You can't win."

"No?" Challon smiled pleasantly. "I just saw Anse out front. He's sweating already, Marce. He asked me where you'd come from in the beginning. He had a funny idea where it might have been. I wondered why he thought that. I think I know now, after finding you like this!"

"What do you mean?"

Challon pointed at the copy of the complaint filed at Santa Fe.

"That's just part of it — getting shut of me. The next move has got to be Anse's, now you've cleared the way. And all of a sudden he's begun to realize he isn't playing a game with somebody else's chips any more. He's just realized his shirt tail is up on the table, along with everybody else's. He's slept with you. Now he's just realized he's supposed to marry you. A kind of a permanent thing. He's got to take you over the mesas to meet his old man on at least his next trip out along the Santa Fe. He's got to take you East to meet the rest of his family and his friends. And I don't think he likes the idea as well as you'd like to believe he does."

"He tell you that?"

"No."

"What did you tell him, then, Marc?"

"About where you came from? The truth, as far as I know it. I could have gone farther. I could have sent him to Trinidad to see Lou Patterson, to backtrack you from the night Lou introduced me. Personally, I've never cared. Roots don't make a person. Mostly it's what's inside of them. I want Anse to discover the rot in you himself."

"He won't discover anything. I handled you for five years, Marc. You didn't see anything until I deliberately showed you. For what it's worth to your vanity, Arson isn't Marc Challon. I'm not worried about his family. Why do you think I had to have the XO? So I could be more than a nobody. Not because I give a damn about raising cattle, that's sure! So I could bring Anson a hundred thousand acres of land. A hundred thousand acres — that's big, Marc — even in a Chicago mansion it's big. Marcy Prentice will get along all right in the East, and to hell with Anson's family. He won't have any trouble when he takes me home."

"If he does."

Anger flared in Marcy.

"You didn't get homesick. Not for me. What are you doing here, Marc?"

"Making trouble, I hope. All I can. Mostly I wanted to tell you your hired boys are playing a little rough. They killed Buddy Eastman out on the lava today."

"What did you expect?" Marcy snapped. "They've got their orders. I'll fire every man, including Van Cleave, when you leave New Mexico, Marc."

"If you won't fire them before that, you're going to have to bury them," Challon said softly. "You better get a crew going on graves in the morning. I filled a couple of them this afternoon and I'm just getting started. For five years I gave you everything you asked for. I can't change. You've asked for this. When you've had enough, you'll find me camped at Tinaja."

Marcy's voice was soft. It had pleasantness of tone. But there was an obscene ugliness to her profanity. Challon stepped into the hall and pulled the door of her room closed behind him.

Prentice was not under the ramada in

front. Night was down, heavy and clinging. Challon thought Van Cleave and the XO crew had had more than enough time to pick up their dead and come in from the eastern end of the mesa. He was uneasy as he crossed to his horse and mounted. The ranch was quiet. It was too quiet. A sharp letdown from Marcy's vitriol.

Challon headed his horse at a fast walk toward the gate. He had nearly reached this when he heard a rider approaching from the opposite direction. He turned aside. It was one man, hunched far over the horn of his saddle and hatless. As the fellow came abreast Challon was jolted by a sudden, hard-hitting admixture of recognition, incredulity, and shock.

The rider's clothes were thick with dust. They were stained with blood. He rode by a dazed fixation of will. The left side of his face was terribly torn away. Marc Challon had held his rifle sights a little too high in the afternoon sun.

The man was Tom Halliard. He was not dead.

The bite was not in this mischance of marksmanship, not in the certainty that Halliard would hear from Marcy as to who had nailed him from the canyon rim, not in the inevitable personal vendetta the man from Lincoln County would swear against Marc Challon if he recovered. What was important was that Halliard was coming in alone, unassisted, under his own power. Van Cleave and the others had not circled back for their dead as Challon had believed they would. And their present whereabouts was a dark, imperative question in his mind.

He lifted his horse into a full run toward Tinaja before the faint dust of Halliard's passing had settled in the roadway.

6

Hugh Perigord was squatting with Hank Bayard and the rest of the boys about the night fire at Tinaja. As he swung down from his sweat-stained horse Challon saw that only one of his riders was missing, understandable since Buddy Eastman's body was gone from the cooking shelter. One of the boys was packing the kid home. Marc Challon would be a bitterly hated man on one homestead tonight. It had hurt old man Eastman when his son had begun riding for the XO. It had been trading with the enemy. This was payment to satisfy the old man's hatred. Challon felt again regret and a measure of self-condemnation, but both were overridden by his relief that Van Cleave had not jumped this fire here.

He moved in toward the light. Playing a face-down hand without knowing what lay under the top card, Hank Bayard had done what he could with Perigord. He had fed him and he had gotten him drunk, fairly well lighting up himself and the rest of the boys in the process. It wasn't good. Challon wanted Hank's blunt levelness tonight. He wanted a crew which could ride. And Perigord drunk was more dangerous than Perigord sober.

"Who got Buddy, Marc?" Hank asked as Challon came up.

"Van Cleave's bunch."

"On the leases, eh?" Hank grunted. "The dirty sons! It looked some that way when we rode past his position, coming in. I doubled back and pulled the night riders off to save them the same thing. Seemed wise." Challon nodded approval. Hank indicated the fire. "Chow's in the kettle, Marc."

Perigord rose to his feet, his heavy, triangular head thrust a little forward.

"It can wait," he said shortly. "Marc, you got some talking to do."

"Not now," Challon said.

Perigord had come out of a couple of the first and worst of the Kansas rail towns. He knew all of the patterns of the great — Hickok and Masterson and the rest — and there was enough of their showmanship in him for it to surface occasionally. It did so now. He put his weight into nice balance on the balls of both feet. He slanted a little forward. He hung his arms limply, straight from the shoulders, with the elbows out at a slightly exaggerated angle.

The firelight drew a hawk's shadow alongside his sharp features and turned the whites of his motionless eyes to a truculent ruddiness. His voice went eastward five hundred miles for a peculiarly toneless twang. He had been a man beside a fire. Now he was a man with authority — and a gun. A gamecock posturing which would have been ludicrous if it had not also been deadly.

"Now, Marc!" he snapped.

Challon did not underestimate the man. He knew him too well for such a fundamental error. The XO had elected every county officer since the organization of the Territory. Pierre and himself had sent a long way for Perigord. He had been the right man to keep order in Red River County. He was wise enough to recognize the source of the votes which continued to re-elect him and guarantee his generous pay. The need had been for a hard man and a direct one. Perigord did not bluff.

He was not bluffing now. Challon had made him trouble and Challon had quit the XO. He was no longer a bloc of votes. He was just one man. And Perigord was tired of waiting beside this fire. He wanted to talk.

Caution had always been a poor restraint for impatience in Challon. He started past Perigord. The man snagged his shoulder with his left hand in a harshly arresting gesture. Challon broke the grip with a quick fling of his arm, ever so little destroying Perigord's fine balance, and he leaned into another stride. He heard Bayard's quick exclamation of warning and he saw Perigord's right hand snap closed on the grips of his loosely holstered gun.

What occurred then was instinctive. Maybe something Pierre had learned of necessity and which he had so thoroughly schooled into the juice of his being that with stature and shape of the head it became a part of the physical heritage Challon had drawn from him. It was an involuntary, unconsidered movement, far more swift and finely calculated than any consciously directed one could have been. The forward stride became a pivot which had whiplash acceleration. With all the instinctive precision of his body behind the blow, Challon's right hand drove into Perigord's belly two inches above his belt.

The impact made a soft, ugly sound. Perigord explosively belched air, staggered back, doubled, and tilted forward onto his head and face. His neck rolled and he spilled over onto his side. He lay there, conscious and in agony, his eyes curiously mirroring simultaneous bewilderment and anger. Challon took a step forward and with his foot pinned down the wrist of Perigord's gun hand. With his other boot he kicked the drawn weapon from Perigord's fingers. The gun skidded through the dust. Hank Bayard picked it up, punched the shells from its cylinder, and tossed it down beside the fallen man.

Perigord rolled onto his back with an effort

and drew his knees up high, almost to his chest. The sharp, gripping paralysis of Challon's blow eased after a moment. Perigord pulled air into his lungs in a dozen irregular breaths and climbed back to his feet. He dusted himself unsteadily, lifted and holstered his empty gun. His face was still gray with shock. He tried twice before he could speak.

"Talking would have been easier, Marc," he said raggedly. "You're not running the county any more."

"Meaning you are?"

"Might give it a try, since you've given me the chance by quitting the XO. The railroad is anxious to have the right kind of a man in my office. And the railroad doesn't like you, Marc. It doesn't like anybody out here east of the XO. I won't be alone the next time I ride this way — and I won't want to talk. You're finished on this grass. You and the rest of them out here that you figured on using as aces in the hole. Pass the word, Challon. I'm cleaning out the lava!"

"I'd put Pierre against you any day, Hugh," Challon said. "And he's been trying to do that for fifty years!"

"Pierre's in Denver, Challon," Perigord said shortly. "If I owe you a warning, you've had it!"

The man turned and walked unsteadily around the corner of the cooking shelter. A moment later he reappeared beyond it, mounted. Hank Bayard took off his hat and parted his thin hair with his fingers.

"You're going to kill a man someday with that hand of yours," he said. "Your hide's going to look good on the floor of Hugh's office after this. Words are cheap. I'd have spent a few to keep Perigord off of our backs. Why didn't you give him his say? He had a fair enough reason for prodding and he'd been waiting since sundown."

"He'll never have a good enough reason for prodding us," Challon said. "And if he comes back, he'll have to come back alone. He'd have a hell of a time finding a posse in Range that would ride after a Challon. . . . Seen anything of 'Lena since you came in?" Bayard shook his head. "Or the XO bunch?"

"Only the tracks they cut through Buddy's position on the flats. Been nobody near and nobody in sight since we came in. They give Buddy a chance?"

"No," Challon said. "Saddle everybody up, Hank. Fast. And see they bring rifles."

"What's up?"

"Trouble — at Pozner's, I think. And I'm afraid we're going to be too late. That's why I couldn't take time for Hugh."

"Too late?" Bayard echoed. "Then why go? You got enough fire on your tail now, Marc. The Santa Fe climbed down the pass today and gave Perigord a charge of buckshot in the backside. A pay train was held up out of Trinidad last night. Lost nearly eight thousand dollars. Kind of a bungled job. One of the bunch drew a hole in him, and the lot of them barely made it back to this side of the mesa, with a clear enough trail behind them. That's what Hugh hunted you up for."

"Why me?"

"Why not? He's smart enough to know the boys that blocked that train must have come out of the lava or out of the Strip, one or the other. Prentice's old man is a director on the road. The whole damned county knows Prentice stole your keys while you were gone this spring. Half the Territory knows you're sore at Prentice and your wife and that you've quit the ranch. And you've been talking to Jim Pozner. A swipe at the road would jolt Prentice. One of your boys died of gunshot wounds today. Why shouldn't Hugh figure you were a good place to start?"

"Because he knows me, Hank. If I was after the Santa Fe, I wouldn't stop at a pay train. I'd take the works — rails, roadbed, and right of way — while I was about it. Perigord's pulling feathers for his own nest."

"Sure. Right off your chest! He's got a posse, all right, Marc, whenever he wants it. You've forgot the ringy bunch Prentice put on the XO."

"The hell I have. If I can jar enough of the whisky you loaded into the boys out of them,

Hugh may never get a chance to swear in Van Cleave and a couple of the others, at least. Come on, Hank, stir them! Get leather up!"

Challon took the ridges, trading the easier going of the lower trail for time. He didn't know what he expected to find at Pozner's. Certainly not the appearance of quiet surrounding the homestead when the party from Tinaja slanted down the low slope behind it.

Saddle animals were in the corral. There was no displacement apparent in the litter of the yard. A lamp was lit in the little stone-and-piñon-log house. Challon had an uneasy feeling that he was at a disadvantage with Cy Van Cleave. His estimation of the man either fell short or overshot. He wondered if Marcy was shrewdly playing upon her knowledge of Challon nature and giving Van Cleave orders she knew would pull Marc up short. He discarded the thought as it was born. He knew Marcy, too, and even with the devil's due, she was not this much of a perfectionist. She could see the ends clearly enough, but the means would necessarily be sometimes beyond her. Van Cleave was weaving his own pattern within the loom Marcy provided.

Hank Bayard discovered the first sign of trouble. He reined his horse in with a sharpness more arresting than an outcry. Challon pulled up beside him. Jim Pozner's big dog

112

lay in the dust of the yard with its back broken by a bullet fired at close range. Challon urged his horse on, pulled up, and hit the ground in the dooryard. Bridging the front steps with a long stride, he tripped the latch, shoved the door open, and flattened against the outer wall beside the frame. He was not challenged. He ducked on through the opening.

The embers of a fire still glowed with considerable heat in the fireplace. Frank Germaine was sprawled on the floor, his feet on the hearth and so close to the embers that the sole of one boot had been blackened by the heat and had curled away from the upper, revealing a scorched sock and swollen foot. The unpleasant acridity of hot leather was in the air. Germaine had a gun in one hand. Blood stained the floor under him. He was dead.

The room was a little disorderly, looking disarranged by the surprise of its occupants rather than by struggle. A partially eaten meal was on a table set with four places. The doors to both the bedroom and the kitchen were open. The lamp Challon had seen burning from outside was in the bedroom. He crossed to this. Tia Pozner sat huddled in a diagonal corner. One side of her face was livid, swollen. Her mouth had bled a little, and the red line from its corner made a thin, ugly scar down across the roundness of her chin and throat. Such clothing as remained on her was in ribbons, its disorder evidently not of her doing and more callously revealing than complete nakedness.

Her back was against the meeting of the walls in the corner. One leg was bent under her. The other was thrust out along the floor. A cramped, unnatural position into which she had obviously been flung. Her eyes were widely open, staring across the room with an intense, unfocused fixity. For a moment Challon thought she, also, was dead. Then he saw the movement of her breathing. He stepped back to the front door, signaling Bayard.

"Frank Germaine's in here. Dead. Get him out and clean up behind him. Light a fire in the kitchen. Find Jim's whisky and put some water on to heat. Then wait outside. And keep the boys quiet."

" 'Lena?" Hank asked.

"No. Pozner's wife."

Challon returned to the bedroom and closed the door. The woman in the corner had not moved. Bending, he lifted her gently and put her on the bed. In spite of her being the girl's aunt, Challon thought Tia Pozner was not more than ten years older than 'Lena. She had the same fine, delicate shape of head and feature and body, although she was shorter than her niece. The proudest kind of Spanish-American beauty, without

114

grossness in middle life.

As he removed the shreds of the woman's clothing Challon swore silently and steadily. There was a little modest lace on the undergarments and primness in their fit and fastenings. A merciless malice had been behind the treatment given Tia Pozner. A malice capitalizing on the knowledge that a woman of her race and kind would rather have the secrets of her soul turned out to public gaze than the clothing next to her skin; that she would not even appear before her husband in a lighted room in undress. The legend of wantonness in Spanish-American women was not something which had grown on the grass itself, but among those who came onto it as outlanders. And beyond the exceptions which proved the rule, it was wholly untrue.

Challon found a scarf on the dresser and a long kimono and slippers in a clothespress. He put these on the woman, wrapping the kimono well around her. He kicked the torn clothing he had removed well out of sight under the bed. And he spoke softly, steadily, gently, in Spanish. A knock sounded at the door. Bayard stood in the opening, holding a big, steaming china mug.

"Thought you'd be ready for this," he whispered. "Couldn't find Jim's whisky, but I had part of a bottle on my saddle. She all right?"

"I think so. Thanks, Hank."

He pushed the door closed again. Tia Pozner's eyes were still out of focus, her body limp, unresisting. Challon put the mug to her lips. She drank obediently. He continued to speak very quietly and with comfort in Spanish. The heat of the toddy began to take hold. The fixity in the woman's eyes faded. They moved slowly to Challon's face and seemed to reach through him. Suddenly they dropped to her own body, to the kimono wrapping it. They searched the floor swiftly, then darted back to Challon. He answered their unspoken question.

"I came in alone. The others are still outside. You'd fainted. I'm sorry we were late. Terribly sorry, señora. Tell me what happened."

A flimsy enough pretense to a woman who had never fainted in her life, but Tia Pozner's pride clutched at it. A little color returned to her cheeks. She raised her hand and explored the ugly bruise marring one side of her face. She used one of the crackling, multisyllabled expletives so rich in Spanish. And she began to talk. Slowly, at first, then with an accelerating rush. A stark account, without hysteria.

The three of them had been at supper: Pozner, his wife, and 'Lena. The Hyatts and Frank Germaine had come pounding in, all hard-eyed over a brush with the XO crew. Pozner cursed them roundly for their at-

116

tempted drive of XO stock so early in the game, calling them damned fools to go so far out on a shaky bridge. The Hyatts had bowed up under his lashing and had ridden off. Frank Germaine, with his eye as much on 'Lena as on Tia's supper, had stayed.

A few minutes later the dog had barked and was silenced with a shot. Riders poured into the yard. Germaine and 'Lena went out to investigate. 'Lena vanished and didn't return. Germaine ducked back into the house. The riders were from the XO. They had the Hyatt brothers tied in their saddles. They wanted Pozner and Germaine. Such was the woman's story, with her husband's innocence of the raid on XO cattle sworn to with righteous courage. The pattern of subsequent events within the house was hard to determine. Tia herself seemed uncertain. Challon filled in the gaps with angry, swift surmise.

Cy Van Cleave was not overly anxious for more prisoners than the two he already had tied in their saddles. From the doorway he demanded the surrender of the two men within the house. Germaine, too young to be afraid of man or god, had drawn his gun. Van Cleave had shot him. Efficient murder, whitewashed with the patina of tradition which took into no account the variance in skill between one man and another. Germaine had drawn first.

What followed had all too obviously been

an attempt to drive Jim Pozner into the same defiant flush of anger which had cost Germaine his life. Not quite as ruthless as it seemed, in inception at least. Tia Pozner was Mexican. To many men in the Territory, a Mexican woman was once removed from a Navajo squaw, and a Navajo woman was a poor trade for a stringhalted horse — not an individual, but one of a kind.

Tia had her courage and Pozner his. In the end she had been slapped into a corner and Pozner had been led out to be pushed into a saddle along with Ed and Simi Hyatt.

"They were taking them back to the XO?" Challon asked.

The woman shook her head.

"To Range. They said they were taking them to Range."

"And 'Lena? They must have gotten her too."

Tia's shrug was expressive. "They'd have been fools not to try. But they couldn't take that one quietly, and I heard no noise from the yard."

Challon pulled open the door.

"She'll be all right, then," he told the woman without surety. "You get some sleep. I'll have Jim back here in the morning."

"You?" Tia asked woodenly. "Why? He's been a burr in your back since he came here. You've wanted the lava open, and Jim has kept it organized and closed. It's open enough now, with him out of the way. And your hands are clean. Doesn't anything ever go wrong for a Challon?"

"This is wrong enough for me. I'm leaving a guard around the house. You better come into the town in the morning if I don't make it back."

Challon stepped on through the door and pulled it closed after him. Bayard was on the porch. The others were hunkered down in the yard, the whisky gone quietly out of them. Bayard straightened as Challon came out of the house.

"Put the boys in a ring, Hank," Challon ordered. "Don't let anybody near the house. Don't let Mrs. Pozner out till it's light. Start for Range with her as soon as you can after daybreak. But take it easy. They really gave her hell tonight."

"You're biting a big chunk, pulling out of here alone, Marc. You ain't Pierre."

"No," Challon agreed, "I'm not Pierre. I had Van Cleave square in my sights this afternoon and I let him ride out of them. That's a mistake I've got to correct."

"It'll be your last, then. I'll split the crew and come along with part of it."

"With Van Cleave and Perigord both sitting behind eared-back hammers in Range, waiting for me to come bowling in with you boys behind me? No. This I've got to handle alone. You're staying here till morning."

Challon swung into his saddle. Bayard hooked his stirrup leather.

"The hell with town, Marc!" he said with sudden savagery. "Get Prentice and that bitch at the XO. That'll choke off the rest. You've waited too long already!"

Challon heeled his horse without answer, and Hank's grip fell away.

7

It was a strange compulsion which drove Anson Prentice away from the ramada fronting the XO house. First he accused the soft night wind which came up as light failed. Then restlessness and uneasiness resulting from his talk with Marc Challon. A civilized man's instinctive reaction to the harsh brutality masked in Challon's quiet anger. Perhaps fear, but a physical fear. He would admit to no more than that.

Challon's anger, for all its unexpected quiet, was a physical anger. Finally, Prentice thought the reason he could not remain at the house was a principled courtesy within himself which demanded that Challon and Marcy have privacy for the talk Challon so obviously desired. They were, by the mere mechanics of long association, still at least partially man and wife.

But all of these things were self-delusive and a deliberate avoidance of fact. As he walked slowly across the ranch yard in the growing darkness, Prentice forced himself to this admission. He had given the relationship between Marcy and her husband no consid-

121

eration in the beginning. It was not be-
coming that he attempt to do so now. The
real reason he had quit the front of the
house was an uneasiness he always felt when
in or near the building. It was as though the
house were the heart of the Challon ranch,
with a pulse and life of its own, and the
ranch itself the entity to which the Challon
name belonged, rather than specifically to old
Pierre and his son.

He had taken Challon's wife. With Marcy
he now held legal title to the ranch. But
there were shadows within the house beyond
his reach. He had not touched the springs of
Marc Challon's existence. Perhaps he didn't
even understand them. And the house would
not accept Anson Prentice. He was alien to
it. He thought he would always remain so.

A slight edge had worked into the wind.
Prentice turned from the yard up onto the
porch of the ranch store. The door was pad-
locked. He felt the ring of keys at his belt. A
symbol of possession. He wondered what he
actually had here beyond this meaningless,
jangling ring of metal blanks. He fingered
through them for the one which fitted this
lock.

Anson had ordered the store closed when
Marcy and himself had come out from their
meeting with Challon in Treadwell's office in
Range. He had a purpose. The store was one
thing on the ranch he intended personally to

change. In the days of the Challons it had been open to every man on the pay roll and to such small neighbors as might find it convenient or necessary to trade on XO credit. Actually it was the root of an occasionally used system of peonage, and shrewd enough for that reason. Pay-roll hands were paid in cash only the difference between their earned wages and their account at the store. Neighbors who could not meet their account paid in land when there was nothing else with which to settle their bill. And land was always acceptable tender to a building ranch.

Sound enough business except that there were accounts as much as fifteen years in arrears with day-to-day purchases steadily increasing their totals and with no evidence of an attempt at collection at any time. Friends, Pierre Challon had once explained. Pensioners, Marc had called them. Both men had spoken in the same tolerant tone, apparently unconcerned at the swelling liability the store accounts represented.

There was something else wrong with the store. The XO bought in wholesale quantities for it, but from local suppliers in Range, agreeably paying the Range markup instead of dealing directly with big houses in the East. Yet those who traded in the store could buy any item on the shelves at a price as low or lower than that posted by the mercantile houses in town. An additional loss and deliberate ignorance of a potential source of profit. Challon had tried to explain this once too.

"Something as big as a ranch needs friends. The store costs something, of course, although I don't think we've ever figured out just how much. But it brings some folks onto the XO that might not come otherwise. And the prices we charge makes friends of them. Maybe that doesn't show on the ledgers, Anse, but it's important. You can fight like hell with your neighbors down here, but they're still neighbors and have to be treated as such. That's the grass. You'll see."

Anson did not see. Marcy had not allowed him as much time as he would have liked, but he had been thoroughly over the store books since he had ordered it closed. And he was close to the completion of a new plan of operation under which it could be made to show a profit. This plan was important, although he couldn't explain its importance to Marcy.

He had put a great deal of money into Marcy's scheme to take over the XO, but not wholly for Marcy herself. There was little accord between Anson Prentice and his father. What tie there was had been built on wealth — the desire of one to produce an heir capable of handling the paper empire and the power he had created; the desire of the other to be sufficiently suitable and in grace to inherit what the first had produced. Jason Prentice would understand about Marcy, all right. The woman part of it — her desirability. Before wheat trading and the railroad and advancing years had absorbed all of his energy, there had been body fires in Jason Prentice.

What the old man would not understand, what he would not believe, was that a sane man would pay a hundred and thirty thousand dollars for a woman for the single reason that she intoxicated him with a belief he was more virile and a more satisfactory companion than the man from whom he had taken her. Yet Anson was aware this was essentially exactly what he had himself done. The thing he had to avoid was the sacrifice of the balance of his inheritance for that same woman. And it troubled him gravely when he was apart from Marcy.

His work on the store books was behind this. Marc Challon's careless appraisal of the XO had worked to Anson's advantage. The old man would back him up on the figure at which he had bought Challon out. The old man would likely even be vastly amused that a woman had come along as boot in the deal, since the acreage involved made the thing financially sound beyond a doubt. But Marcy wanted more than just another man. Anson was aware of this. She wanted more than just the share Challon had granted her in the XO. She wanted full control — legal ownership of the man who held the balance of the title. She wanted a recognized claim on whatever Anson Prentice would have from his father. She wanted marriage. And the old man would raise hell at this.

There was one solution. If Anson took hold of the XO, if he showed management skill in its operation, the old man might concede Marcy was bringing his son something in compensation for what she wanted. Compensation was the keynote of Jason Prentice's life. If Marcy made a businessman out of his son, he would accept her on her own terms.

There was gall in this kind of thinking, but Anson knew himself and his father too well to avoid facts. And he knew his own limitations. He had no interest in the XO. He would not learn the cattle business. What he had seen of ranch management smelled too strongly of sweat and hard seasons. He had acquired the ranch only to acquire Marcy. If the XO was run, it would be by Marcy and the men she hired. But the matter of the store was no more than simple arithmetic and a little bookwork, and it could be dressed up into an appearance of shrewd thinking and an evidence of a flair for efficiency. As a beginning project it would make an arresting impression.

Prentice turned the key and the padlock fell open. He folded the hasp back and pushed the door inward. The dark interior of the store reached out with its mingled odors of foodstuffs confined in motionless air. He rasped a match to flame and lighted the tall lamp at one end of the counter. Almost immediately he saw the bedding shelf had been stripped of blankets. Raising the counter gate, he stepped through it. The displaced blankets had been loosely spread on the floor behind the counter, out of sight from the windows. A man lay huddled on them. One of the new hands who had arrived on the ranch with Cy Van Cleave. His dirty shirt was thick with hardening blood. Prentice knew by the color of his face that he was dead.

He tried to remember when he had seen a dead man before. Never like this, certainly. Not without the softening and impersonalization an undertaker achieved. Not when death was so bloody and ugly and there were neither tapers nor music in the background. He looked curiously at the man on the floor behind the counter because he had never really thought of death before, and it took him time to realize it could be like this.

Backing slowly through the counter, Anson returned to the door and closed it, shooting the night bolt on the inside without knowing why he did so. He trimmed the counter light a little lower and stepped back through the gate, kneeling beside the dead man with a steadiness which surprised him.

This was an XO hand. He was dead of a gunshot wound. A companion or companions, presumably also XO men, had hidden him in the locked store on the obvious assumption that his discovery here was unlikely. Prentice judged the man had been alive when he was carried in. The scant offering of comfort afforded by the blankets on the floor attested to that. Sometime during the previous night, probably very late. Not today, certainly, as the crew had quit the ranch early in the morning, immediately after a talk between Van Cleave and Marcy and a couple of brothers from out on the lava. And the crew had not returned. This man had been hidden here with Van Cleave's knowledge. There were only three keys to the lock on the door. Van Cleave had one of them.

Anson remembered a sharp question Marc Challon had asked him in front of the house. Something about looking in the XO corral for horses winded by a hard night ride southward over the mesas. Tensing with aversion, he searched the dead man's pockets. Cigarette makings. A knife with the bone gone from one side of the handle. A jumble of loose matches. Three clanking silver dollars and some change. In a breast pocket, stained along one edge by blood from the wound which had killed him, a thin packet of crisp bills in a wrapper bearing the imprint of

128

Donaldson and Kane, Kansas City — bankers to Jason Prentice and the Santa Fe.

Anson took only these, shaking out a fresh kerchief and wrapping them in it before shoving them into his own pocket. His breath was unsteady. After blowing twice across the chimney of the lamp without killing the light, he turned the wick down until it snuffed itself. He did not refasten the hasp and padlock on the door.

Coming up through the yard, he saw a big man swing onto a horse before the house. Recognizing Challon, he was momentarily tempted to call to him, knowing Marc would have an answer for this and an instant's decision. It was the decision Anse didn't want to make himself. But before he called Challon's name he remembered the chill and bitter hatred in Marc's eyes and he knew the time was past for help from a Challon in anything. For the first time he began to think beyond himself as far as Marcy was concerned. For the first time he stood in Challon's boots. For an instant he saw fully exactly what he had done to the man. He stood without movement, very quiet in the quiet yard, until Challon vanished toward the main gate.

When Marc was gone, Anson moved on toward the front of the house. He had nearly reached the ramada when another rider appeared out of the darkness. He must have passed Challon near the main gate, but, there had been no exchange of greeting. Anson lengthened his stride. The newcomer did not pull up at the head of the gravel path but came on diagonally across the carefully kept lawn. Prentice realized the man's horse was picking its own way without attention from its rider, that it was taking the shortest route to the corral. As he reached the lower end of the ramada, Anson heard Marcy's voice and realized she had come out of the house to watch Challon's departure.

"Quién es?" she asked in the universal night query of the country. The man in the saddle stiffened, lost his balance as a result of this shift, and spilled down. Marcy spoke again, something Anson did not clearly hear, and she leaped forward to half catch the man as he fell. The horse shied away and trotted across the lawn toward the work yard. Prentice reached Marcy as she straightened the man's body on the ramada flagging.

"Who is it?" he asked, repeating her question in English.

"Tom Halliard. Shot. Get his feet. We'll take him inside."

"How, Marcy?" Anson asked as he hooked the man's ankles.

"With a gun!" Marcy snapped. "Marc's gun!"

"I just saw Marc leave. There wasn't any shot."

"This afternoon, someplace on the lava. Not here. Marc was boasting about it to me. Here, get him up. He's too heavy for me."

Anson shifted his grip on Halliard's body and swung it up with a pulling effort. Marcy held the door open, then led the way swiftly back through the house to the kitchen. At a gesture from her he rolled Halliard onto the big kitchen worktable. Marcy came around with a lamp, and for the first time he saw Halliard's face. His gorge rose and the room tilted. He gripped the edge of the table hard. Marcy put the lamp down. She bent close to the injured man and began probing with forceps fashioned of thumb and index finger in the terrible wound which had opened Halliard's cheek. Anse clung to the table while she plucked out two brightly stained white fragments which he recognized with horror as teeth. Marcy slapped him hard with her eyes.

"You asked me if Marc was serious in his shooting talk the day we told him about us. He had his gun in his hand. He could have done this to you, Anson."

"My God, you mean this was deliberate?"

"A Challon can hit a fly on the wing with anything that will shoot. Bring me a sheet out of the press and a bottle of your whisky."

Anson reeled out of the room, thinking of mountains which exploded, raining rock over half a county, of grass as endless as the sea and in many ways as baffling, of a tall old man who went a strange place in search of a bride, and of a man so ruthless in anger that he would inflict on another the kind of wound Tom Halliard had brought back to the XO.

An hour later Halliard was in his bed in the bunkhouse with the yard boy sitting beside him, alternately listening to the unintelligible flow of his pain-laced profanity and helping him get the neck of the whisky bottle far enough into his shattered mouth to drink a little of the universal narcotic of the grasslands. Prentice had come back to the main house. Marcy, misunderstanding his purpose, had disappeared into her bedroom. He sat in the living room, hunched deep in a big chair, listening to the sound of water splashing in a basin as Marcy washed the marks of her crude, dispassionate surgery from her hands and arms.

There was war in Prentice. He had asked for some of this. He had believed there was hunger in him. He had thought he had a taste for the elemental and that contact with it would lift his pulse. Only Marcy had done that. What he had wanted in New Mexico he had not found. The one thing he might have wanted — the friendship of Marc Challon — would have cost him Marcy, and he had believed the price was too high.

The rest of this grass country was no different from Kansas or Missouri or Illinois. Essentially unfriendly, distrusting him for no better reason than the tailoring marks on his clothes and his father's name on the letterheads of the Santa Fe. Small and busy people, engrossed by their own way of life, unwilling to open a door to it for him, and both unwilling and unable to understand his need. All but Marcy. He was grateful to her because of this and at war now because, for the first time, he was forced to take a stand he knew instinctively she would oppose.

She came out presently, smiling a little because she believed she knew not only his features but his thoughts. She had dressed in a soft white blouse and a plain skirt cut at shoe-top height. Her arms and face glowed with soaping and toweling. She looked young almost to a point of girlishness. Almost, but not quite. The full challenge of a woman's wisdom was in her eyes. She dropped onto the arm of his chair. The fingers of one hand slid under the uneven lie of his thin hair, ruffling it.

"Poor Anse," she said softly. "It takes such a long time to get used to the grass."

"I've got to go into Range tonight, Marcy."

The fingers retraced their path across his scalp, ending with a quick, gentle tug on the cowlick which would not lie straight from his crown.

"Why? There's nothing you'd want in Range tonight you couldn't find here on the XO, even if you did lock up the store."

"Halliard — that face — he ought to have a doctor — tonight!"

"What could a doctor do that we haven't already done? Marc is thorough. I've told you that before. No doctor could do anything for that face. Even Halliard doesn't care about it now. He wants it to stop hurting him, maybe. But mostly he wants to get back on his feet so he can go hunting for Marc Challon. That's all. Ask him. He'll tell you."

"The shooting ought to be reported — and Marc — if he did it."

"Is your nose turning blue, Anson?" Marcy asked. "What ought and ought not to be done! From you! We'll do best to keep all the XO business we can out of Range. Having everything that happens out here talked about in town won't help any. Van Cleave and the crew will show up sometime tonight. They'll take care of Halliard and anything involving him that needs attention. They're his friends. Give them time. They'll take care of Marc. They understand their business. They'll earn their pay. You and I have no need to take any night rides."

"Just how do you take care of a man like Marc Challon, Marcy?"

She frowned a little. "Break him. Hit him hard and break him into a million pieces that can't be put together again. If he won't break that small, you drive him. You drive him hard till he quits the country."

"But if he doesn't quit?"

"You kill him, Anse. I told you Cy Van Cleave knows his business."

"You're talking murder!"

"I'm talking common sense, and you know it. We quit worrying about Marc Challon months ago, both of us. We're the ones who are important. Marc can't scare Van Cleave, Anse. He can't scare us while Van Cleave is on the XO. A man doesn't get to be called a rattlesnake in this country for nothing!"

"I'm not worrying about Challon. I'm worrying about us. Halliard isn't the only man on the place with a bullet in him tonight. There's a dead man behind the counter in the store. One of Van Cleave's men. This was in his pocket." Anson unwrapped the thin stained packet of bank notes. "My father's in Trinidad. You read the letter he sent me by messenger about the holdup last night. You remember he said he was writing Sheriff Perigord too. I'm sorry, Marcy, but I've got to go into Range tonight. Perigord has got to know about this."

Marcy ruffled the bills, then tossed them onto a table.

"Can't the railroad take care of its own business? Haven't you enough to keep you busy here, Anse?"

She leaned farther on the arm of his chair. Her eyes lengthened. Her lips parted a little.

"Haven't you, Anse?"

She leaned still farther on the chair arm, farther toward him. She repeated her question, softly and insistently. Prentice did not know if she finally lost her balance or if he pulled her toward him. Her hair was in his face, choking him.

"Yes!" he said hoarsely. "Tomorrow, then. Tomorrow I've got to see Perigord. . . ."

Marcy laughed softly. She straightened a little. He thought it was a sigh. It wasn't. It was an intake for a sudden explosion of breath which blew out the lamp.

8

The fire in Marc Challon's camp under
Tinaja was in embers, a red eye in the night.
The acrid, unpleasant odor of burned wool
was in the air. From the last ridge 'Lena had
been certain the camp was deserted, but she
approached the stone fire circle cautiously.
The dust about it was heavily tracked. A
fused crust overlay the coals. Bedrolls, spare
blankets, duffel, even a saddle, retained their
shapes in ash. She moved down to the
cooking shelter. The meager supplies and
equipment within it had been methodically
destroyed. Beyond, a gap had been torn in
the brush corral.

Challon's cavvy of horses was gone. They
were XO stock. They were good animals,
trained for rangework. They had undoubtedly
been scattered, but by morning they would
be standing against the XO fence nearest the
home coral. They would be hard to retake.
Cy Van Cleave had been as thorough here as
he had been at Pozner's, although the work
was different.

'Lena moved away from the unpleasant
odor of the fire and sank down on a patch of

grass. She felt steadier. The sting of her brush burns and scratches was subsiding. The fear which had run with her through the barrancas from her aunt's place was something she could now take in her hands, containing and compressing it, so that there was room in her mind for thought.

Marc Challon and Bayard and the others had been in the camp earlier in the evening. Supper sign was about. That it had not been cleaned up was evidence of a hasty departure. Then the XO had moved in, likely passing her in the malpais and coming here direct from Pozner's. Challon and Bayard and their crew could have been traveling in the opposite direction, but on a higher and shorter track. Challons were direct men in a hurry, and Bayard and the others would have learned from them.

Waiting here was difficult, yet there was nothing more to be done. The horses she had hoped to find were gone. And even with a saddle under her, there was no further place to go. Range, perhaps, and small people there who would share her fury but who would not buck the XO under any management. Small people who would talk much and earnestly under their own roofs but who would say nothing in defense of a man from the lava on a street where Hugh Perigord walked. The shadow of the Challons was deeply etched across the doorways of Red

River County. Only a Challon could change its pattern.

This was 'Lena's belief. It was for this that she had ridden out of Range with Marc Challon. A belief that in the quiet, towering anger of his battle for his pride and his land against a woman who had been his wife Challon could be made to see that, while he and his father had built much in this country, others had built, also, and that the XO iron was not burned into the mortar of every mud wall between Tinaja and the foot of Boundary Mesa.

It was a belief for which 'Lena had to fight, even within herself, for she had not lied here under Tinaja when she had said that all who knew her knew also that she had always wanted Marc Challon. Not the XO. Not the ranch. What could any piece of land be to a woman but a roof over her head, a right to a little pride among her neighbors, and a source of living? It did not take a hundred thousand acres to enclose her desires. Four walls would do as well. Four walls and Marc Challon. A physical want, like that for food, with its own kind of hunger. And sometimes as intolerable to bear.

Still, she could not quite sacrifice her belief for the man. And her greatest fear was that this decision would be forced upon her. She had not thought in the beginning that Marc

Challon was married to so dangerous a woman.

'Lena had been fifteen minutes in the camp — she had barely steadied her breathing after her stumbling run through the brush from Pozner's — when she heard horses on the slope above her. Alarm clamped tightly about her throat. She had expected one horse returning, or a dozen; not two. There was no shelter. She flattened on the grass where she had been sitting. A moment later Challon rode down from the ridge, leading an unsaddled animal.

With her cheek pressed against the sod 'Lena watched him ride toward the dying embers within the fire circle with a duplication of her own cautious approach, his big and loosely built body almost shapeless in the saddle, completely masking the fact it was a tightly coiled spring, requiring only a trigger touch to explode.

The lead horse, she thought, was one of those released by the XO from the breached corral. A rangeman's skills were his instincts. It was not hard to understand in this moment why the two Challons had been able to build an empire while others who sprang from the same roots built nothing.

'Lena knew she didn't understand all that was at work within Marc Challon's mind, but she understood enough to realize the burden with which he rode tonight. Yet the working man within him continued to function, perhaps automatically. In the middle of a hurried ride from one place of violence to another he had found time to work a stranded, drifting horse from some brush pocket and trail it in with him on a lead rope. He knew the animal was his own. That it was drifting in the night when he had left it securely corralled with others could mean many things. But this was certain in his mind: a drifting horse, pocketed in the brush, was valueless, while one at hand, ready to ride, had worth. So he had noosed the animal and trailed it in.

While she watched, Challon went directly to the corral, studied the breach in the fence briefly, and tethered the strayed animal to a post. From this he went to the cooking shelter and then to the fire. 'Lena lay in the grass, watching him and silent. This had been his camp. His enemies had done this damage. And she knew a man was universally like a child, wanting privacy when he was hurt. Perhaps a woman was comfort. She wasn't sure just what a woman was to this kind of man. But not in the first moments, when the sting was sharp. Later. Perhaps later.

'Lena lay motionless, holding a tight check on her own uncertainties, her fears, her almost certain knowledge of what had happened at Jim Pozner's place after she had herself slipped into the brush. She lay motionless until Marc Challon straightened from the tracked dust about the fire, turning slowly through the full arc of a circle, and called her name. Quietly, experimentally, but with a deep concern and perhaps a fear. She didn't move even then, until he had called a second time and she was sure of the concern and the fear and of something else. Then she rose and answered him:

"*Aquí*, Marc. Here."

Challon came swiftly toward her. Big hands closed on the points of her shoulders with savage tightness. There was so much a man could say to a woman without words.

"You were looking for me?" she asked. "You expected to find me here?"

"I didn't know when I came in. I was just hoping. Your aunt didn't know where you had gone — what had happened to you."

"But you called my name — twice."

"Your tracks were down by the fire, on top of all the others, fresh."

A little brightness dimmed in 'Lena. A rangeman's instincts again. Footprints in the dust. Not a need which had to be voiced because it could no longer be contained.

"Tia?" she asked, afraid of the answer to this question. "Tia is — is —"

"All right," Challon said quietly. "Roughed up, 'Lena. Roughed up pretty badly, inside and out. But she had more sand than they did. She's all right now. Bayard and the boys are with her. They'll stay with her."

'Lena exhaled slowly, letting out the tightness which had been threatening to choke her. Cy Van Cleave had won in many ways the name attached to him. And one of these had been with women. Tia Pozner was young enough for beauty still, and her tongue was Spanish-Mexican. 'Lena had not thought Van Cleave would be in such a hurry as this — that he would not have time for anything beyond roughness. She would not herself have run so desperately through the brush if she had known there would be only this.

Tia would have fought at anything beyond mishandling, and all the Territory knew that Van Cleave could not resist a woman who fought.

"Jim is all right too, I think," Challon went on. "They loaded him into a saddle, the same as the Hyatts, and took him off with them. But not hurt."

"Frank?"

"Germaine is dead," Challon said bluntly. "He wasn't as smart as Jim, as your aunt. He bowed up. Van Cleave got him. Frank should have known."

A flat and dispassionate condemnation of a dead man. A man who a few hours ago had been sitting across a supper table from her, talking about the year after next and the one beyond that, when everything would be different. When there would be rails into Range and the XO would be cut down to size. When Washington would have done something about inclusion of the orphaned Strip in some neighboring state or territory so that it would be no longer a lawless haven. When more people with the stain of the soil under their nails and the shine of a saddle on their pants would have come down over the pass into New Mexico, some of them even into the lava.

A time when the law would no longer be a personal thing of one man against another and there would be justice which weighed evenly on both sides of the scales. Frank Germaine had talked eagerly about this time when a man could do well enough on even a small piece of ground if he worked it. 'Lena had known as he talked that he would never see these things because he had no roots and would grow none and because there was a monotony to labor he could never endure.

Still, he talked of a time which would certainly come, and it had been good to listen to such talk in a homestead on the lava from one of a kind of men whose existence delayed its coming. It had been good to sit erect, keeping her shoulders squared and her shirt tight, knowing Frank Germaine wanted her to lean a little toward him so that the collar of her shirt would slacken and he could watch the changing shadow in the

144

hollow of her throat as he talked. He was personable and talked well and he laughed easily.

Now he was dead and Marc Challon was condemning him without resentment as a fool because he had not known, as Tia and Jim Pozner and Challon himself knew, that life was more important on the grass than pride or principle or belief. You swallowed these when there was necessity, or you died. And the kind which stood against a challenge for one of these could not survive — because they were fools. They died when they should have known that a struggle here was a grim thing and only those strong enough to control themselves were strong enough to exist.

Marc Challon had surrendered his ranch because he played at poker and intended to win on the last turn of the cards. Jim Pozner watched the hands of other men on his wife without releasing the protest livid within him because he wanted to live. Tia was roughed — roughed badly, Marc had said — without whimpering or retaliation of her own because she, also, wanted Jim to live. 'Lena Casamajor rode into the lava with a man she loved, knowing she was involving herself and her friends in the malpais in that man's personal quarrel, because she wanted him in the end. They were the strong ones. Frank Germaine was a fool.

"You're going back to the ranch, Marc?"

she asked. Challon shook his head.

"No. I was there once today. That's enough. There's nothing to do at the ranch. Not now. Van Cleave was taking Jim and the Hyatts into town. Now that I've located you and you're all right, I'm going into Range. You go on back to Pozner's. You stick with Hank and your aunt. You'll be all right. Hank's got his orders."

"There's nothing you can do in town, Marc," 'Lena said softly. "You must know that. Jim wasn't with Frank and the Hyatts. He was angry as the devil with them for trying that drive. But they did and Van Cleave caught them at it. It can be proved. This is the thing Perigord's been waiting for. The day the law could put a loop onto Jim and the others out here. The day you and your father have been waiting for. The day the XO could ride the lava as freely as it rides the rest of the grass. Nobody is going to believe Jim's story. Nobody is going to believe he wasn't with that drive along the trail into the Strip."

Marc Challon flexed his hands and began drawing on the gloves he had peeled off as he came up to her.

"The hell they won't!" he said. "Jim's got a good witness. I was on the rim above that drive today!"

'Lena felt muscles across her belly tighten. Germaine and the Hyatts had speculated on

146

the identity of the rifleman above the trail who had broken up the XO trap into which they had been driving. At supper Germaine had concluded the marksman had been a drifter from the Strip who had bought himself a few chips in the game opening up below him on the off-chance of edging into a claim on a share of the stolen beef when it was safely across the mesa. Neither Jim Pozner nor Germaine had considered Marc Challon.

He was, they believed, bluffing. They were convinced he would lose his shirt in all of this because he had been too long accustomed to hiring others to build what pressure he needed. It was a strange thing that Tia's husband and Germaine and the rest could hate a man as long and battle him as constantly as they had Marc Challon and still have no real measurement of him. Marc was not bluffing. It was doubtful he had ever bluffed in his life.

"You're not the XO now, Marc," she said earnestly. "They won't believe you in town, either. Van Cleave is the XO — Van Cleave and your wife. Range will listen to the two of them. Unless the rest of the men out here in the lava bunch together strongly enough to break them out of jail, Perigord will hang the Hyatts and he'll hang Jim. Don't go into Range tonight. There's nothing you can do alone!"

"Maybe not with Van Cleave; maybe not even with Perigord. But I can do something with the town, and Perigord and Van Cleave can't either one of them buck practically every vote in the county! I promised Tia Pozner I'd have her husband back for breakfast. After tonight, that's a promise I'd like to keep!"

"I'd like to see you keep it," 'Lena said. "But, Marc, don't be a fool — like Frank Germaine! There isn't anything in this county but the XO. Don't you understand? The Challons made it like that. People in Range won't listen to you, even when they know you're telling the truth. They have forgotten how to buck the XO and they won't listen to you if you try to tell them how, now. They won't follow you if you try to show them. And if you did succeed in stirring them up, you'd finish forever your chance of getting back the same ranch you released to Anson Prentice and your wife. They're my people in town; I know them."

"Then I won't persuade them to back me. I'll make them do it," Marc said bluntly. "If I helped make them knuckle to the ranch, I can make them knuckle to me, at least long enough to get Jim clear — and to hell with the XO beef the Hyatts tried to steal! It isn't their first try and the first time they failed; I want them clear too."

"Listen to me, Marc, please," 'Lena

begged. "It wasn't your fists or the men you hired that made the XO what it was when you left it. It was something inside of you. Something a lot of folks hated, maybe because they were afraid of it, but something they admired, just the same. Bigness, I guess. I don't know another word. Your father had it and you had it. The knuckling by the rest was to that. Now it's gone. You've given up your ranch for no reason anyone can see well enough to believe in. You've run your father off to Denver, and Pierre Challon's been as important to Range since anybody can remember as the road over Boundary Mesa. You've cozied up with Jim and the rest out here on the lava after publishing everybody out here for years as outright outlaws.

"Folks trusted you, even when they hated you, because your judgment was sound. You're off the XO and they've got nothing but recollections to hate you for now. But they won't trust you. There are only two people in Red River County who don't think you're a damned fool, and I'm not even sure of one of those. You're one and I'm the other, Marc. I tell you, you can't do anything in town and you'll be walking right in where both Van Cleave and Hugh Perigord want you!"

Challon frowned, pulling again at his gloves. Suddenly he turned and headed back toward his horse. 'Lena walked beside him, hoping he could see what she had tried to tell him. She didn't want an admission of understanding from him, only the knowledge that he knew she had spoken the truth. He gave her no sign.

"You head on out to Pozner's," he said abruptly. "Ride that bay I brought in from the brush. You can handle her. Tell Hank Bayard we're burned out here. Might as well head-quarter at Pozner's now. We're all in the same kettle, for fair. Tell Hank to have a couple of the boys salvage what they can here in the morning. Then sit tight. Tell him I've changed my mind about his bringing your aunt into town in the morning. Tell him to stay out here with the boys until he hears from me."

"Will he believe a message I deliver?"

"He better!" Challon said grimly. He swung into his saddle. "You tell him that too. *Adiós, chinita*." He reined away.

'Lena waited patiently until he was out of earshot, then quieted the bay he had led in out of the brush and climbed onto the animal's back. She could think of only one thing which could be done now. A thing which would take precious time but which could be shortened by driving straight for the pass, missing Range altogether, relying on people of her own blood along the way.

Marc Challon needed help, and in 'Lena's mind there was only one source from which it could now come. No man was ever sufficient unto himself.

9

Range lay on the grass at the foot of the mesa, lights down, like a woman waiting for a man; silent, eyes closed, and slow of breath, but expectant and so very awake. Marc Challon paused at the willows at the edge of town where 'Lena had met him at the beginning of their ride into the lava. The courthouse, containing Perigord's office and the single row of barred cells across the back in which Jim Pozner and the Hyatts would be waiting in bitterness and with little hope for eventual release, stood slightly apart from neighboring buildings.

Across the street, so wide here as to be almost a square, was the Palace Hotel, in which a lobby light burned. Two doors away, its rack lined solidly with riding stock, much of it bearing the sear of the XO iron, was the Red River Saloon. There was a glow from it, also, although the light inside was reduced to a single lamp or the others were trimmed low.

It was strange that, when men were uneasy or facing something which forced a decision of which they were not sure, they wanted little light about them. A man could fumble in movement or judgment in dim light and the error would be invisible to others. Van Cleave would be in the Red River. There would be Van Cleave men in the lot behind the courthouse. A man like Van Cleave clung to life only by precaution, and attention to this sort of detail became second nature to his kind.

Perigord was different. Perigord had no men behind him; only a star. Perigord would be in his office. On occasion one man could be harder to face than a dozen, but the prisoners in the cells were Perigord's prisoners — as long as he could hold them. Challon reined out from the willows and rode into the street, keeping close to the walk which passed before the courthouse and leaving a wider distance between himself and the door of the Red River, so that his intention was plain.

The tip of a cigarette glowed brightly in the shadows at the corner of the courthouse as Challon dismounted. A boot scraped on the walk across the street, and he knew without turning that at least one man had come out of the Red River. Somewhere farther into town, at some distance, a man whistled — a brief, single note in the night air. Challon felt for a moment as he had at meetings of stockmen in years which were gone. Casual meetings and purposeful ones, involving Pierre and himself. Meetings in which the talk was in part of the times, the grass, and the beef, and in part of the growth of the XO when others could not increase. Talk on the lips of resentful men who saw before them, day by day, the Challon way of building, but who did not build, themselves.

It was the same thing now. The fleeting of opportunity. Two men in Range tonight would gratefully buy all the whisky the town could hold in exchange for Marc Challon's death. One had been hired by a woman to break Marc Challon and would add enormously to his own peculiar stature by killing Challon. The other had been elected to office by the XO and could easiest break the domination which had actually made him for years an XO employee by putting a bullet into Challon's body. This was their opportunity. There was no legality in Challon's presence or purpose here. Yet both of these men were waiting — one because he lacked confidence, and the other because he owned too much.

This was not the Challon way. A man's death was the last necessity in the building of the XO or in its preservation. But when that necessity arose, the man died. And there was no calculation, before or afterward, as to whether he should be shot in the back or shot in the belly. There was no waiting.

Perigord's door in the face of the courthouse was not locked. Challon pushed it open and stepped into the darkened room. The one gleam of light traveled the length of a connecting corridor from a bracketed lamp on the wall outside the cell gates. Challon wanted to do Perigord justice. As nowhere else in Range tonight, this dimness was not out of a desire for cloaking darkness but because a man within an unlighted room could more clearly see through his windows the movements of others on the night-shrouded street. Perigord was behind his desk, hunched a little forward, stiffened with resolve, but wary. When the door latched closed behind Challon, he spoke.

"Marc, you've got no business here!"

"I think so," Challon corrected. "A lot of it. I didn't have time to listen to you out at my supper fire on the lava tonight. Hank Bayard convinced me. The Santa Fe sent you out for the pelts of the outfit that sprung the road's pay chest last night. Hank claimed you believed one of those pelts was mine, and you wanted it tonight. That sure as hell is my business!"

"That isn't what brought you in here now."

"No. But we'll settle it first."

Perigord leaned back a little. "All right, Marc. Were you up on the Santa Fe line in the pass last night?"

"Have I ever wanted another man's money — another outfit's money — enough to go after it with a gun? You know me better than that, Hugh. Land, maybe, never cash. I don't want the Santa Fe hurt or its line slowed. Those rails mean a lot to the XO —"

"But not to you, Marc. Not now. Prentice has a stake in the road through his old man. You hate Prentice. I don't judge that, but you're going to have to prove where you were last night when that holdup was pulled. If you can't, I'm going to lock you up. I have to."

"Tonight?"

Perigord smiled a little, deprecatingly.

"Kind of operating a full house out back tonight," he said. "No, Marc. I'll come after you when I want you. Now, line out of here. Get back out on the grass. Don't stack the tally against you any higher than it already is. Get out of the Territory!"

"I promised Jim Pozner's wife his company at breakfast, Hugh. I run a little short on time. Give me your keys — or open up those cells back there. All kinds of tallies are being stacked tonight. Be careful you don't draw the steepest count."

Challon lifted his hand and let Perigord see for the first time the gun which he had drawn as he swung down from his horse at the rail outside. A soft exhalation escaped the sheriff of Red River County, as though this was satisfaction — the thing for which he had been waiting. He pushed slowly back from his desk and rose to his feet.

155

"You can't do this, Marc," he said without real meaning in his words. "I'm holding those men on a proper complaint."

"Signed by Cy Van Cleave!" Challon cut in sharply. "You're wrong about something, Hugh. Nothing has changed so much you can start telling me what I can't do. Pozner wasn't with the bunch that tried to drive some XO beef today. And the drive broke up, anyway. I want those men back out on the lava. That should be enough for you. Open the gates, Hugh."

Perigord shrugged. Turning, he walked back along the corridor toward the cells, moving into the light. Challon followed him. Simi Hyatt was pressed against the gate of his cell. He had heard them coming. He said something softly. Ed Hyatt and Jim Pozner appeared at the next two gratings to the left of him. The three of them eyed Perigord and Challon with wooden faces. There was a small, musical, metallic sound as Perigord pulled on a belt chain, drawing his bunched keys from his pocket. He stopped and looked at Challon, respecting the gun in his hand but wholly unafraid of it. Jim Pozner spoke through the bars of his cell gate.

"You cut it thin, Challon," he said. "There's light in the east already!" Then, his mind shifting to another channel, "Tia?"

"All right, Jim. Worried about you, but all right."

Pozner dropped his hands from the bars in front of him and stepped back as Perigord approached the lock. Challon shoved his gun back into its holster and watched Perigord finger unhurriedly through his keys. Simi Hyatt spat through his grating.

"Hank and your boys sure come in quiet, Challon. How's it feel to have a town so hand-whipped it won't chew at you, even when you're left without a leg to stand on?"

"My legs are all right, Simi. I came in here on them. Damn you, Hugh, get a move on!"

"Alone!" Jim Pozner grunted. "You wall-eyed fool!" He thrust through the grating at Perigord, shoving him a little off balance. "Get away from that lock! Challon, can't you see they've been waiting for this? You're the same breed as we are now. Lava dust is on you. Hugh, here, and Van Cleave, and the whole damned town — waiting! Hugh and Van Cleave with their reasons and the town with its own. The lava bunch trying to break jail. An easy way to wind up a lot of trouble the whole county is fed up with."

Hugh Perigord caught his balance and swung around so that his back was flat against the panel of plaster between the cells occupied by Pozner and Ed Hyatt. His keys had dropped from his hand and hung a little above one knee, swinging on their chain.

"*Ley de fuga*," Pozner continued bitterly. "Law of escape. Odds are better for us before a bribed judge than they are now, Challon! If you'd brought your boys in —"

Pozner was angry and afraid. A hard, honest fear, with no cowardice in it. It poured through the cell gate like something tangible, washing about Challon and penetrating him. Range was his town. His shadow was on it. There was bitterness under that shadow and resentment and perhaps certain injustices, but there was also respect. He had believed this was the one thing of which Marcy could not strip him. He had always been a hundred thousand acres, but he had also been a man. The land was gone, but the stature remained. He was Marc Challon.

He looked now in a swift instant of appraisal at Hugh Perigord and saw that to this man Marc Challon was now only a substance of bone and sinew and blood, an obstacle and an enemy. So there was a trap here. And Range, knowing it, feigned sleep, waiting for it to close — waiting for a little fury and the end of the lava bunch — the end of trouble which had bred steadily there for a generation between small and stubborn men who did not love the law, and the expanding body of the XO. To Range, the end of the Challons had already occurred; Pierre had gone to Denver and his son had surrendered what he had built to a woman.

Somewhere up front there was sound. Dawn wind against a loose casement — or a door latching softly open. Perigord's shoulders were tight against the plaster panel behind him, his hands hanging loosely at the ends of slightly bowed arms. His eyes were steadily on Challon's face.

A breath of outer air made the flame in the bracketed lamp waver. It did not change the quality of the light, since dawn was half over the eastern horizon and gray brilliance was visible beyond the small, high windows in the cell row. Somewhere on the street outside a man swore suddenly. The single lip-shaped, clearly whistled note Challon had heard earlier sounded again. This was followed immediately by the hammer of running horses on hard adobe street earth. Hugh Perigord tipped out a little from the wall, unrest suddenly in his eyes.

"Marc, I'm halfway sorry —" he said.

Jim Pozner shouted. Perigord reached for his gun. Challon flung himself a little aside in a flattening twist which carried him into the mouth of the corridor, and he snapped his own weapon upward from his belt. He knew he would be hit, but he had an instant of hard, sure satisfaction that he would kill Hugh Perigord in this exchange. Then, before Perigord fired — before Challon himself was braced for hurt — a tremendous blow struck the flat of his back, driving him stumblingly and helplessly forward onto his knees and then onto his face. His lips were crushed

159

against the worn pine flooring before he heard the shot, and then only dimly, echoing and re-echoing in ragged cadence in the corridor, in the street outside, and in his head.

10

Prentice did not sleep. The narcotic of Marcy's lips, her embrace, failed in effect when he needed it most. The room was hot, oppressive. There was no air movement, although he could hear a breeze stirring outside. He remembered an evening during his first weeks on the XO. Marc Challon and Bayard and the crew had been gone, working high meadows on top of Boundary Mesa. The bunkhouse and the yard were empty. Marcy had left half a bottle of whisky where the cook would find it and had sent the yard boy on a needless errand to Range in the buckboard.

It was full dark, a soft night, and warm. They were sitting on a rustic bench under the cottonwoods on the east side of the house, watching a moon of enormous size pull up out of the lava country. His impatience and eagerness in those first weeks made Prentice vaguely sick in recollection now, but they had been things he could not contain then. He had touched Marcy and she had risen abruptly, returning to the house.

It was an hour later, in Challon's study,

with the night securely shut away behind closed doors and windows, that he learned Challon's wife had not been retreating from his caress, but from the openness of the night. He had known then that there was a dark and privy corner of Marcy's nature which could not bear the free inspection of the night wind and the dark sky or so impersonal a witness as the yellow moon. She required full dark and walls and a ceiling and the certainty of closed doors. It was not modesty. What Marcy cultivated in the night darkness of the house was a thing which could not flourish in open air.

The windows of the house were tightly closed now. Prentice stirred restlessly. He could hear Marcy's breathing, deep and steady, a little stertorous for one so young and slender of body. She was at peace, secure from the night and from consideration of the problems alive on the grass. A clear conscience could sleep so soundly, and Prentice understood. There was no conscience in Marcy.

Moving cautiously, Prentice rose. Carrying his clothes, he moved down the hall and dressed in the study. He smelled sweat and remembered this was a big man's room — Marc Challon's room — that he was an alien in this house, regardless of his position with Marcy, the money he invested here, or the documents which had been signed. Time

162

would not change this.

He was nearly dressed before he realized the faint, acrid odor of which he had been aware came from his own clothes, and the realization tightened a muscle in his throat, as though his gorge was unsteady there.

Wind outside came across the corral, and there was another odor. He had been on the grass long enough to have become accustomed to it, even to realize there was a sweetish quality to it which could approach pleasantness. But it was the odor of dung, and when he moved into the dark barn to take his usual saddle horse from its stall, he realized he had been careless in stepping and had dung on his feet.

He felt unsteady under a wave of mental nausea. Over the pass, at Trinidad or somewhere along the Santa Fe division to the eastward, a grim, gray old man was building miles of track in his mind tonight. Track which would be put down across this high, barren country and across which Santa Fe trains would roll. Track which would funnel even more profits into the Prentice fortune.

And somewhere in the back of Jason Prentice's mind he would be thinking of his son. He was a tired man and old, and if the building of the Santa Fe was for anything, it was for the boy he had raised. Young Anson, whom he did not know — whom he had never known. Young Anson, for the first time showing evidence of the complete willfulness and strength which had made his father a wealthy man. Anson wanted a woman. Neither the fact that she was the wife of a powerful and dangerous man nor that she was probably a thorough bitch had made any difference. Anson had faced down the husband, buying him helplessly and completely out of the way, and he had taken the woman.

Not Jason's exact way of doing things, but similar enough. Not the kind of woman Jason had ever wanted, but a decisive action, and therefore good. The first broad stroke Anson had ever made. Not right, perhaps, but ethics were something a rich man and the son of a rich man could not afford. There was iron in Anson or he could not have done this. There was courage. And time would temper iron into the steel a man needed to stand on his feet and cast his shadow apart from others.

This was Jason Prentice's thinking. This was the satisfaction he drew from his son's presence on the XO. And knowing these thoughts, Anson felt fouled by more than the dung on his boots. He knew the thing within him. Not iron. Not steel. Not courage. With utterly ruthless self-analysis, he knew he was a complete coward.

He had feared his own desires when he had first met Marcy Challon and he had acceded to them. He had feared Marcy's confident dominance and had ensnared himself

164

further in it because he could not escape. He knew he didn't love Marcy Challon — only the feeling of virility and strength she engendered in him — the elation of possessing something a titan like Marc Challon had been unable to hold.

That it seemed to him now his possession had been empty, that Marcy spent favor as he had been raised to spend his father's money, prodigally, if necessary, to accomplish an end, made no final difference. He was afraid to afford pride now. He was afraid he would lose the empty thing Marcy had given him, and the fear was of the losing, not the loss.

His horse saddled, Prentice rode cautiously across the ranch yard. The crew had not come back, Van Cleave and the others. A light still burned in the bunkhouse where Tom Halliard lay, cursing with the pain of his torn face. The door of the ranch store was still unlocked, and a man lay dead behind the counter there. Abreast of the house, Prentice drew up for a moment.

Marcy was sleeping inside. He could return to her. Shelter was there for as long as there was money in his accounts and influence in his family and no greater opportunity arose to tempt Marcy into another stride along the road she traveled. There would be no demand made of him and no recrimination offered, and he would still encounter the

165

occasional lust of a kind of woman he had never known before and would never know again.

But there was also emptiness. A realization had come with Marcy's deep and steady breathing with him in the room tonight. He had never owned her. Marc Challon had never owned her. By a queer obtuseness of event, he had hurt Challon a great deal less than he had done him a service. Marcy was using one of them as she had used the other, savoring neither as a man and seeing only usefulness where each had fancied strength.

Prentice money had bought nothing on the XO. The Prentice mark was on nothing about the ranch now. And without an actual personal stake in it, Anson recognized fully for the first time that he was deep into a vicious struggle. He feared the impending violence of this more than he feared anything else. He had to find a way out while there was a way still open to him.

Gigging his horse into motion, turning his back on the first faint promise of day already beginning to lighten the eastern horizon, he took the road to Range.

There was a willow clump at the eastern edge of town. Prentice pulled up there, reaching into his pockets. He regretted he had not reordered the expertly fashioned Turkish cigarettes a Chicago tobacconist had

166

been making up for him for years. Hank Bayard had made a comment about them once, and Anse had tried hard to fare with the sacked leaf choppings and loose cigarette papers of the Territory since. However, his hands were too unsteady now. On the third attempt he gave up, wryly admitting to himself he had no desire for a smoke, but was instead wrestling with indecision.

What he did now took him out of the audience of the interested, where he had been sitting, and shoved him out on the stage, in the middle of whatever might come from here on. A private corner of the stage, he was afraid, where he would have to stand alone. And maybe it was the prospect of that aloneness which troubled him most. As he had felt much earlier in this interminable night, he experienced a desire again to talk to Marc Challon — a need for Challon's blunt, curiously direct counsel. But Challon would be hard to find and harder to make listen. There was only Sheriff Perigord left. Perigord was the law and he had made overtures to the Santa Fe people. The letter from Prentice's father concerning the pay-roll robbery had expressed wary confidence in the officer.

Anse knew there would be only Perigord here. He had known it when he left the ranch. But still he did not ride on past the willows marking the outer limits of Range.

167

He studied the street, seeing many horses he thought belonged to the XO racked in front of the saloon and the hotel across from the courthouse, and a single big-bodied animal in front of the courthouse itself.

He saw a man beyond the county building and another under the awning fronting the saloon. The XO horses meant Van Cleave and the new XO crew were here. Anse wondered if Perigord would be a sufficient defense against Van Cleave and decided he would, here in town at least. But still he made no move to ride on up the street.

He wondered if the sheriff of Red River County, even with the weight of the Prentices and the railroad behind him, would possess enough raw sand to serve a warrant on Van Cleave and those who had ridden into the pass with him when he learned of the proof against them lying dead behind the counter in the XO store. He decided there was only one way to find out about this, but still he didn't ride into the street.

He was wondering about nothing but the sickening depths of his own fears when the sound of a bunch of hard-ridden horses rose behind him, coming in with the increasing dawn-light along the road from the east. Anse had no choice then other than to be flushed out by those behind him as they came through the willows.

Traversing the lower hundred yards of the

street with the party from the grass rapidly overtaking him, Anse heard a man swear suddenly. Farther along another man whistled a single, sharply clear note. And the man who had been under the saloon awning trotted briskly across the street to the door of the sheriff's office in the courthouse, disappearing inside. Anse saw the man was Cy Van Cleave.

The party from the grass slanted into the foot of the street. Hank Bayard's lean, forward-slanting figure was in the saddle on the first horse. Anse heard Bayard's harsh, flat-toned voice rise in a yell. And Range, which had been so soundly sleeping, was awake in an instant.

Anse pulled aside, taking his horse up over the uncertain planking of the walk into a lot to clear the street for those behind him. Within the courthouse he heard a single shot. There was a long pause, as though for emphasis, followed by three more shots in rapid succession. Almost immediately the door of the sheriff's office burst open. Van Cleave appeared, moving at a full run and closely followed by Hugh Perigord. They sprinted together for the stone front of the Palace Hotel. As they ran, Van Cleave shouted something.

Men poured from the saloon and ducked hurriedly for the hotel. One dropped to a knee and fired twice in the direction of

Bayard's approaching party. The gunfire made Prentice's mount restive. The animal danced back across the plank walk, fighting for the better footing of the street. Bayard's party swept up, some returning the fire of those holing up in the hotel with Perigord and Van Cleave. One of Bayard's companions veered toward Anson, gun recklessly high.

"Here's Prentice!" he sang out.

"Grab the bastard!" Bayard yelled. "But keep moving!"

Anse thought his horse went with the others without conscious direction from him. He felt picked up by a wild wind, carried along, and dropped by a sudden eddy before the door of Perigord's office. Gun sound had penetrated him until it beat in the hammering of his pulse. He heard the swift anger of driven lead, and a man to his left, as he hit the walk, was looking at a red fountain spraying out inches from his side and uttering his protest in a conversational tone which made his words the only sane sound in a bedlam of the impossible:

"Jesus! Oh, Jesus!"

Somebody seized Anse by the shoulder and thrust him roughly through the door. Then the street and its violence were behind and he was at the end of a corridor, staring at three cell gates, unlocked and standing open. He stared at the gates because four men lay in their own blood on the hallway floor. One of them was Marc Challon,

A man ducked into the cells and out.

"Cut 'em down through the bars, then unlocked the cells and dragged 'em out here to make it look like they were breaking clear. Van Cleave and Perigord. Both of them ran out of here as we came in."

"Pozner's still alive, but going fast. A bullet clean through his head. The Hyatts never finished the breath they were working on!"

Hank Bayard was on the floor, lifting Marc Challon's powerful body. Anse looked at this, his attention drawn unwillingly by the soft, concentrated fluency of the most virulent profanity he had ever heard on a man's lips. Bayard had Challon half upright, cradled against him, and Challon's blood generously on him. Hank swore from the heart, and there were fresh furrows on his dusty cheeks. In a kind of revelation Anse realized they had been cut by tears.

Challon's lips were injured. Anse could not tell if the blood on them was from these surface abrasions or from an internal flow. Challon's strength, his vitality, was evident. His shirt covered a terrible wound in his back, but after a moment of support against Bayard his eyes opened. They focused on Bayard and flinted in accusation.

"I told 'Lena to tell you to stay at Jim's, Hank," he said faintly.

171

Bayard blinked. " 'Lena? Hell, I ain't seen her!"

"She didn't show up?"

Bayard shook his head. Challon closed his eyes again and put his hands down flat on the floor on either side of him, supporting the sagging weight of his shoulders on them. He opened his eyes once more.

" 'Lena —" he said in a stronger voice. "Hank, get me out of here!"

Bayard looked up at the men bunched above him.

"Three of you give me a heft with the boss," he said. "The rest of you get out front. Clean the street. Drop everything that moves. And take this with you." He nodded savagely at Prentice. "When we're back on the grass I want to hear what he knows about this! Keep him in talking shape."

A gun dented Prentice's ribs. It hurt. He thought of the hurt in Marc Challon's body, and his stomach surged upward. Only a second ramming blow from behind prevented him from vomiting. He staggered back down the corridor toward the office in front and the street. Behind him, Hank Bayard and three others lifted Marc Challon from the floor.

11

Marcy rolled over. There was no head on the pillow beside her. Flat on her back, she stretched: her toes, her calves, her thighs, her torso, her arms and neck. A luxuriant awakening awareness which stirred her blood and chased the last haze of sleep from her mind. Anson was gone.

He was not an early riser. He had never voluntarily left her before. She scowled. Rising, she crossed to a window and, brushing back the heavy drapes with which she shut out the night but never the day, she opened the casement. The sun was bright outside, the hour perhaps eight. No movement was visible in the yard. Anson was not in sight. Marcy leaned far out of the window for a view along the side of the house to the ramada. He was not there either. Morning chill was rising from the ground. It stung her bare skin. She turned back into the room and swiftly dressed.

The yard boy was dozing in exhaustion on one of the beds in the bunkhouse. Tom Halliard lay in a deep-breathing stupor, an empty bottle beside him on the floor and the odor of whisky so strong above him that the flies avoided the clotting bandage with which Marcy had swathed his torn face. The other bunks in the building were empty. Cy Van Cleave and the rest of his men had not returned during the night. With her lips compressed Marcy moved on down to the store, remembering the blood-spotted bills Anson had brought so worriedly up to the house to show to her. The door was unlocked. The dead man, discovery of whom had so shaken Anson, still lay behind the counter. He had no whisky-laden breath to keep away the flies.

He was an ugly thing to survey before breakfast. A Lincoln County man, like Tom Halliard; a reckless kid who was trying to make big tracks because another boy was making them down around Fort Sumner, gathering a useless kind of glory as Billy the Kid. Marcy thought this one had been named Ben Freeman. And Anson had been right about him. He had unquestionably been alive when he was dragged in here. He was, however, very dead now. Marcy rummaged through his pockets, found nothing of interest, and tossed the corner of a blanket across his rigid face.

Finally, in the barn, she found the stall usually occupied by Anson's horse empty and his saddle gone from its peg. She knew then that he had ridden into town. She was concerned, a little amused by this sudden quiver of righteousness in him, and angry. She'd been a little too easy on him. She'd let him become a little too sure of her. Too much acquiescence. She should have kept him in enough turmoil over the course of his affair with her to have no time or energy for consideration of the broader problems of the ranch and his father's interest in the Santa Fe. This was something she'd have to remedy when he returned.

He was a thin man, pale of body and pale of emotion, and he moved in an orbit as small as the circumference of a silver dollar. She knew the usefulness of this narrowness, but she hated Anson Prentice for it. She hated the necessity of her own ambition which compelled her to heat this shadow of a man with the furnace within her when a dulled ember would have seemed as recklessly searing to his thin-blooded perceptions. She hated having to foster a feeling of dominance in him when in fact she could crush him in an instant. The justice of God Almighty, riding into Range against her orders, because she had made him believe there was a man and a man's guts within his narrow-shouldered frame!

Because of her hatred Marcy was suddenly glad Anse Prentice had moved against her wishes. The barb she had set in him would not pull out, no matter how he twisted and squirmed. She was sure of this. And with this ride to Range to invoke the law against an XO thief as an excuse, she'd make him crawl. She'd make him whimper. She wanted hurt and fear in him and tears in his eyes. She wanted to see them. In some way this might afford her repayment for the prodigality of waste she had spent on him to lift herself from the roots of this dusty New Mexico grass.

Returning to the house, Marcy made a pot of coffee, stirred a couple of piñon knots into the coals in the firebox of the stove, and sat down to wait for the coffee to boil. The poor judgment in Anson's ride to town was, she thought, strictly a personal matter between them, of no particular malice to her position in the county, or to her plans. However, the evidence Anson had stumbled on in the pockets of the dead man in the store — evidence that at least a part of the present XO crew had been involved in the Santa Fe holdup in the pass — this was something else.

For all his ardor and willingness to move onto the XO as she had suggested, Anson had not gone as far as she would have liked. He had been content to stay on the ranch. In spite of the fact that his father had several times been no farther away than Trinidad, across the pass, he had shown no desire to visit him. Once, when she suggested she invite Jason Prentice to the ranch during one of Marc's convenient absences, Anse had been amused.

"My father can bear life in our Chicago place on the lake when all the servants are there." He had laughed. "Or he can exist after a fashion in his suite at the Palmer House. Or, with plenty of work on his hands — if he's not out for too long a stretch at a time — he can make do in his private car along the rails. But he'd disown me cold if I brought him down here — and this house isn't too bad for comfort. You've got to get along with the old man sooner or later, Marcy. You want to start him off hating you for fair? Leave well enough be."

Anson, in his joking, had been mercilessly right. Marcy knew she would have to get along with Jason Prentice and get along with him well if she was eventually to move into the glittering circle of gracious and idle women such men supported. His father, in the last analysis, was more important in her scheming than Anson was.

It was because of this — not because infringement upon the law greatly disturbed her or because she was concerned with the ethics of theft or the gossip of the county — that Van Cleave's involvement of the XO in the holdup troubled her. Jason Prentice, in his own mind, was the Santa Fe, and the theft was a personal blow. This had been evident in the letter he had sent swiftly and expensively across the pass by messenger to his son.

Anson's father could quite obviously accept the alliance of his son and another man's wife, but Marcy knew the old man would buck if he became convinced that woman's ranch was being used as a base of harrying operations against his rails. Whether these operations, regardless of their nature, were with or without her knowledge would make little difference to him.

Sipping slowly on hot coffee which had always made Marc swear at the scalding temperature at which she served it, Marcy revised plans. With Anson gone to town, Hugh Perigord would know about the dead man in the store and the blood-marked money Anson had found in his pockets. Perigord was swift and shrewd in his thinking. He would know instantly — as Marcy had known — that the theft had been Van Cleave's work — an evidence of the readiness of Van Cleave's kind to trade a little riding and risk for a quick, substantial profit at someone else's expense.

Marcy thought Perigord might have been courting the rails since the sudden withdrawal of the Challons from effectiveness in the county. Such a man needed the support of the influence of others to bolster some shallow rooting in his own nature. He would be able to shift from the Challons to the Santa Fe without losing balance. And within reason, he would be able to shift his motives as deftly. It seemed unlikely that he would act hastily on Anson's information, even to make an impression of efficiency on Santa Fe officials. He would be certain to see that Van Cleave had involved the XO and that the XO involved young Prentice. Perigord was too wise to go directly to the father until he was certain the son was clear. Therefore, Marcy thought she would have opportunity to rectify this mistake and to bring Van Cleave to heel.

Strangely, it was this which troubled her. She had wanted a hard man to pitch against the hardness in Marc Challon. Van Cleave was hard. But she didn't know the man. She wasn't sure that she could ever know him. Like herself, he wore none of the brands by which men as well as animals were identified in this country. Like herself, he preferred to look inward with one face and outward with another. Marcy thought she would be very afraid of Van Cleave except for one thing. He was a man, and she had been born with the means to handle any man.

It was paradoxical, perhaps, in some ways a step in retreat, to use the same implements upon a strutting little grass-country bad man as upon the son of a major stockholder in a great railroad. But any artisan used the tools

179

with which he was most adept in accomplishing a piece of work.

Warmed and completely awakened by the coffee and with her spirits brightened by the brightening sun outside, Marcy began preparing breakfast. The Challons had a taste for thin, aged breakfast steaks, and Marcy had learned to like them too. She kept a few always ready in the tightly screened meat box hanging inside the outer screening of the back porch, and she was hungry this morning. Alone, with her problems ordered in her mind and her confidence unshaken, she hummed as she worked.

It was never more apparent to her than when she worked in this kitchen that a woman had built the XO house. And curiously, Marcy could not resent Belle Challon's hand here. It was a big room, with a huge, shelved pantry in an ell and a table and chairs in another ell, opposite. It was arranged so that a woman didn't have to walk the equivalent of a length of line fence to prepare a meal. But its pleasantness was not all a matter of efficiency. It caught morning sun and was therefore cheerful. Its builder had known that a kitchen is really the heart of any house — a place of companionship, gossip, and occasionally even idleness. There was room for all of these here.

Marcy was setting a single place on the table in the ell and two small steaks were smoking in a skillet on the stove when the back door opened without a knock and closed again. She turned. Cy Van Cleave had come in from the yard. He had not removed his hat. He was standing motionless, looking at her. And the devil was laughing in his eyes.

A small, compact man with a towering surety. A man physically engineered to be exactly what he was. No softening quirks, no flabbiness, no impracticality. As cleanly efficient, as dispassionately ruthless, and as repellently beautiful as a honed blade of steel. Marcy returned his stare for a long moment, wondering why she had never seen him as a man before — why he had not knocked now before he came into her house — why she was not really angry that he hadn't done so. And with the answer to these things came a sudden, unfamiliar flush which stung her cheeks.

He removed his hat then and dropped onto the corner of the table. He pulled out a chair after a moment and dropped into it with a faint shadow of weariness.

"Breakfast ready? I'm hungry as hell!"

Marcy went onto the back porch and took two more of the individually wrapped little steaks from the meat box. While there she studied the yard. Five horses were at the corral rail, dusty and hard-ridden. Van Cleave's horse and four others. No more.

And twenty men had left the ranch with her new foreman.

The four riders were washing up at the trough. Their weariness was more marked than Van Cleave's. And they were silent. The spirits of range hands could be measured by their yard talk. When there was none, it meant something. Marcy returned to the kitchen, forked out the two steaks she had already cooked, and dropped the fresh ones into the skillet. She reached silver from a drawer and another cup and plate and saucer from a cupboard. When she bent over the table beside him, placing these, Van Cleave spoke.

"You aren't going to like this."

Marcy was thinking of the magnet of flesh to flesh she had suddenly discovered in this man. Her mind was reaching swiftly, uneasily ahead, trying to discover what changes this would work in her long planning.

"I don't like it now," she said almost absently.

Van Cleave shrugged.

"Things sort of went to hell in town last night," he said.

Marcy returned to the stove, still thinking more of the man than of what he was saying.

"We picked Pozner and the Hyatts up late yesterday and hauled them into Range for bait," Van Cleave went on. "It worked, too. Challon came in early this morning after them. Alone, like I figured he would, trying to avoid a big showdown. Counting on the size of his breeches in Range and not much else. Come close to getting away with it, at that."

"But he didn't?"

"No." Van Cleave's satisfaction in this, at least, was apparent. "Perigord's tired of wearing a Challon lead rope. I signed a complaint for him, charging Pozner, the Hyatts, and Challon with pushing XO beef off toward the Strip. Dropped a hint, and Perigord was plenty anxious to hang the holdup in the pass onto them too. Gave him the excuse he wanted. When Challon hit town he didn't have any breeches at all with Perigord, and the rest of the town didn't count — not with our boys on the street to keep it indoors!"

"Marc's in Perigord's jail with the others, then?"

"That isn't what you want to hear!" Van Cleave protested with knowing sureness. "You've got to run this ranch, now you've got it, whether you want to or not. You don't want those lava hellions just behind bars; you want to be rid of them, permanent. And a bullet is a hell of a lot faster and cheaper than a long-winded divorce trial. Challon could have been trying a singlehanded jailbreak. Perigord is going to claim he did, and it's against my principles to call the law a liar — this time, at least. We got them all."

Marcy burned her hand on the skillet handle, turning.

"Marc?"

"Dead," Van Cleave told her bluntly. "As dead as I know how to make a man."

The burn on her hand hurt. Things could end so swiftly! Marcy wet the burn with her lips. Marc Challon dead!

It had been inevitable. She had known it from the first night she had seen him in Trinidad, with Lou Patterson standing beside them, making an awkward introduction. Perhaps she had known it from the first time Ed Bennett had talked of the men who owned the XO. She had known she would be able to climb past Marc Challon but that she would be unable to leave him alive behind her. She had dreaded this instant, knowing it would come. Now it was here — it was past — and like all things past, it made no difference.

Van Cleave rose, passed her, and returned to the table with the coffeepot. He poured both cups full and sat down. Not even Marc had possessed this man's sureness, his steadiness. Marcy, needing steadiness in this instant, recognized the core steel in Van Cleave. She forced herself to speak slowly, accepting the news of Marc's death as casually as it had been offered.

"You said things went to hell in town —"

Van Cleave nodded wryly, as though events

had been the result of error on his part. He spoke briefly. Marc had not been expecting reinforcements from the grass. Van Cleave was sure of that. But Bayard and the old XO crew had come into Range. Too late to help Marc, but riding like thunder rolling down from the mesas. They had plowed into the courthouse and they had brought Marc's body out with them. Not the bodies of the others; just Marc's.

Marcy drank her coffee slowly. The curious sentiment of the grass country . . . No more practical a man than Hank Bayard had ever lived, but he could not sever his devotion to Marc Challon with death and so blindly took the risk involved in retreating under gunfire with the burden of a dead man's body. That this kind of sentiment was wholly missing in Van Cleave added immensely to his usefulness — and to the queer attraction Marcy felt toward him. The old story of the snake and the bird — she smiled inwardly at the simile. A hawk with ready talons, she thought, was safe enough from even the rattlesnake of Mora, for all his serpentine charm. She straightened in her chair.

"Anson found one of your men dead in the store last evening," she said. "Some of the money stolen from the railroad was in his pockets. You weren't hired to hold up trains."

Van Cleave upholstered his gun and put it down on the table between them.

"That's what I was hired for, and we both know it," he said imperturbably. "You expect me to ride calluses onto my tail for just a foreman's pay when I can see the stakes you're playing for? I'm keeping you in your game; you're going to keep me in mine. And railroad money spends as easy as any other."

"Anson rode into town early this morning to talk to the sheriff about the dead man in the store," Marcy said.

Van Cleave smiled.

"I saw him. That's the part I said you weren't going to like. Prentice showed up in the middle of things in Range. Not soon enough to know what was going on. But he'll find out now. Bayard snagged him and took him along when the old XO bunch quit town. With those boys in the mood they're in, I'd hate to be in Prentice's shoes!"

Marcy recognized the malice in this. Quick anger and fear collided in her. Men like Hank Bayard were direct and they clung to an old belief that what a man did in this country he did out of his own will and desires alone. A woman could bend a rangeman more easily than any other because of his peculiar chivalry toward one kind of woman and his staggering hunger for the other. But no power on earth could make a saddle man believe he had been bent by a feminine hand, before or afterward.

Defenseless and in a measure guiltless,

Anson Prentice — who had slept in the Challon house and now had part title to Challon land — was in the hands of men whose loyalty to the Challon name had been a life's work. And this morning Marc Challon had been murdered! With her lips pulled flat, ringed by angry lines, Marcy leaned accusingly toward Van Cleave.

"You could have kept Anson clear of Hank and the rest in town!"

"Maybe, if I'd tried," Van Cleave admitted. "But I had to have a talk with you first."

"You swaggering, stupid fool!" Marcy said intensely, the colossal ruin Anson Prentice's death now could work rising before her. "If anything happens to him —"

His eyes hard and his voice roughened, a deep sensitivity obviously trodden upon, Van Cleave touched the weapon between them on the table.

"There's some talk I won't hear, even from a bitch!" he snapped. "Just because you lived with a Challon, don't get confused by size. Just because you slept with Prentice, don't get confused by a million dollars. This equalizer has made me as big and as smart as any man I ever met. It made me as big as Marc Challon this morning. And because I'm here and Prentice isn't, it's as important to you as his bank roll right now. We going to have that talk — civilly?"

Here was fundamental fact. Marcy knew

187

how to accept it. She nodded slowly.

"This county is like a horse with an empty saddle," Van Cleave went on quietly. "You knocked down the rider it was used to when you ran the Challons off this ranch. Perigord's sold what little soul he has to the railroad, figuring the Santa Fe'll give him a leg up to the empty seat. But I want it and I aim to beat him to it. The XO is going to be my stirrup."

"The XO belongs to Anson Prentice and me."

"Now," Van Cleave agreed. "But you figure on marrying Prentice and getting to hell out of here — with the getting out the thing that's important to you. The big cities and plush living. If it wasn't, a woman like you wouldn't have traded what you had for what you've got now!"

"You want something," Marcy reminded him.

"I'm getting to it. I want the XO when you've made your take. The chance to make men jump without prodding them with a gun barrel. The chance to leave a hell of a lot I'd as soon forget behind me. Maybe the same things you want, only not so much of them. And don't tell me you'll have to take it up with Prentice. You may not get the chance."

"What makes you think I'd keep a promise like that if I made it?"

Van Cleave refilled his coffee cup. With his

head slanted downward he looked at her. His intolerable confidence surfaced again.

"I know this country and the fools in it; you don't. I'll take the chance."

An oppressive sense of repetition crowded in on Marcy.

She had heard this before. This bland assertion she was an outlander and so could not figure the people on the grass into the equation of her desires. And once before she had heard a tremendous larceny involving the XO as calmly expressed as this Van Cleave now proposed.

It's really very simple, Marc. We want the ranch. . . .

"That all?" she asked Van Cleave. "That's all you want?"

He had crossed to the stove and was serving their plates with the steaks smoking in the skillet. He studied her over his shoulder, thoroughly, line for line and shadow for shadow, with an infuriating deliberation. Finally he shrugged again.

"Depends on how good you cook. I'm done eating with the crew in the cookshack. I live here now. Maybe I'll like it. I don't know."

Marcy lifted knife and fork when he set her plate in front of her. Here was her language. Here was her way of thinking. Here was a challenge no man had offered her. Van Cleave was thin, shabby, worthless enough by most standards, but he was completely ruthless. And she needed him now as she would not need the XO when she had married Anson Prentice. She had occasionally felt vastly alone here under the mesas. She did not now. Here was her own kind, and to be done with posing was like wriggling free of corset and stays after a day of being dressed for town.

"Sit down, Cy," she said. "Breakfast is getting cold."

Van Cleave spoke around a mouthful of steak.

"We'll have a line on Prentice in a couple of hours. That's where the rest of the boys are now. I sent them out from town to pick up Bayard's tracks. When we know where he's gone, we'll go after your million dollars — honey."

12

The sun was hot and it hammered in from all sides, making a furnace of the interior of the coach in spite of the tall stands of timber on both sides of the road and the fact that this was near the summit of the pass, almost eight thousand feet above the sea. Elena Casamajor understood this heat as she understood most things in this country — because she had long lived with them. The sun itself, backed by the inverted azure porcelain bowl of the sky, was hot enough. But it was the mesas which occasionally made the heat become close to unbearable. The mesas were capped with dark rock. Rock outcroppings thrust out here and there through even the heaviest stands of piñon and pine. It was lava rock, without the color or appearance of a reflector, but it had been glazed by volcano heat to an incredible smoothness, and it warped the sun's rays in from a thousand new angles of reflection with every changing moment of the day.

It was not the heat which made 'Lena's stomach churn over and over again beneath the tight, upward-swelling bodice of the dress

Pierre Challon had bought for her in Denver. A sickness she miserably wished would become nausea, but which she knew would not. It was not the heat which drove impatience through her like the sharp wincing of a sprain when one tried to walk upon it. It was not even the heat which made the palms of her hands moist and unpleasant to her own touch — which beaded the flesh above her straight brows and her upper lip with an uncomfortable dew of perspiration — which darkened the underarm fabric of her new dress.

There had been Territory news at Trinidad. News hard to believe and harder to doubt. Shocking and terrible news. And the road was so long over the pass into New Mexico.

"Hurry — Mother of God, can't you hurry it more?" she cried out the door window to the driver on the box above. The man on the reins made no answer, and she sank back onto the seat. Gravel rattled in a steady hail against the underside of the floor boards. Gravel sprayed widely at each of the incessant turns of the road. The coach rocked wildly. A magician was handling the spans ahead. But wings would have been slow.

Beside her, Pierre Challon dropped a great, mottled hand onto her knee. The long, once powerful fingers closed exerting strong pressure through the fabric of her skirt.

"There's plenty of time, *chinita*," he said

quietly. "The need for hurry is past. You need a drink. Lean back. Breathe deep. I'll fetch you one."

Chinita!

Marc had called her that, falling easily into the endearments and diminutives of her own tongue. In the camp at Tinaja, when he was riding in one direction and she in another, he had called her that. And now his father. She looked at the man beside her and wondered if at the end of so many years Marc Challon would have been so great a man, with so much of life carved into the lines of his face and deepening the shadows of his eyes. They were so much alike in other ways that she thought this would have been so. Now she would never know. Marc was dead.

Leaning back as she had been directed, 'Lena watched old Pierre Challon removing the double stoppers from an ornate, astonishingly large pocket flask. The faint, pleasant odor of good whisky rose from it as the stoppers came free. Whisky was a man's antidote to shock. 'Lena wondered if there really was an antidote for a woman in a like case. If there was, she didn't know it and neither did Pierre Challon. She took the flask when he handed it to her, noting the unsteadiness of his hand. She drank little but was careful to stifle the choking burn in her throat, mindful of the adage that those who could not drink whisky should not.

Pierre Challon watched her anxiously, as though he expected a miracle from his flask. 'Lena was sorry she must disappoint him. She thought no man could know less about women than this old giant. A wiser or more embittered man would not have gone to Denver in the first place. And 'Lena was certain that if Pierre Challon had remained in Range his son would not now be a week dead.

The churning began again in her. Her ride northward swept back over her in retrospect. Without money, without extra clothing, with a horse to which she could prove no right of use. Riding hard across the mesas and the high, sandy grass along the base of the mountains — grass unaccountably so much poorer than the rich grama beyond Boundary Mesa. Fording the Huerfano and the Arkansas, threading the sandhills. Hitting the arid course of Cherry Creek beyond the gaunt spire of Castle Rock, and so trailing dust on into Denver.

Riding from friend to friend, *casa* to *casita*, learning names she had already almost forgotten. Sandoval Plaza, the sheep camp of a cousin of the Archuletas, a woodcutter's place on the outskirts of ugly Walsenburg, a section shack along the new, unrusted rails of General Palmer's Denver and Rio Grande Western. Her ticket for meals and bed and passage, her guarantee of freedom from molestation and delay, no more than her face, her figure, and the Spanish of her name.

A hard enough ride for a toughened man at the constant speed at which she had traveled. And at the end, a day far harder than the worst of those in the saddle, attempting to convince Pierre Challon he had not outlived his usefulness and the affection of his son. Breathing life again into clay which had become dust. There was something terrible about having brought a dying man again onto his feet. But she had not known in Denver that her resurrection of the old man was only for him to face another death with the news waiting for them at Trinidad.

Riding, pleading, hurrying until fatigue was leaden within her, a burden she seemed to have carried for an eternity. But always one buoyancy, called to mind as she needed it. Thought of Marc Challon. The bigness of his body. The clearness of his skin and its sun color. The high, healthy sheen of his hair and the clearness of his eyes. The way his hands could close irresistibly, but as gently as a caress. The magnificence of his hatred and the superb justice of his revenge. The pride and strength of his country and hers in his aggressive, swinging carriage. The warm man flavor of his breath on her lips. So pitifully little to know of a man, in reality. She had built more out of her imagination as she rode. Things she could feel in her heart, in her head, in the currents and sinews of her body. Now none of it was left. None of it was left but ashes decaying in a narrow pit somewhere under New Mexico sod.

Pierre Challon drank deeply from his flask, not out of need but out of relish, and he recorked the silver container. With the automatic gesture of long habit he wiped his lips with the back of his hand.

Disconcertingly he smiled. His hand again gripped 'Lena's knee. Not cavalierly, but with a comradeliness 'Lena had not thought possible in a man toward a desirable woman, regardless of the variance in age between them. Not an insinuating creation of senility, either — the knowing, ugly, half-childish leg rubbing with which a grandfather too often apologized for failing glands and a misspent youth. This was something containing beauty. 'Lena Casamajor could not remember her own father, and Pierre Challon had never had a daughter, yet the touch of his hand and the tired and gentle smile in his eyes created such a relationship in an instant. 'Lena leaned wearily and gratefully into it, her head tilting to one side until it rested against the still square angle of Pierre Challon's shoulder, and her hands closing over the bony one at her knee.

There had always been people of two bloods on the high grass in the minds of those who lived upon it. But this was not really true. A people in any place upon the face of the earth was one people. The same blood flowed from the hearts of them all. Here was proof. The ends of the earth could produce no more opposite a pair than Pierre Challon and the Mexican girl who sang a couple of songs of a Saturday night at the Uncle Dick, living apart with her pride, yet common blood could not have made them closer than this.

"You know, honey," Pierre Challon said slowly, "it's funny about Marc and me. We got along. A man that's busy manages to do that. Things come up he'd like to sift out with them he regards, but time runs along and he's got to sleep and there's work to be done and something else that won't wait to be talked about. Maybe that didn't make as much difference with Marc and me as it might have with some. We were close. Close, but different. I used to wonder what the difference was."

"Now you know?"

"I think so. A woman, honey. I married her. She borned Marc. She was wife to me, but she was mother to him. That was the difference. A woman's got pride in her husband — the kind of a woman that Belle was, that you are — but she's got more than pride in her son. A husband ain't perfect; he's already built when she gets him. But a woman is kind of like God; she can create in her

own image — in the image in her mind —
with a boy. Belle did that with Marc. She
sort of took up with him where God left off
with me."

"There wasn't so awful much room for im-
provement, Pierre," 'Lena murmured.

The old man smiled widely.

"Honey, this is in private. We can talk free.
You was raised in and around Range. You
know exactly what kind of a bastard Pierre
Challon has been all of his life. What I've
been is what has killed Marc. Folks expected
him to ride like a wild, damned-fool lightning
bolt, same as his old man did, when the
wind got strong. And one of them acted ac-
cordingly. They forgot his mother had taught
him another way of getting from the north
bank of the stream to the south. He took a
bullet that had ought to have been meant for
me."

"We'll know the truth in another hour or
two," 'Lena said. "You're guessing now. And
not cleverly. Think of this. Uncle Jim and
Simi and Ed Hyatt were all in the jail section
of the courthouse with Marc. Sheriff Perigord
was there. And they said in Trinidad that Cy
Van Cleave came in to help him when the
trouble started. If Marc was trying to break
Uncle Jim and the Hyatts out of jail, like the
story we heard goes, wouldn't the four of
them have gotten farther than the corridor in
back of the sheriff's office? Could Hugh

Perigord and this Van Cleave have stopped four of that kind of men without taking a mark of hurt on themselves — if there was actually a jail break and the odds were anywhere even?"

"You make Marc sound like a handy man."

"He was! He was your son, grown out of the same grass as you. He wasn't killed; he was murdered!"

Color receded from Pierre Challon's lips, and the stained old ivory of his enormous, even teeth showed briefly. His hand turned under 'Lena's clasping pair, crushing them savagely together.

"You wouldn't let a man drag his tail, would you?" he growled. "If I can't lie to you, I sure as hell can't lie to myself! If Marc was shot, he was shot in the back. I've made enemies in the last fifty years, but, by hell, I've made friends too. The kind of friends a man seldom gets nowadays. And I've never asked a sou from any of them. Somebody in Red River County has got an idea the Challons never amounted to more than a big hunk of land — that a bitch with more itch in her palms than in her flanks could stringhalt them. It's going to be a mean, ornery, downright unreasonable surprise to that somebody to find out different!"

Pierre leaned forward and spat forcefully out the window on his side of the coach.

"You know a sight of folks in town too," he

went on. "Some I never had on the XO and never had a call to know. I could do with some help."

'Lena shook her head.

"Not now. Later, maybe. They said Hank Bayard took Marc out onto the grass. I have to find him out there, Pierre. There were some things I never had a chance to tell him. He said once that he had one too many women. I want him to know he never had a woman — a real one — as long as he was on the XO. I want him to know he had one in the lava, even if she rode away from him the night he was killed. He'll hear me, wherever he is, and I have to know Hank Bayard took good care of him. A man is clumsy at things like that, and Marc would need a lot of grass over his heart, just like he used to need it under his feet."

Pierre nodded.

"I'll want to talk to him, too, when I'm finished up in town," he said. "You mark the place where you find him. Belle will want to be moved out there too — it's where we all began. And there's got to be enough room left for me."

"Yes," 'Lena agreed. "I'll let you know."

Pierre leaned out the window and called up to the driver:

"Haul up on this side of Goat Hill and let the lady out. I've got a yellow-gold double eagle in my pocket with your name on it if you've forgotten she rode with us by the time you've rolled into Range."

The driver grunted assent. Pierre leaned back and looked at 'Lena.

"Hank Bayard didn't ride out onto the grass just to bury Marc, honey. I know Hank from a long ways back. He's near as much Challon as I am. He's aiming to take a swipe at whoever done Marc in. And this Van Cleave — or Hugh Perigord, or whoever it was — they'll know that about Hank. They'll be watching for him and looking for him. Hank'll know that. He'd be almighty hard to find if you started out from town and maybe somebody followed you, hoping you'd lead them to Hank. Better do your looking on the quiet. Tell Hank I want to see him. If you need me, I'll be at the Palace."

13

There was a thin, steady morning wind coming across the potholed lava. Farther back from the mesa rim piñons broke up the wind, diffusing it so that its chill was not uncomfortable. But on the very lip of the break there was no shelter.

Anson Prentice rolled from his blankets, painfully aware of their strong horse smell and the unpleasant odor of his own body, unwashed for too many days. He stood up. He was stiff. His eyes were leaden. The thin scrawniness of his beard pricked irritatingly under the line of his jaw. In two places hair had ingrown, raising red, angry pustules he could not treat because there was no mirror, no surface bright enough to give him a reflection by which he could work. He could only finger them occasionally when they gave him the most trouble, irritating them further. He fingered them now, curiously relishing the stinging hurt.

Al Carlin was still asleep a few yards away, his breathing heavy and his body relaxed, as though rough stone were a sufficient couch for any man. Hank Bayard was crouched over another of the tiny, smokeless dry piñon-twig fires above which all the indifferent cooking of this camp had been done. A kid they called Lou — a pimply, testy, foul-mouthed youngster who talked of little but sleeping with women — was on lookout on a rounded crag which overlooked the mesa face a hundred yards away. The others were below somewhere, down in the hazy blue void in which lay the grass, the XO, and the New Mexico Anson had thought he had known — still untouched by the rising sun.

He moved toward Hank Bayard at the fire. When he had first come onto the XO he had thought Bayard one of the indestructibles of the country. He had been wrong. A man could not wear much thinner than Bayard was worn now. Anson Prentice had never hated a man. He didn't hate Bayard. But he had come to find satisfaction in watching the man break down. He had come to pushing Bayard a little because he had discovered he could.

This was the kind of living Bayard should know, and he should have been able to take it in his stride, but he was breaking. He was breaking faster than his prisoner, yet Anse knew Marc Challon's foreman had brought every pressure to bear against his prisoner that he could find. Bayard's bitter scorn had been monumental, but the man he scorned was making a fool of him.

As Anson reached the fire, picking the matter of sleep from the corners of his eyes with a fingernail, Bayard grudgingly swung the skillet out to him. Smoking bacon lay in it; thick, whitish, lean-streaked slices, floating in half an inch of their own grease. Anson could taste the thickness of cooling grease against the roof of his mouth — the grease of yesterday's skimpy bacon breakfast and that of the day before and other days beyond — how many of them? Ten, he thought. At least ten, with the whole party of them crouching here on the mesa rim, hiding from searchers from town and searchers from the XO, waiting to know whether Marc Challon would live or die of his wound.

Anson fished out with his fingers the two slices of bacon which were his ration. The grease was hot and burned. He shifted the bacon carefully to his other hand and quickly licked at the smarting places. There was grime on the fingers he licked and under their nails. Water here was for drinking, and little enough even then. He licked his fingers again and suddenly laughed softly. Bayard looked up quickly at him.

"Something's so damned funny?" he snapped.

"They'll find us today," Anson said. "They'll sure as hell find us today. They were close enough when they quit last night."

"They get any closer and you go over the

edge," Bayard said raggedly. "Right down on top of them. It's a thousand feet. You'll make a splash that'll stop even Van Cleave. Now, shut up, damn you! And stay back from the rim. Any signal —"

"They don't need a signal," Anson said surely. "And nobody is putting me over the edge. That would take guts you haven't got, Hank. Marc is still alive and I might be useful to Marc. You got to know about that first. You got to keep on waiting —"

Bayard swore with a sullen, bearlike shake of his head and made a threatening swipe with the skillet. Anson moved away from him, chewing on a limp strip of bacon. When a man got this hungry — not the full gripe of starvation, but a savage awareness of long having been only half fed — even the taste of his own saliva was good. Bayard couldn't hang on up here much longer, even if the camp remained undiscovered. Bayard and the others had to be getting hungry too.

The bacon gone, Prentice shoved his hands deep into his pockets for warmth. Finding an eddy in the wind after a little search among the potholes, he hunkered down close to the rock to let the warming sun strike his back. This was instinctive and it startled him that he had learned how to do it. There was so damned little he had learned in this country. So very damned little.

Carlin had awakened and was moving out

toward the rock from which watch was usually kept. Relieved, the kid called Lou was in and on his knees beside Bayard's tiny fire, trying to thaw out the chill driven into him by the dawn wind. None of the three was watching their prisoner.

Prentice eyed the only shelter in the camp — the crudely improvised brush lean-to in which Marc Challon lay — and he speculated on his chances of reaching it. They were better today, he thought, than they had been yesterday. And yesterday had been better than the day before. Today he might make it.

It was not so hard to look back on now, although it had been intolerable the first two days. Two days in which the thickening stain on the blanket under Marc Challon's body had continued to grow and the best man in the crew stared helplessly at the ugly blueness of Challon's slowly swelling wound.

The bitterness in this old crew of Challon's had been at Hugh Perigord and Van Cleave, but they could do nothing toward either until they were sure, one way or another, that there was no risk Challon would again fall into the hands of the men who had tried to kill him. Still, Bayard and Carlin and the rest could not wholly contain their bitterness, and Prentice was at hand in their camp.

In the first hour here on the mesa rim after the incredible ride out from town, Bayard and the others had learned that their prisoner knew nothing of the stupid but singularly effective trap into which Marc Challon had walked. His own shock and evident aversion when he learned the truth of what had happened in town had cleared Anson of complicity in it. But still there had to be an outlet for the impotent anger in the others.

These men of the saddle, who had bought the women any of them had ever known, had beaten him for buying Marcy Challon. They had kicked him for buying the XO, knowing well enough that Challon had been content to let the ranch go. They had roughed him from one to another and back again until their unsqueamish bellies were full and a coroner would have as readily chosen him as Challon to work upon.

His bruised and swollen groin and buttocks had made walking impossible for two days. These men had known where to kick to punish. Breathing was still occasionally sharply uncomfortable, reminding him of boots driven against his ribs when he lay sobbing on the ground. Curious that he should remember the sobbing when the hurt was nearly gone — that the sobbing should stir his anger when thought of the boots no longer did so.

The lengthening stubble on his cheeks and about his mouth hid drying scars, and his tongue was already accustomed to the gap where two teeth had been. Frightened men were savage, and these had been frightened men. They had been afraid Marc Challon might die.

Afterward, by some common accord, they had kept their hands from him. Except that he knew his own cowardice, Anson would have believed those first few hours had been a physical trial, by surviving which he had won the grudging admiration of those who had mauled him.

But they had not let him see Challon. They had not let him add his efforts and hopes to their clumsy ones. Their world had only a wrong and a right where two men and a woman were involved. There was no room in it for a fool who had taken too long to see the enormity of his mistake. They could not understand that, although Anson Prentice owed the man nothing approaching the staggering fixity of their own loyalty, he, also, desperately did not want the man to die.

Al Carlin had vanished into the scant, shallow shelter of some pothole on the lookout rock. Lou and Hank Bayard, at the fire, were mixed in one of the heated, meaningless quarrels over nothing which often flare briefly among men too long alone together under pressure and strain. The sun was higher and the air warmer. The blue night haze was lifting from the grass far below. Prentice rose stiffly to his feet and crossed to the open face of Challon's shelter. His movement was not seen.

Two or three days before, when the wind was right, Anson had caught a strong odor of putrescence from Challon's shelter. He had thought then that the injured man could not long survive such an atmosphere, let alone the decay feeding on his body. Ducking under the low brush roof, he caught the odor again, fainter but unmistakable.

He would not have known Marc Challon. The man's face had been craggy, supported by a plaited underlay of muscle which had set hard lines and strong flat planes among the features in repose and had provided a curious, fierce mobility under duress. The face he saw now, fevered and with the jaw sagging in exhaustion, had something of beauty, of which he had not before been aware. The underflesh was gone and the skin drawn taut. The beauty was in the modeling and proportions of the bones now so evident. Prentice saw that Marc Challon had been a handsome boy.

Squatting on his heels, aware of the flies still too chilled to be stirring and so clinging to the powdery leaves of the crude roof thatch, Anson ran back in his mind over the smattering of theory and science with which even a moderately conscientious student involuntarily emerged from a big university. Not medicine, as such, but half-forgotten

209

shadows cast by study of allied sciences into the medical field.

Bayard and the other boys, within the limits of their knowledge and the materials at hand, had provided homeopathy, at least. Whisky — empty bottles were about — consumed by patient and ministers with about equal effect. A tumble of brass shell cases from which the charges had been painstakingly emptied. Anson shivered. He had heard of this cautery and credited it as an old wives' tale, yet here was evidence of its use. Gunpower poured onto torn flesh and ignited there to seal off bleeding and discourage infection.

There were quantities of refuse bandaging in a corner, appallingly stained. Shirts, underdrawers, even blanketing when the supply of fabric apparently ran low in the camp. It seemed incredible that a man could have lived through this. But Challon was alive. His breathing was steady and strong but markedly labored. And the heat of his fevered body seemed to warm the interior of the shelter to oppressiveness.

Anson reached for Challon's arm, remembering to set the balls of his fingers against the underside of the wrist, rather than his thumb, but he could not recall the proper pulse rate, if he had ever known it, and his watch had been broken during his first night here so that he couldn't measure time.

Challon lay on his side. It was not difficult to raise his dark, stiffened shirt and to slip the shoddy knots of his bandages. However, the cloth stuck and would not come free. Anson explored under the edges, finding red, angry flesh, hard to his touch, as though callused. The hardness of internal pressure.

Rocking back, Prentice tried to remember what this meant but could not. Such of the wound as he could expose resembled a huge pustule, ripe enough to be opened. But a bullet hole was not a boil. There seemed little that could be done except to remove the filthy, adhering bandage. Anson was working gently with this when Challon suddenly broke the deep, labored rhythm of his breathing and turned partially away from him.

Something broke with the movement. The bandage came away. And with it came a great deep core of mortification. The bullet, which had most certainly been so deep as to avoid any but the most skillful probing, lay where Anson could lift it clear with his fingers without touching flesh. Challon's wound was no less staggering in size, but the pressure was gone from it. Prentice thought with elation that, if the man had lived for ten days with this slough in him, he was bound to recover now it was gone and the wound clean.

A limp evidence of habitual fastidiousness, Prentice had in one hip pocket a folded, unused square of linen kerchief from which the starch and freshness were long gone but which offered the closest approach to cleanliness he could find. He packed this over the open wound and had just bound it in place with strips torn from the cleanest edge of the blanket under Challon, when Hank Bayard ducked angrily under the open side of the shelter and slammed a half-opened hand at him.

The blow caught Prentice across his ear, spilling him onto his hands and knees. Bayard caught his collar and dragged him outside. Anson twisted free and scrambled to his feet.

"What the hell you doing?" Bayard demanded unsteadily.

Prentice pulled at his banged ear.

"Cleaning up the mess you made of him," he said with a jerk of his head toward the shelter.

Shaking and livid, Bayard caught his arm.

"I told you to stay away from him!"

The rangeman's hand slammed across Anson's face with loose, biting knuckles again, reopening a half-healed cut in his lip. He tasted blood and something else. Something which surged up out of a dry well within him.

"God damn you, Bayard!" he said very distinctly. And he hit Challon's foreman.

Maybe it was a clumsy blow. He didn't

know. But it gave him the same kind of release removing the crusting bandage and its load of rot had given Marc Challon's body. He had an instant's awareness of relief and inward cleanliness. Then Bayard came in with a crouching cat's bounce, his gun high. The barrel chopped downward and the sun collided with Prentice's head.

14

The strong sun of midmorning was in Prentice's face, the stiffness of clotted blood in his hair. Heat rose visibly from the dark rock about him. He raised unsteadily to his elbows, then to a sitting position, cradling his head with his hands. The rim of the mesa was before him, beyond, a blue void of space. Bounding it on the far side was the truncated cone of the volcano, flanked a little farther to the south by the tall, slender spire of Tinaja. Orientation was an effort which made him wince.

All of the old XO crew was now gathered here on the rock. Those who had been long out watching the parties searching for them had come in. And their horses had not been left, as before, farther back on the mesa crown where timber would screen them from discovery. The smell of good cooked meat was in the air. Bayard's usual cautious fire had been replaced by a huge one which sent a tall, careless column of smoke into the air. And the crew was eating. Prentice saw a young steer had been hazed in from the timber grass and killed and butchered.

Searching for the roots of this sudden change in the mood of the camp, Anson had a bad moment of fear that he had done Marc Challon a final violence in dressing his wound. Then he saw Hank Bayard straighten as he came out of Challon's shelter, and the former XO foreman was again the man he had been the first time Prentice had seen him. Bayard was laughing. Challon was all right.

Puzzled, Anson rose unsteadily to his feet, found his hat and replaced it, and started for the shelter. He was yards short of this when the cause of the change in the camp materialized in Challon's doorway. A woman. A girl. In this first instant, guided chiefly by dress and manner, a Mexican girl. One of a kind apparent along every street and nearly every roadway south of the Arkansas. Then Anson saw her face. Radiance was short of the rapture shining in it — the eagerness and tremendous joy and relief apparent in every excited movement of her body. Prentice could not tell whether she might be beautiful in repose, but there was a beauty in her now he had never seen equaled.

He was completely baffled for a moment. Then he remembered Marcy had told him with unconsciously bitter amusement of a cheap little Mexican saloon wench Marc Challon had taken out onto the lava with him.

215

"Marc's a fool," Marcy had said. "He thinks I cost him something! Maybe I did, but he got nothing in return but a bad smell and disease. I hope this one fixes him right!"

Prentice saw this had again been one of Marcy's dark visions. This was no saloon girl. The look of freshness was about her, and the smell of freshness would be about her too. And there could be no disease in a body with so light a heart. Looking at the girl, Anson felt weary, diseased, himself, and as alone as he had ever been since his mother's death. The girl had thought Challon was dead. He was alive, and her rapture was over this. He wondered if something like this hadn't been what he had wanted from Marcy — at least there was no mockery in it.

The girl stopped him a rod from Challon's shelter.

"I want to see Marc," he told her.

"Why?" she asked.

Startled, Prentice tried to reach an answer out of his still ringing head. To his surprise he could find none which would be valid to either the girl or himself.

"Marc has already told Hank to give you a horse and start you down the mesa," the girl went on. "You'd better go."

Prentice knew he had lain a pair of hours untended in the sun with his scalp split open. Granted her attention was all for

Challon, surely this girl must have known where he lay and why, and that he was hurt. But she hadn't come near him and she had sent no one. There was hard and uncompromising unfriendliness in her eyes now. Not enmity, not accusation; only disapproval and dismissal. Marcy had said she was a saloon girl, but Anson Prentice was beyond her pale.

"Marc doesn't want to see me?" he asked unsteadily.

The girl smiled without humor.

"You can't be that big a fool!" she told him.

Prentice fingered the dried split in his scalp and replaced his hat. He was thinking far, far ahead.

"I don't know," he said. "I don't know. Hank's got a horse for me?"

The girl nodded. Prentice started to turn away, then swung back.

"I thought Marc was the fool," he said softly. "I really did. A damned poor trader. I was crazy, I guess. Crazy as the devil, miss. I didn't know about you."

The girl's eyes warmed a little.

"Neither did Marc," she murmured. "Not then." Her voice strengthened. "Why don't you get out of New Mexico before you're really hurt?"

"I don't know," Anson said slowly and with complete honesty. "Be damned if I do!"

There was nothing more to be said. There

217

was no way to explain the feeling in him that if he could see Marc Challon, now the man was conscious and mending — that if Marc could see him — somehow Challon would know the bad days were past. Maybe even that Challon would understand he had known almost as little of Anson Prentice as Prentice had known of Challon's wife the day they had all sat in the office in the XO house, putting their cards down for each of the others to see.

Prentice turned away and approached Bayard at the fire. The smell of food made him uncomfortable and more aware of the lingering pain in his head, but he asked for none of the meal the others were enjoying so ravenously.

"You've got a horse for me?" he asked Bayard. Challon's foreman nodded toward the bunched animals.

"Saddled and waiting."

Anson saw among the others the short-coupled bay he had ridden from the XO into Range and from Range here to the summit of Boundary Mesa. Bayard fell in beside him and they crossed to the animal. Not surely and without real purpose except to cover his own uncertainty, Prentice tested the saddle girth.

"You thought Van Cleave would find us today," Bayard reminded him. "I wish I had busted your damned head in!"

"You tried," Prentice said. "Maybe I half wish you had too. What's happened to Van Cleave?"

"Nothing, yet!" Bayard said with a wicked grin. "But his pay is on the way, for sure. And Perigord's. Hugh's got to climb back into his traces, and that means he's hauling against Van Cleave from here on out instead of with him. 'Lena brought us near as good news as we had waiting here for her. The Old Man is back. She brought him down from Denver. Pierre's in Range and pawing dust, for sure. I know him. Van Cleave and Perigord are both going to have to walk the top strand of the wire or they'll have the whole damned county on their necks. You'll see. Now, how about getting to hell off this mesa? We could do with some clean air up here!"

Prentice pulled himself into the saddle, wondering if any old man could be equal to the ambitions and combined malice of Hugh Perigord, Van Cleave, and the woman to whom he was himself now returning. He didn't think so, but he knew Hank Bayard wouldn't listen.

Challon felt like he had unwillingly been born into a new body. A limp length of bony flesh with which he could do nothing. And the change was not in his body alone.

He knew now who had fired without warn-

219

ing into his back. Marcy had done it. The man she had hired with probably just such a shot in mind had done it. There was little difference. And the bullet had shattered more than the bone and muscle of his back. It had ruptured the canals of his confidence as well as his energy. He was heavy with weariness, and the thing he had wanted to do seemed to have lost the imperative challenge it had once offered him.

His values were all shot to hell, and the important things were now those he could reach and secure most easily. 'Lena, before and beyond anything else. A place to light, then. Not in this county. There were too many complications, too many things left undone here. On the Taos side of the range, maybe; perhaps even up in Colorado. There was a hell of a lot of room left. He had a fortune in cash banked in Range. A small one by most standards, probably, but enough. He needed only a piece of land to buy. Then an exodus with 'Lena and Hank and the boys — and Pierre. A soon exodus, before Pierre stirred up any hornets in town he couldn't tame.

The whitefaces were out on the lava. Tia Pozner was out there. The stock would flourish on new grass as well as old. And he owed Tia Pozner something. He had thought he could take her husband out of jail and had gotten him killed in the attempt. He had forgotten that all snakes did not rattle before they struck. Tia would go with 'Lena and himself. They'd all go together. A fresh beginning and no trouble. A new iron which would not take all of a man's time and all of his energy.

There would be protest. He knew that. But 'Lena would understand. She would have had enough. Between them they could make the others see it too. Maybe it was a retreat. If so, then it was the discretion which the saying posted above valor. But it was even simpler than the saying made it. It was plain horse sense. Plain good judgment. Even Pierre would have to admit this. Pierre was as old as Challon felt now. Pierre would see the sense of it, all right. There was too much to be done here. Too much which might be impossible. A man didn't give his life to a ranch — and to an idea — and to a revenge. He had to save a little for himself. He was entitled to a measure of quiet and the simple problems.

A man was a damned fool who asked twice for the same ticket to hell. A man was a damned fool who didn't quietly admit when he was beaten.

Outside the sloppy shelter over his head Challon heard 'Lena talking to someone. Her voice was still a little unsteady. The day they had ridden out into the lava from town he had thought she was drawn to him. When she had returned to his camp with Jim Pozner and the Hyatts and the others, he thought the liking was strengthening. Then, under Tinaja, when he was starting for town, he thought it could be love.

Hell, he hadn't known then what love was! He was not sure that he did now. Something bigger than the desire by which he had once measured it. That much was certain. And 'Lena had taught him this in the last hour.

He had believed sentiment a woman's device for coloring the life she lived to an acceptable hue — a sort of gilt lavishly splashed onto the ordinary and the habitual to lend them a self-deluding charm. A man could be injured physically, he could have the devil scared out of him, he could be made angry, but the inside of him could not be hurt so that it would show. Not a man. Still, Challon recalled the hot tears which had run from his eyes this morning when Hank Bayard brought 'Lena into this shelter and he could see the grief which had been in her — when he could see her joy and the heartbreak that was now gone, and her excitement — and knowing it all sprang from him, from the fact that he was not really dead.

Hank had seen these tears. And Al Carlin and the rest. And they had thought nothing of them, seeing them through tears of their own. They were a hard bunch of boys, too — big enough men for any breeches. So a man

222

was a damned fool to think he knew even the currents of his own nature. 'Lena's hurt had hurt Marc Challon and he had wept.

He remembered cursing Marcy Bennett. But no tears. Not in all of the five years they had shared the same house. None of these tears today had been for her, either. The hell with Marcy. The hell with the XO. This was a new beginning; be damned if it was a retreat!

Challon stirred restlessly. A moment later 'Lena bent and entered the shelter.

"Perigord rode out to the XO this morning to tell Van Cleave to give up looking for Hank," she said. "I met Paco Encelador, the yard boy, out east of the house, and he told me. Pierre talked to some folks in town. They talked to Perigord. The bank was broken into Tuesday night. Mr. Stuart says several thousand dollars were taken. He and some of the others think the sheriff ought to worry about that instead of about where Hank's been hiding. Perigord couldn't claim the bank job was yours this time, Marc. You're dead. Mr. Stuart was stubborn with the sheriff. Mr. Stuart's a good friend of your father's, Marc."

"He should be," Challon said. "Pierre set him up in business twenty years ago because he thought the county needed a bank. Stuart's made a good living off XO deposits alone, since."

"Van Cleave will have to listen to Peri-gord," 'Lena went on. "If he doesn't, Hank and the rest of the boys can take care of him. They've got something to fight for again."

"You're forgetting Marcy," Challon said wearily. "It's Marcy Van Cleave will have to listen to. She'll make him. Prentice is here and she won't have been sleeping nights since he's been gone. Marcy doesn't like to sleep alone."

"She's got Van Cleave," 'Lena said bluntly.

This was ugly. Shabby estimate though he now had of his former wife, Challon knew where Marcy's pride began and the heights toward which she was driving it. The thought of Marcy lowering her sights as far down the scale as Van Cleave left a string of dirty eddies in his mind. The charge didn't become 'Lena. Marcy needed no tarring from either of them.

Then he saw there had been no malice in the statement. 'Lena was voicing conviction, nothing more. He wondered if while he lay here on the rim of the mesa, recovering from his wound sufficiently to admit defeat, Marcy had also lost something of what she had gained. Curiosity prompted the thought, and it passed swiftly. Nothing concerning Marcy any longer made a difference.

"I've taken care of Marcy," 'Lena said softly. "I've sent Prentice back to her just now. She won't have to send her little killer out to look for him. And you're done with this kind of care. We're going back down into the lava, to Tia's place. There's a house, at least. Tia's alone, and you have stock down there that needs attention."

"They'll think on the lava — the rest of them — that I got Jim and the Hyatts killed. It wouldn't be good there."

"Didn't you?" 'Lena asked. "What difference does it make? Since when have you given a damn what other men thought, if you knew you were right? Could anything be much worse than it's been here since Hank piled this brush up over your head and started praying because he couldn't do anything else?"

"That's just it," Challon said. "There's been enough of this — for you and Hank and Pierre and Tia Pozner. Enough for me too. I was wrong as hell. It's time I turned right. Tell Hank to come here, will you?"

'Lena stepped outside and called to Bayard. He came over in a moment to grin down, hat pushed back, at Challon.

"We turned that Prentice loose just about in time," he said. "He's beginning to get his belly tanned up a little. I tell you he took a swing at me this morning."

"The hell with Prentice," Challon said, feeling creeping into the statement involuntarily. "We're done with him and all the rest of it. You boys have been up against a tough pull. Now the easy row is ahead. We all got enough mud on our boots. Get word to Pierre, Hank. Tell him to transfer everything we've got in Stuart's bank over the pass to Trinidad and then come along himself and meet us there. You and the boys bunch what whiteface stuff you can gather in a cut through the lava and start it moving through the mesa on the Branson Trail. We'll meet Pierre in Trinidad and drive out west of there. Ought to be some good starting range over Trinchera way."

"Marc, you crazy?" Bayard grunted in astonishment.

Challon grinned.

"No. We're done here, that's all. Me, I want to see what kind of a house 'Lena can build — without somebody else's underwear already hanging on the doorknobs."

'Lena bent solicitously, brushing her hand across Challon's brow. Her fingers strayed caressingly down the slope of his cheek to the hollow under his ear, to his shoulder, following his arm to his wrist, and stopping there. Challon eased. He didn't know why. Perhaps because she understood what he was trying to tell her so readily. Perhaps because her acquiescence was so swift. She looked up at Hank Bayard.

"Too much excitement," she said solemnly. "A touch of fever back, I'm afraid. Delirium.

Clear out of his head. You get on, Hank. Get camp broken and on the move. The sooner we're settled at Tia's, the better it'll be for Marc."

Challon choked in astonishment and partially raised himself. 'Lena pushed him back strongly. Hank Bayard eyed him with a transparent enough commiseration.

"I about got the horse litter rigged, 'Lena," he said. "Reckon I better rig some lashing to hold him in it too. A man that's out of his head —"

Anger burned through the listlessness hazing Challon's mind, and the strong, heavy note of his voice startled him.

"Who the hell gives orders around here?" he demanded.

"I'll get the boys on the move right away, 'Lena," Bayard said. He shook his head, not wholly getting away with the staginess of his regret. "Sure hate to see a relapse like this set in on Marc when he was doing so damned well!"

Challon swore but with little fury. He was too tired. And it appeared there were two women whom he could not beat.

15

Prentice had never been able to grasp the
method by which people of this grass found
their way so readily from one place to another. There were plenty of landmarks — the
mesas themselves, Tinaja and the volcano,
the ever-present white-capped horizon line of
the mountains to the west — but intervening
distances were so great that the slightest in-
accuracy in bearing multiplied itself in an
hour or two into a huge error. He experienced this trouble working out a way down
from the cap of Boundary Mesa. It was, he
supposed, no more than fifteen miles in the
saddle from Bayard's camp to the home
buildings of the XO. Three hours at the outside, allowing for the steepness of the first
part of the descent. But at noon he was still
threading the long, slanting ridges, the deep-
cut arroyos, and the tumbled lava ruin which
formed the talus footing of the mesa.

His horse sweat with the dogged pace at
which he held it, and the afternoon died
overhead before he reached a low promon-
tory, an XO fence, and a view of the home
buildings. There were lamps already alight in

the main house when he found a gate in the fence and passed through it with his usual difficulty in refastening the hooped wire barrier. A number of horses were saddled at the corral rail, but they were dry, their coats free of dust, and he thought none of them had been ridden during the day. Two or three of Van Cleave's men were in the yard. One of these took Prentice's horse when he swung down in front of the corral gate.

The rider eyed Anson, his eyes widening at the beard, the thinness of the face, the limpness of clothes worn ten days without removal, but he said nothing. Tom Halliard, again in boots and saddle clothes, his face more supported than bandaged by a swath of cloth encircling it from under his chin to the crown of his head, was sitting slump-shouldered on a bench outside the bunkhouse. He looked up but also said nothing as Prentice passed him.

With weariness something he carried like a burden across his shoulders Anson angled on across the yard to the back door of the main house. Van Cleave was smoking at a table in the kitchen. His boots and shirt were off. He looked as if he might have shaved half an hour before and had not redressed. He looked comfortable. He looked at home.

"Turned you loose, eh?" Van Cleave asked. "Bayard must be pretty damned sure of himself with the old man back in town!"

"I could have escaped from Bayard," Anson suggested.

Van Cleave grinned.

"Anybody else, maybe; not you. Perigord was here about noon. He said Hank would turn you loose with Old Man Challon back in Range to stiffen his back. I been waiting to see if Hugh was right."

"Funny," Anson said shortly. "I had a notion maybe the sheriff was out here looking for the gang that held up the Santa Fe pay train and the bank in town. He ought to have been smart enough to have come to the right place the first time."

"Word gets around, doesn't it?" Van Cleave asked easily. "Prentice, you got a dirty mind! Sit down. Marcy's dressing."

"Supposing you dress and get the hell out of here," Anson suggested, anger beginning to pulse in him like liquid over steam. This was the last time he was going to come home to this house, and he wanted a different reception.

Van Cleave agreeably drew on his boots, stamping each foot sharply against the floor to set the leather, and he stood up.

"Why don't we understand each other right now?" he asked pleasantly. "You want something on this ranch. So do I. Two different things. But we're both here and we're going to have to make a trade. I'm going to get what I want. If I don't, I'm going to have to take what you think you've got. I can do it. I know. I've had ten days to find that out in."

"Marcy?" Prentice breathed softly.

"Is there anything else you want here?"

Prentice stared at Van Cleave's torso in half-sleeved gray underwear with a row of stamped ivory buttons, each bearing the initials of a trade-mark. He had been camped halfway into the sky with a different kind of man for the last ten days. A kind which worked in the sun and was colored by it. A kind with ridged biceps and deep chest. A bigger kind than this. Yet there was something repellently beautiful in the slender perfection of Van Cleave's body and the chalk whiteness of the skin on his upper arms and hairless chest. This man did not take his shirt off in the sun, only within the shelter of a house. And he bred fear where another might have bred respect. Anson felt sorry for Marcy. Her attack was her defense. She had no other.

Turning, he walked wordlessly out of the room, leaving Van Cleave grinning imperturbably beside the kitchen table.

A man long drunk would feel like this on his first sober day. A certainty of wrongness inside, at first; self-condemnation for an obvious excess which had not been at all apparent during its commission. The old saying that no man knew he was drunk until he could see the bottom of the bottle. This was

231

the bottom now; these were the dregs. Their taste was in Prentice's mouth. His tongue was thick with it. And the whole machine of his thinking was churning against the poison he had poured into it.

It was easy for a man to quit the bottle when he was prostrate with the after-nausea of a bout. Prentice wondered if it would be like this with Marcy. He hoped not. He wanted a cleaner break than that.

She came out into the main hall of the house when he was half along it on the way to the living room. She was in a fresh dress with the top starched and her hair was newly brushed. The light of the wall lamp between them was good to her. It was not hard to read motives he wanted into her flooding relief when she saw him. For a moment it was easy to believe that here was exactly what he had hoped to have in this house when Marcy told him she was willing to divorce her husband.

Then she was running toward him and her relief was all too plainly from a personal desperation rather than from a concern for him. The lamplight was in sharper focus on the lines about her eyes and mouth. Marc Challon was at Tia Pozner's, recovering from a shot in the back and nursed by a woman who loved him. Old Pierre was in Range, urging the people of his county to indict a man and a woman who had walked impatiently through barriers they all honored. Cy Van Cleave was in the kitchen of Challon's house, counting stolen money in his mind and calculating how little of it he would have to use to take over the XO from the two who now had it. In Range, Hugh Perigord was polishing his star assiduously, measuring two titans against one another in order to choose the stronger for his own support — a railroad and an old rancher now without land. Tom Halliard had no face. Jim Pozner and the Hyatt brothers — men from Van Cleave's crew and Challon's — were dead. There would be other wounds.

One man had the fuse to all this in his hands, to snuff it out or fan it to more furious burning. It was curious where and when a man could feel strength and the sharpness of the cleavage which could occasionally develop between the right and the wrong.

"Anson!" Marcy cried as she ran against Prentice. "Anson, I've been half crazy!"

"I'm hungry," Prentice said.

"You poor dear, you look it!" Marcy told him, backing a little away. Her lips smiled tenderness, but her eyes were restless with speculation. So much could have happened in ten days. "Sit down," she said. "I'll bring you something. Kick out of your boots. Maybe you'd like a bath and your pajamas first. You look done in."

"I'm hungry," Prentice said again.

Marcy half pushed him into a deep living-room chair and ran down the hall toward the back of the house. He heard her speak there and knew Van Cleave was still in the kitchen. Her voice rose in pitch and he could feel the tension of argument, if he could not hear the words. As Marcy neared the door, returning, one phrase was distinguishable:

"Not tonight!"

It could mean so many things. Prentice sighed heavily. Wisdom was hard come by. But when a man knew an answer, a decision was ridiculously simple.

Marcy came back into the living room. She brought him the coffeepot with no mug from which to drink the half-warmed stuff and two slabs of bread concealing a slice of meat, the lot having been cut so hurriedly and under such duress that no ordinary jaws could have attacked it. Prentice put the sandwich down on the arm of his chair.

"I'm going out to Trinidad in the morning, Marcy," he said.

Obviously startled, she was a moment regaining control of herself.

"Business?" she asked guardedly.

"Business. Yes."

"Alone? You don't want me to go with you?"

"No."

Silence for a moment, then more quietly:

"How long will you be gone?"

"I'm not coming back."

Prentice was forced to admire again the hard-rock ribbing of her nature. There was now none of the false hysteria with which she had greeted his return. She turned her back and walked to the fireplace, her mind, like a man's, functioning best in a difficult moment while she was in motion. Before the mantel she turned.

"I hate a coward," she said.

"Meaning me?"

"Anson, you're exhausted. You must have been through hell. We both have. Tomorrow —"

"No, Marcy."

Her jaws clamped shut. She recrossed to him and stood looking down.

"Hate you?" she asked quietly. "You try to leave the XO in the morning and you'll find out just how much I hate you! How much I've hated you since the instant you first touched me!"

"There's more than just the two of us involved," Prentice said patiently. "There's the ranch. We'll have to talk about that."

"What are you afraid of that's making you quit — me?"

Prentice didn't have to lie. "No."

"The country — the people?" Marcy went on with a tight smile. "Talk? Listen, no young couple off the grass ever got married because they were in love and spring was in the air, but because they had to. No baby was ever born down here but calendars in every kitchen and pool hall and store got marked back to the week and day to see if a preacher had got the parents hitched in time. No woman ever went north to Denver or east to Kansas City or even across the pass to Trinidad for medical attention without everybody knowing why she went. Cancer, woman's complaint, anything — it's always been a cover-up for abortion. You actually give a damn what people who think like that think of you, Anson?"

Prentice thought of Stuart, of Treadwell, of Hank Bayard. He thought of Marc Challon and Challon's father and the dark-skinned girl out on the grass with Challon now. Marcy's accusation wasn't just. Not against such as these.

"Yes," he said slowly. "Yes, I'm afraid I do."

"Why didn't you tell me?" Marcy demanded. "We can make them crawl. We should have already, but being married would have made it easier. We're the XO ranch. We're as big as the Challons ever were, and for the same reason that they were big. These people down here are a funny kind, sort of bullying in their thinking. If we hide, they talk. But come out flat in the open and make them like it, and they will. It's their way.

"We'll have us a party here at the house, a big one. They'll all have to come. The XO puts bread onto too many of their tables, one way or another.. And they won't talk after that. Not after they've seen your ring on my finger!"

"Not my ring, Marcy."

She clamped her hands until the knuckles whitened and strode once more to the mantel and back.

"You're afraid of Van Cleave!" she charged.

"I'm afraid of what we've done to Marc Challon and his father and Hank Bayard and the rest of the XO people. I'm afraid of what we've done to the ranch and Range and the whole Territory. I didn't know in the beginning how big a ranch like this was — that it was something which belonged to more than the Challons alone."

"Ah!" Marcy said. Prentice thought she would spit, but she did not.

"I'm afraid of what we've done to ourselves. I thought I loved you, Marcy. I think I tried hard. But there's nothing —"

"You should have seen me when I was eighteen," Marcy cut in harshly. "You should have seen the kind of life that was facing me then. I've done a lot in the last ten years, but I'm ashamed of none of it. And I know as well as you do that love is for kids. You're dodging. You're afraid of Van Cleave!"

Prentice made no answer. Marcy's lips

twisted bitterly, but the edge of the blade was still toward Prentice, not herself.

"You needn't be, Anson," she murmured. "I've taken care of him."

"I'm afraid I don't envy the man."

She struck him then. Not a woman's tolerated prerogative of a quick, wiping slap when words failed. This was the hard, swing blow of a balled fist, with deep malice behind it. And it hurt. Prentice tasted blood. He reached for his kerchief, then belatedly remembered he had used it to dress Challon's wound on the mesa. He swabbed at his lips with his dusty sleeve.

"We better talk about the XO, Marcy," he said quietly again.

The lamp over the desk he had occasionally used in the ranch store was smoking heavily, but Prentice did not trouble to trim it, once it was alight. He wouldn't need it long. He brushed aside the accumulation of figures which represented his work on the store accounts. They had no value now, either to the ranch or to himself, as evidence of industry to offer his father.

Drawing out an envelope, he addressed it to Jason Prentice, care of the Atchison, Topeka, and Santa Fe Railroad, Trinidad, Colorado. He thought the mails as good a way as any to let his father know what had happened here. He wrote a terse note with the very bad pen on the desk. Folding this, he slid it into the envelope with the document he had earlier written in the house, subsequently signed by Marcy and witnessed by the Mexican yard boy then cleaning up in the kitchen. It was curious that his signature should have been more graceful and legible than Marcy's — *Paco Encelador.*

Sealing the envelope, Prentice dropped it in the metal slot in the top of a locked mail sack hanging on a peg on the wall — a mail sack stenciled with the point of its origin: *Challon, New Mexico Territory, U.S.A.* It would be riding in the candy wagon to Range before breakfast in the morning. This done, Prentice returned to the desk, lighted another of his eternally unsatisfactory wheat-straw cigarettes, and stared at the smoky lamp.

In a way he had offered Marcy a fair enough deal. So fair it was doubtful Jason Prentice would ever tolerate his son again — unless he could be shown that by quitting now Anson had affected the course and ownership of the XO and inevitably the mood of the whole country about Range to a degree which would benefit the Santa Fe when it built across the grass. The old man might not figure the price too high for this, in the long run.

Marcy had been a good trader, even in this last hand. When she realized that he was himself no longer any part of the consideration and that it was beyond her power to make him so, she had listened to his offer. She had a full third interest in the XO, transferred to her by Marc Challon in the beginning. Anson himself had another third as forfeiture on the loan he had made Challon. And he had bought the remaining third at the time of their settlement.

It had been plain that with wider and brighter dreams now dead, Marcy would not relinquish her share of the ranch. Perhaps out of her own desperation; perhaps because of Van Cleave. Prentice had not known and he didn't want to know. But he couldn't give Marcy his two thirds outright. Some pride remained and it overrode his impatience to be done with the dealing. The measure of that pride was in the figure he had asked; a demand note for fifty thousand dollars. A total salvage of less than the amount of his original loan and actually a total loss, since he would never enforce its collection. But it was an anchor to hold Marcy in place, to insure that she would never cross his path again. And the note was something to show his father. To have come out of this with at least something on paper might mollify Jason Prentice.

Marcy had signed — sullenly — but she had signed, already doubtless planning feverishly at a new tangent. Her carriage was not

Marcy's only feline attribute. She had a way of landing always with her feet under her. Her pyramid was reversed now. She didn't know that Marc Challon was alive. But in Challon's good time she would find it out. And Cy Van Cleave, who had been merely a buttress she had flanked in against her original scheme for additional support, now became the focal point on which the whole structure precariously balanced.

When Challon was once more on his feet he would turn again to the task of repossessing his ranch. This was certain. The XO was in the man's blood as it was in his father's. And Marcy had her limitations. She could hold the ranch against the Challons only as long as she had Van Cleave. Anson had told her he didn't envy the thin, soft-voiced little man from Mora. He could have gone farther. He didn't envy Marcy, either.

When his cigarette had burned his fingers and spilled its fire on the floor at his resultant start, Prentice rose and snuffed the lamp with a gusty breath across its chimney. There was still much to be done, but he would not do it. A talk with Perigord in town on such facts as he knew concerning Van Cleave's part in the holdup in the pass. Mention of Van Cleave's evasive answer to his direct charge that the XO foreman had a part in the more recent robbery of Stuart's bank. A threat to relay this information on to his father and the Santa Fe, thereby almost certainly forcing Perigord's hand. A few minutes with Old Man Challon to tell him Marc was alive and recuperating at Pozner's place.

He was too tired to ride farther tonight, but things were finished here. He would go on to Range, but he would speak to no one there. This was the measure of his cowardice. It was not as large here at the end as he had been afraid it might be, riding down from the mesa in today's noonday sun.

Van Cleave was leaning against the corral rails when Prentice crossed over from the store. No others of the crew were visible in the yard. The bunkhouse windows were dimly alight, but the main house was now wholly dark. Prentice passed Van Cleave without greeting and went into the barn, heading for the saddle rack. Van Cleave followed him in, pulling the big door shut. Prentice put his back to the rack and waited for the other to come up. The restless sound of the animals in the big building was about him. The sweet smell of meadow-cured hay. Oiled harness and riding leather. And the dung-littered straw underfoot.

"Riding?" Van Cleave asked.

"Yes."

"Alone?"

"You said there were two things on the ranch a while ago. They're both yours now."

"So you quit!" Van Cleave breathed. "Curled up your toes. Riding out all clean-shanked and to hell with the rest of us. Giving her the whole thing without even letting me have a chance to bid for your share of this place — and you knowing I want this ranch like you never wanted anything in all of your damned, fat-bellied life!"

"Make your bid to Marcy."

"I will," Van Cleave agreed. "I'll make even a cleaner deal with her than I could have with you, before I'm through. But there's something else. I've had a few men spill from their saddles when they were riding with me. Enough of them to be used to it. But I've stuck to an old rule of mine; I've never left any of them in shape to talk about me behind my back after I'd moved on."

Van Cleave had come very close to Prentice in the darkness. Anson could hear the quick, light tempo of his breathing.

"Leave me alone!" he said.

"There was Ben, dying over there in the store before I could get back to take care of him."

"Leave me alone!" Prentice said again.

"You got into Ben's pockets and found some money. You wanted to talk about that in town once. You might want to again."

"It'll be dawn before I'm in town now," Prentice said rapidly. He could hear his own voice with a peculiar detachment. A voice warped upward in pitch. It was hot in the barn with the door closed. He was sweating. "I'm catching the daylight stage to Trinidad. I'm not talking to anybody!"

"No," Van Cleave agreed. "When the buzzards start to swing, somebody is going to find you out somewhere between here and wherever Bayard has been hiding on the mesas."

"My God, please leave me alone!"

Prentice's voice was an entity of its own now, disembodied and beyond volition, shaming him with its thinness.

"It'll look like you escaped Bayard," Van Cleave went on steadily. "It'll look like one of his boys trailed you and got you. There isn't a man on the XO tonight would dare admit you'd been here after I pass the word."

"No, man, listen! There's something you ought to know. Bayard isn't on the mesas now. He's at the Pozner place. And Challon isn't dead. He's alive. He's alive, I tell you!"

"So's Jesus — they say," Van Cleave answered. "But nobody reliable has seen him since he was nailed to a cross quite a spell ago. Takes something I can see to scare me."

There was a soft, almost caressing metallic click. The hard muzzle of a gun rammed an inch into Prentice's belly. It was then that he realized his voice was still in his own throat — that he could speak with it — that he had to.

"For the love of God, don't do it!" he screamed.

The gun grunted, making no louder sound because its muzzle was embedded in the soft flesh above his belt. A harsh violence and an exquisite agony flung Prentice up against the saddle rack on the points of his toes. He caught one of the pegs and hung by it as rigidity rushed from his body through a great hole where his bowels had been.

"Marcy," he said very distinctly, "Marcy, help me."

The peg in his hand broke and he fell heavily. His face struck a hard boot toe which was hastily withdrawn. There was a rushing wind of compelling velocity and no hurt. As from a great distance and rapidly receding farther, he heard Van Cleave's voice:

"God almighty!"

And he found comfort in the lifting wind. Here at last was something of which he was wholly unafraid.

16

Tia Pozner had ordered the most comfortable chair in her front room nailed onto the seat platform of the buckboard. Blanket-wrapped and held in place by a band like a saddle cinch passing across his belly from one chair arm to the other, Challon rode on this. 'Lena drove for him. Pierre flanked them, astride a lava bronc two hands too short for his great frame and twice too ornery for a man of his age. Swinging with the springy jolting of the buckboard, Challon was warm in the sun. He thought he was farther along toward complete recovery than the others would admit. Damaged springs of energy were again nearing full flow within him. And he could feel the workings of his body steadily storing away again the reserves against which he had once been able to draw at will — reserves of strength which had made it possible for him to cheat death when all of the jokers in the deck had been skull-faced.

The heaviness which had burdened him in the first conscious days of convalescence had lifted. An old, familiar restlessness was again stirring in his blood. Old objectives were again in place and an old determination locked in mesh with his will. It seemed incredible to him now that there had been days when he had been willing to let the accomplishments of a lifetime slip between his fingers as unprotestingly as life itself had nearly slipped through them. It was hard to believe he had lain upon his back so exhausted that it had been easier to consider a whole new beginning than to look ahead to final settlement of the hand he had sat down to play out with Marcy Bennett.

Marcy Bennett . . . He remembered again a recollection which had come to him as he dozed on the feather mattress in Tia Pozner's bedroom. A recollection which had eluded him all of the years he had lived with Marcy. Something he would have liked to ask her about.

Three or four years before she had come to the XO there had been a rider on the ranch named Ed Bennett. A tall, good-natured kid with a kind of a lonesome way about him and an unusually even temper for a saddle hand. A good boy. Good enough to be remembered a long time. He had quit to start himself a shoestring jerk-line freight outfit up in the Kansas rail-construction trade. About the time Marcy had showed up in Trinidad, now that he thought of it, Ed Bennett had died of lung fever in La Junta. Left unconscious and hemorrhaging in a shack there by a woman who skipped with all his cash.

It was some time before he heard the story, and when he did it didn't mean much. But it meant something now. Marcy was using the name of Bennett when he met her, and she had said she had come from Kansas. If this was true, then she had come through La Junta. He'd see Marcy again. When he did, he'd sure as hell ask her about Ed Bennett.

It was good to be thinking about Marcy again, to be tasting his own sureness and the inevitability of her defeat. Defeat she would create with her own hands, without intervention from him except in the right of self-defense. Challon glanced at the girl riding the seat of the buckboard beside his cumbersome throne. He wondered if his swing from surrender to hostility again had troubled her. He thought not. There was a strong current of the physical in 'Lena. She would understand better than most that his earlier passiveness had been only his shattered body trying to shed the dual burden of bitterness and hatred — a burden so heavy for a time that the prospect of eventual benefit to the XO from Marcy's tenancy had failed to counterbalance it.

Certainly Hank Bayard had been troubled, and Pierre. He had seen their spirits rise daily as his strength grew and his determination returned. Among those two and himself it was difficult to know who was the most devoted to the grass the three of them had ridden so long.

This drive today was a thing cooked up in secrecy between Hank and Pierre. The result of many murmured parleys in Tia's front room when Challon's lamp was out and he was supposedly sleeping. A step in some sort of scheme they had rigged between them. Pierre was the guide. Hank and the rest of the boys were waiting for them out here someplace in the malpais. And Marc knew he was going to have to be surprised as hell.

With Pierre riding as loose in his saddle as a boy and grinning near as wide, they pulled up out of the sand-bed arroyo they had been following and rolled over a low rise. Pierre pulled up, and 'Lena halted the buckboard. In front of them lay a bowl of green patch grass in the lava, maybe four miles out from Pozner's. In its center, apparently relishing this attention after so much neglect, were the whiteface breeders Challon had excepted from the XO herds and about which he had been much concerned in recent days.

While dust settled about the motionless wheels of the buckboard, Challon looked at the cattle with an almost sensuous possessiveness. They had not fared badly for having been scattered so long. Brush-burned and scarred some. A few lamed by the bad footing scattered through this malpais.

Gaunted a little because they needed more water than range beef and had not known how to find it. But apparently intact and the same potential wealth they had been on XO meadows.

Hank Bayard came jogging across to the buckboard, grinning widely. He pushed back his hat, swabbed at his white forehead with a dirty kerchief, and indicated Challon's chair with a tilt of his head.

"That outfit would look better on the back of an elephant," he said.

"This is something, Hank!" Challon told him. "Really something! Takes a load off my mind. You get a full tally?"

"Down to the last head," Bayard agreed with satisfaction. "If I never believed in Challon luck before, I do now. Say, Pierre — offhand — how much you suppose this bunch would be worth in cash money, set down on the rails at Trinidad?"

Pierre gave the question elaborate consideration, although it was obvious enough to Challon that this whole thing had been thoroughly rehearsed. Pierre duplicated Hank's hat-tilting and brow-wiping ritual, except that his kerchief was white, silk, and immaculate.

"Blood stock," he said slowly. "An easy average eight hundred a head, on a broker's market and asking for quick money. Eighty thousand for the bunch, Hank. And I was noticing, they're so toughened up now from ranging on their own that they'd easy take the drive through the mesas on the Branson Trail."

It was transparent as hell.

"Eighty thousand is a sight of money," Hank murmured, as though he had not known at all what the stock was worth.

"With what Marc's still got on deposit with Stuart in Range, it's damned near half the money God ever made," Pierre agreed solemnly. "But money in the bank is like beef in the air, Hank. It ain't worth much of a damn by itself. A man has got to have land. If he's got that, he can raise stock again quick enough and make his money too."

"Now take a woman that likes a soft bed," Bayard said. "One that's looking for the easy and the fancy way to live. A ranch ain't the best answer for her. But she could use the kind of money you're talking about, Pierre. And an outlander with a yellow belly ain't hard to buy off." He swung toward Challon. "Marc, listen. We all got to get back on the XO! Throw in this stock and your cash and let me try to make us a deal. We're not getting anywhere out here."

Challon felt suddenly hot and irritable and more tired than he cared to admit. He didn't like Hank and Pierre stacking their weight against him like this. They were feeling their way, all right, careful-like, but putting on all the pressure they dared. 'Lena stirred beside him.

"We can talk about it back at the house," she said swiftly. "We've been out here long enough. Marc's had enough of this sun."

Challon shook his head. He scowled at his father. "There's a million dollars in that bunch of blood bulls and you know it. Eight hundred a head!"

"They cost about that," Pierre protested.

"They cost us five years, building the bunch up. You figure that in?"

"The XO cost us fifty years!" Pierre answered. "Did you figure that in, boy? Look, I want to be inside, looking out over my own wire again. Damned if I care what it costs!"

"All the cards aren't down in my deal for the ranch yet, and you know that too!" Challon said sharply. "Sell the whiteface stuff — let Marcy force me to that too? Pierre, what's the matter with you and Hank? You think I'm a complete damned fool?"

"We got an almighty nasty suspicion, boy," Pierre said bluntly. "Hank and me are reasonable. So are the rest of the boys and folks in town — folks in Trinidad and Santa Fe and maybe even Denver. And so is the railroad. But it's got to know whether there's going to be a beef ranch down here, run by stockmen and showing an annual increase that'll furnish it with freight, or whether it's climbing down the pass into a rats' nest of wild riding and trouble stirred up by a crazy, cut-throating woman's itching.

"I got to know whether I'm going to leave a son behind me to keep the birdlime brushed off my headstone when I'm gone. Hank and the boys would sort of like to know whether to figure on dying with their boots on or in bed. You claim we're going back onto the ranch. All right. This is the easiest way. Prentice and that woman will both buy off at the right price. The extra quick money we might need is in the white-face bunch — most of our profits have been going into it for quite a spell. And selling them, we don't have to wait twenty years for them to sire your million dollars, either!"

"If you wanted to pull out halfway through this game, you and 'Lena and Hank made a mistake in hauling me out of the grave Van Cleave tumbled me into," Challon growled. "This is our country — my country. There's nobody on the XO even knows what that means now. But you should, Pierre. The country works slow, but it does a permanent job. I told Marcy that. By hell, she's going to see what I meant. I pulled out here into the lava in the first place to wait. There's still some wait left in me."

"So suicide's a game now!" Pierre snorted. "Hell, standing bare-breeches in a nest of rattlers is common sense to what you're trying! It's been quiet as bejesus since Hank

253

and 'Lena turned young Prentice loose up there on the mesa. Quiet like that is dangerous, boy. A man — or a woman — that don't make no noise is either dead or fixing to stab you in the back. If you ain't had enough of that, I have!"

"You were doing a chore in town before you found out I was still in my boots out here," Challon said impatiently. "If Range closed up like a vise on Marcy and Anse, the break would come quicker."

"Sure," Pierre agreed sourly. "But how can I beat down talk I can't disprove?"

"Gossip —" Challon grunted. "Sand in the air. What is it — that I'm waiting too long?"

"That you're waiting at all!" Pierre said harshly. "You been kicked out of your bed and off your grass. You been shot in the back. Folks are wondering one way or another just what in hell it takes to make you fight, boy. And so am I. By God, maybe they're right in town, after all. Maybe you have lost your priming; maybe you have been plumb castrated by that woman!"

Pierre jerked his bronc around and rode it at a short, high-headed, stiff-legged lope across the grass toward the crew bunched beyond the whiteface herd. Hank Bayard lingered uncertainly for a moment, then followed him. 'Lena snapped her lines and swung the buckboard around. Challon swore with feeling.

"I need a drink!"

"You need rest," 'Lena corrected firmly. "It's home and blankets for you. If Pierre had a bullet in his back, maybe he wouldn't expect you to talk fighting practically your first day on your feet."

"It isn't my feet that are getting calluses from this ride," Challon grumbled as the buckboard clattered over a patch of field stone. "Pierre's an old man. Maybe I forget it sometimes. He sure as hell does. When he's gone, 'Lena, there's going to be a hole in the sky. This country must have hit cover for fair when he came in here with a wagon, a forge, an ax, and half a keg of powder to build him a ranch. Waiting is hard for him, maybe because he's short on time. And that talk in town that a Challon has lost his priming would gall the hell out of Pierre. Is he right about it?"

"That talk?" 'Lena asked. "You care about it?"

"Before, no. Maybe not. But now — yes. Yes, I think I do. What are they actually saying in town?"

"That you've quit. That you had quit before you ever rode into town the night you were shot. That you quit the day you rode off the XO. Folks don't understand that."

"Do you?"

"What you've told me," 'Lena said. "And I can wait it out if you can."

255

If he could . . . The phrase had barbs. Challon tried to shake it free of his mind, but he could not wholly do so. The buckboard rolled on in silence.

A wind had come up. 'Lena held the buckboard to lower ground than she had followed on the way out. The shelter was welcome. Nearly half of the way back into Pozner's a wagon, moving in the opposite direction and obviously following their outbound tracks, appeared suddenly on the crest of a low ridge a quarter of a mile to the east. 'Lena pulled up. The other driver had already done so, staring across at them with interest. Challon thought the rig was a spring livery wagon hired in Range. The brightness of its green paint made it unlikely that it was a working outfit from someplace on the grass. But the distance was too great to make out the identity of the driver.

"Who is it?" he asked 'Lena.

The girl shrugged.

"Looks like he followed us out from Tia's," she said.

"We better get on in, then."

'Lena snapped her reins. Looking back, Challon saw the other driver begin to move again in a moment or so, also, heading on out into the lava.

They had left Tia Pozner alone at her place. Challon could think of no danger which might threaten her now that Jim was dead. No business anybody from town well enough off to have hired a livery rig could have with her, either. Still, he was relieved when they topped a last rise and could see Tia staring off under the shading of her hand toward them. 'Lena obviously shared his relief. She shook the team into a sharp trot and held it until they were in the yard. Tia ran to the near wheel as they stopped rolling.

"Did you see him?" she asked anxiously.

"Who?" 'Lena asked her.

"The sheriff, from Range. Hugh Perigord. He was here. He followed your tracks out of the yard."

"He passed us a quarter of a mile off, Tia. We couldn't tell who it was. What did he want?"

The older woman lowered her eyes sullenly.

"I don't know. He killed Jaime. Could I talk to him? I hid in the house till he was gone."

'Lena unstrapped the band which had held Challon in his seat, and he swung down gingerly from it, finding his weariness was mostly the monotony of enforced time in one position and that he was neither as tired nor as unsteady as he had anticipated. He didn't think he would have to wait a week to try a saddle, after all. A few days. Just a few days.

Tia clutched 'Lena's arm, worry deeply graven in her frown.

"The *cabrón* could have found out Señor

Challon is not dead?" she asked.

Since Jim Pozner's death his wife had reverted almost wholly to her mother tongue. She seemed to find comfort in it. And she invariably now used the señor before Challon's name. Aware that Spanish-speaking people often used this formality as an evidence of polite hostility, Challon had been disturbed. He had been some days in her house before he realized Tia Pozner was using the word to express respect. Not because he was a Challon of the XO, once long her husband's enemy and the biggest man within her horizon, but because he had earned it from her. He had failed in what he had tried to do one night in Range, and his failure had cost this woman her husband, but she respected him for the attempt. Or was it for the care he had shown her the night Van Cleave had been here? Whatever its roots, the respect was sincere.

"It doesn't make much difference what Hugh knew when he left here, *hermanita*," Challon told her gently. "It's about time he found out, anyway, and that throne I was riding would have given me away ten miles off. He was closer than that. Right this minute I'll take any odds that the sheriff of Red River County is sweating blood. When you plow a man under, you kind of like to have him stay plowed instead of popping up through the clods in a few weeks, like spring

258

grass. Hugh's going to be a mite nervous from here on."

The three of them had moved into the house. Jim Pozner's shotgun was standing against the casing just inside the doorway. Challon glanced at it in surprise. Tia picked it up and calmly let its hammer down from its cocked position.

"I wish I had shot him!" she said fiercely.

"Why didn't you?" Challon suggested good-naturedly.

Tia looked at him with mild surprise.

"Why?" she repeated. "Because he's yours, señor. I saved him for you, of course. Surely you wanted me to. He cheated you in Range."

Tia went on into the kitchen, returning the gun to its usual resting place behind the door there. Challon ignored the open door of the bedroom and the invalid's bed waiting for him there and dropped down on the settee in the front room. After an uncertain moment, 'Lena sat down beside him. Challon raised his good arm, and she slid under it. Tia reappeared in the kitchen doorway, saw them, and backed from sight. A moment later Challon heard the outer door close behind her. Another Spanish courtesy. Tia knew privacy could not belong to more than two.

'Lena's heavy hair was a cloud under Challon's chin. The warm currents of her body sped his own. But it was her silence

259

which he relished most. Few women were born with an ability to hold to silence, to use it for their own purposes, so that it became a greater challenge than any which could be built with words. In silence a man could order the run of his thoughts and so know his own desires to a full certainty. This could not often be done in the presence of a woman, and many of a man's mistakes could begin at such a time. There would be no mistakes with Elena Casamajor. She wanted none.

Challon's fingers lay along the roundness of her ribs, tightening slowly of their own volition. Her near thigh lay along his, steadily burning through thick petticoating, the cotton of her skirt, and the fine whipcording of his own breeches. Her breathing was deep and steady, falling more and more out of cadence with his own quickening breath. The house was silent, and the yard, and the whole width of the empty afternoon. Minutes slid by, their soundlessness precious.

It was not planned and it was not completely hunger, since there was a gentleness which did not pull at his knitting wound in the reach which Challon made for her free shoulder with his uncertain left arm. Her head turned and tilted back questioningly, although she must have certainly known the answer. Her lips were there, a little parted and softer than those which had always masked Marcy Bennett. It was a longer moment than any of the rest and equally as silent. It was like others Challon had known often enough, and yet wholly different. At its end Challon straightened a little, touched by a small foreign fear. This was a need he had never known before. This was a closeness of approach no living soul had ever made to him. This woman was of the same dust as himself. Not only was she in his blood; she was the fiber of his being.

'Lena looked for an instant deep into his eyes, and he thought there was a somber sadness in hers. He believed he understood. There was so much time already gone. And on the grass, more than anywhere else, time was short for a man and a woman alike. She put her hand gently against his chest and pushed him away a little. His left arm cramped in an uncomfortable reminder of its lingering stiffness. He swung it back to its own side of his body. 'Lena slipped his other hand from her side, cupped it in both of her own, and smiled. The silence had held through all of this. She broke it now, knowing as certainly as Challon did that no perfection was endless.

"I think Pierre and Hank were right on one thing a while ago," she said, her smile widening. "You're ready to fight now — any time!"

Challon made no answer to this, presently

voicing his own thought.

"There's so much happened. So little time to talk. Never about us — about what we'd do — about when. You've never asked."

"Why should I? I know the answer."

"You're sure?"

"Marc Challon, open your eyes! Do you think you're the only person who can cut the cards he wants from the deck? You think you're the only person with enough patience to get exactly what he wants in exactly the way he wants it? Of course I'm sure! I've had a long time to make certain!"

Challon grinned. His hand slipped from hers again. As it did so a voice spoke from the front doorway:

"You die hard, Challon!"

Marc swung abruptly around, spilling 'Lena from him. A man filled the doorway. For an instant Challon thought he was masked. Then he realized the cloth strips covering most of the man's face were a curious arrangement of supporting bandage. His thick, spumy enunciation indicated a broken jaw, improperly healed. Marc was momentarily puzzled. Suddenly alarm shot through him. He remembered a rifleshot he had made from the rim above the trail leading into the Strip the day some XO cattle were being driven that way. The man had an answering gun in his hand now.

"Be careful, Halliard," Challon said sharply.

262

Tom Halliard nodded. The bandages on his face twisted in a travesty of a grin.

"I will," he said. "A damned sight more careful than Cy must have been in town the other night. You can count on that, Challon. Now, where's Hugh?"

17

Halliard wiped spittle from his sagging lower lip. He rocked the gun in his hand impatiently.

"Perigord?" Challon repeated cautiously. "He's not here."

"I can see that!" Halliard grunted. "Hugh'd like to climb right up into thin air and stay there now. But he can't. Hell is loose in Range. And whatever he does anyplace else, Hugh's got to come back and face it. I'll come up with him if he doesn't."

Halliard seemed vastly amused. Challon could feel sweat on the tight skin of his own face and he could feel the tenseness of Elena's body beside him. Halliard obviously was in no hurry, possibly because he hadn't anticipated this and so enjoyed the additional relish of surprise in having his chance to face Marc Challon on his own terms, after all.

"What's up in Range?" Challon asked.

"Hell, I said," the man repeated. "Loose for fair. Anse Prentice has disappeared. Before he did, he signed the XO completely over to your wife, Challon."

"She's not my wife," Marc said solidly.

"Forgetful as hell, ain't I?" Halliard grinned. "Anyway, she recorded the deeds from Prentice to her and she's got the ranch, lock, stock, and barrel. What she's been aiming at from the first, I reckon. Only one thing wrong. A couple hours after she recorded her deeds a railroad flunky shows up at the county office with another paper. A demand note for a lot of iron, with the ranch as security, signed by Marcy Challon and drawn to Anson Prentice. Signatures too good to refuse, too. Seems Prentice got it off to his old man in Trinidad, maybe in the ranch mails, before he lit off to nowhere. Old Man Prentice shows up next, roweling Perigord to beat hell to find his son. Meanwhile, he swears he's going to shove that note right through to collection; going to foreclose if your wife can't pay, immediate."

"She's not my wife," Challon said again.

"Ain't it funny how I keep forgetting that?" Halliard said.

Challon looked at the man's shattered face and the gun in his hand.

"Not very," he said. "Hugh's troubles don't sound as bad as you claim. The worst trouble sounds like it belongs to Marcy and you boys off of the XO. All Hugh's got to do is find Prentice."

"That's all," Halliard admitted. "Hugh's real trouble is that Cy don't want Prentice found. That makes a difference. Way things

265

are in town now, a man that could bluff out other bidders might stand a chance of buying the XO off of Old Man Prentice for maybe not much more than fifty thousand dollars — a better deal than he could make with a mask and a handgun. And without having to figure your wife into it at all. If Anse showed up again, one way or another, he might knock all that to hell."

Challon let this third reference to Marcy as his wife go. He knew he had to keep Halliard talking.

"Van Cleave's a burr, a tumbleweed. He hasn't got that kind of money."

"Maybe not. But he wants that ranch about as bad as I want you dead, Challon. And he's picked up a little working cash here and there."

"From a Santa Fe pay roll and Stuart's bank!"

"I wouldn't know," Halliard replied with a shrug. "I was laid up. Remember? Anyhow, that's Hugh's trouble. He's got to find Anse for the railroad — and Cy doesn't want him found."

"So Hugh was spotted wheeling this way past the ranch and you were sent after him to see he didn't uncover anything that ought to stay buried."

"I got to earn my chuck, Challon. One way and another. And you've drawn about all the time you've got coming from me. Supposing you tell that blouseful of *chili pinchi* to get off that seat and out of the way."

"Over by the wall, 'Lena," Challon said quietly.

"Marc — Marc, he'll kill you!" 'Lena protested raggedly.

Challon disengaged her hands.

"Over by the wall!" he repeated more sharply. Halliard's gun was swinging up impatiently.

'Lena rose slowly; then, with a sharp exhalation of breath, she drove head-down at Halliard. The man sidestepped and swung his free hand angrily at her, knocking her to the floor. At the same time he tried to retain his balance to meet the almost simultaneous lunge Challon made at him. He failed in this, lost his footing, and they crashed to the floor together. Halliard's gun fired but found no mark. Hampered by shortened wind, unsteadiness, and the stiffness of his wound, Challon fought savagely. However Halliard broke free of him and, spitting vitriolic profanity, surged to his feet.

He snapped his gun down, hammer back, its muzzle a scant yard from Challon's head, but it was not the concussion of this weapon which shook the room. Halliard's jacket and shirt seemed to leap of their own accord from his chest and the arm holding his gun. The man reeled heavily backward. It was not until Challon saw dark blood welling from countless tiny punctures in his skin, so closely interspersed near the V of his ribs that they formed a single, terribly torn wound, that he fully understood this reprieve.

Halliard fell slackly and without outcry into the entryway. His unfired gun clattered to the floor with him. Challon turned toward the kitchen doorway. Tia Pozner stood there, white-faced.

"Mil gracias de mi alma, santísima mía!" he breathed with feeling.

Tia slowly stood her dead husband's shotgun against the door casing. Smoke still drifted faintly from its wide muzzle. She came on into the room, staring with fixed aversion at the dead man on the floor, her nostrils quivering unconsciously at the faint, unmistakable smell of his blood. Challon caught her hand, her arm, and pulled her against him. She was trembling. 'Lena rose from where she had been crouched against the wall and ran into the kitchen. She returned in an instant with a whisky bottle and three cracked china cups. She poured liberally into these from the bottle. Challon raised one to Tia Pozner's lips, then drained his own. 'Lena choked on hers and lowered it, barely tasted.

"Marc, I don't understand this!" she said. "Where is Anson Prentice?"

"He's dead," Challon said shortly. "Take that gun out into the yard and fire three shots into the air as fast as you can load. It'll do for a signal. I want Hank and Pierre in here!"

The echoes of 'Lena's signal shots were barely dead against the low lava hills before Pierre and Hank Bayard hammered into the yard with most of the old XO crew behind them. They had not come in answer to the shots. They had already been on their way. Pierre was the first onto the porch and into the house, carelessly striding over Halliard's body. He pulled up within the doorway, relief easing the clamped vise of his features and lowering the stertorous pressure of his breathing.

"Thank God you're all right!" he breathed with a gratitude which included both Challon and the two women. "I was afraid of something, and those shots scared the hell out of me!"

He stepped back over Halliard's body and impersonally prodded it with his toe as Bayard loped up to the porch.

"See what I mean?" he asked Hank in an apparent continuation of a talk between them. "Hugh don't have a chance, whichever way he jumps, the way it is. The wolves are already at his heels. This is one of them."

Bayard nodded uncertainly. Challon moved outside to face his father.

"Hugh know where Anse Prentice is?"

Pierre spat beyond the porch railing.

269

"He sure does, boy," he agreed. "Prentice is where you should have put him months ago, flat on his back with a tarp over his face. Hugh has got him in the back of his wagon. Found him over in a feeder off of Dry Wash. Dead a week, I'd say. Gut-shot." Pierre spat again.

"Van Cleave!" Challon said with certainty.

His father nodded.

"Everybody on the XO knows about it but that woman. One of the hands couldn't stand the knowing and sneaked off to town to tell Hugh about it. Hugh's got him locked up in a cell now to keep him safe. Ain't it a hell of a note that with all the yahoos calling themselves men on the place it had to be a Mexican — hardly more than a kid, at that — who had the guts to jump Van Cleave's orders? Yard hustler out there. Encelador. Paco Encelador. Seems to me his old man's been a sawyer at the lumberyard for quite a spell. Recollect the family, Marc?"

"His father is a cook at the Palace Hotel," 'Lena corrected gravely.

Challon stirred with impatience. It was curious how people faced with compelling matters could so easily derail themselves in their thinking, what confounded difference did it make what an XO hand's name was or what his father did for a living?

"What did Hugh want with you, Pierre?" he asked sharply.

"When a man's got his shirttail caught on a fence or a rattler hanging by its fangs from his backside or more kids at his table than he can feed, what does he always do in this part of the country?" Pierre asked. "What has he always done? Run like hell, with his tail curled under so far it tickles him under the chin — run to the XO. Only you and me weren't on the XO today, so Hugh had to run this way. And you're supposed to be dead, so he had to do with me. It was a hard enough swallow he had to make, I reckon, but Hugh come hunting help."

Challon remembered the calculating impersonality with which the sheriff of Red River County had drawn a gun on him in the corridor of the jail.

"Kind of late, isn't he?" he asked bitterly. "Kind of late."

"Kind of," Pierre agreed. "Hank and me was just figuring — it's going to push us some to be able to do anything for him now."

"Hank and you are crazy!" Challon snapped. "Hugh's spilled this grease. Let him cook in it!"

"All right, boy. But there's no call for us to lay in the same skillet without trying to flop out of it."

"We're clear," Challon said stubbornly. "That's why I holed up out here in the lava in the first place. That's why I hung onto the whiteface bunch. We got no stake in town. That's why I been waiting. When the frying is all done is time enough for us to move."

Marc saw the choler of impatience which had always made Pierre dangerous and to be reckoned with now begin to rise in his father. Pierre spoke patiently with an effort, but his outrage was evident.

"I can stomach stupidity when there's no help for it, but plain damned foolishness gets my taw, and I've had just about all of it I can handle from you, Marc! Look, there ain't a hell of a lot of things hold a piece of country together. A few folks' ambitions and what they're trying to build — a church, maybe, a school, some decent women. A little profit for them that do it from the work that's done. Kids to take holt where the old ones leave off. But mostly it's the law."

Pierre paused. His huge old head shoved aggressively forward.

"That's what Hugh Perigord is," he went on. "The law. We made him that, you and me. Likely we could have done better, the way it's worked out, but it's too late to change now. That woman on the XO has given Van Cleave and his bunch a taste for something besides sowbelly and beans, and they've turned hungry. Hugh's about all that's left in their way!"

"You're thinking XO and talking XO," Challon said wearily. The thing which was so certain to him seemed obscure to others. "Let a little time go and Van Cleave can no more hang onto the ranch than Marcy can. Besides, she's still there. She's still in his way. She could be more trouble to Van Cleave than Hugh could ever be. I know. You lie down, Pierre. Perigord's got barking at a bear that's in his back yard instead of yours."

"Sure I'm talking about the XO, you stone-headed idiot!" Pierre exploded. "That's the same as talking about the whole county. Always has been. Maybe you don't give a damn who's sleeping in your house or eating your bread, but I got friends to think of. There's a lot of folks that have eaten regularly — maybe cussing us some, but eating, just the same — because we run our ranch according to the best lights we could. That's going to change. Either Hugh slaps iron onto Cy Van Cleave and those brush-runners of his or they're going to whip Range into line and buy out title to the ranch from Old Man Prentice on that note.

"And what about that young hustler Hugh's got locked up in his jail for safety now? What'll Paco Encelador get for having enough guts to try letting Van Cleave's cat out of the bag? The same thing Prentice got — a bellyful of lead. And that woman on the ranch — what can she do with a hellion like Van Cleave? He's beat half the life and all the fight out of every bitch he ever got his hands on. You think she's any different than them? Well, she ain't!"

"Hell, Prentice won't sell out to Van Cleave. Cy killed his son!

"Won't he?" Pierre asked savagely. "He shot my son in the back and he's still on my ranch — that Van Cleave! Jason Prentice ain't never been half as ringy as Pierre Challon, either! Besides, it ain't the note that's for sale now, Hugh says. Prentice got Judge Farrady up from Santa Fe this morning. He sued for foreclosure, and Judge Farrady entered judgment half an hour before Hugh left town. Tomorrow the ranch goes on the block. Kind of irregular, maybe — rushed some — but legal enough. Prentice can't help himself. He's got to sell the XO title to the highest bidder over the amount of that judgment. And if the law is dead in Range tomorrow, you tell me who's going to bid against Van Cleave and live long enough to get his money into the auctioneer's hands. Hank and me and the boys are heading for town, Marc."

"Van Cleave will be there with his bunch," Challon warned. "If not this afternoon, then before morning."

"Then we're apt to find out whether the rattlesnake of Mora can stand the kind of tromping every crawling critter on the XO has been getting for fifty years!"

"We'll take it easy, Marc," Hank Bayard said quietly. "Just back Hugh up a mite. He's going to need it."

Challon caught his father's arm as the angry old man started down the steps of Tia Pozner's house.

"This is the old way, Pierre," he protested urgently. "The thing Van Cleave will be expecting. I tell you, it's better to wait. There'll be blood —"

"Your fingers ain't exactly lily-white for all your round-siding and waiting for time to do your chores! I'm too damned old to wait. You get out of my way!"

Pierre clumped on down the steps. Bayard followed him.

"If you was in shape, you'd be riding with us, Marc," Hank lied. "We know that. Me and the boys'll watch out for Pierre."

It was a loyal untruth. Hank Bayard knew Challon wouldn't take this ride, regardless of his state of health. And it would tax the good Lord to watch out for Pierre in his present mood. Challon watched the old man swing up to leather, then tried a final protest, stabbing at Pierre's practicality.

"Even if you last long enough, you can't do anything at that auction tomorrow," he said flatly. "Neither can Van Cleave. Prentice is no fool about money. He'll bid that note in himself, knowing that way he can get the XO at a tenth of its worth. If he doesn't there's half a dozen pieces of Colorado money around Trinidad that'll come over the pass for a crack at that much New Mexico land at that kind of a price. We've got some money, all right, but not enough to stand up in open bidding."

Pierre sat very stiff, very straight, in his saddle.

"Boy," he said slowly, "you been running the ranch the last few years. This business with that woman has been yours from the start. Maybe you got the soundest idea. I don't really know, I guess. Hank and me tried to show you this morning what we thought was the easiest way. That was the last try I'm going to make far's the ranch is concerned. If there's ever a Challon back on the XO, it'll be you that puts him there. This ride is between me and my God, Marc. When I turn in under the sod — and I'm wore down enough to be ready any time — I aim to sleep good!"

He reined away. Elena came out of the house and started past Challon. He checked her.

"Where you going?"

"To town," she said quietly. "Pierre's right. I've tried to tell you. There's more than just you and the XO here under the mesas. I've got friends in Range. Trouble there affects them. This isn't for you — or for your ranch, Marc. There are folks in town who'll need help tonight and tomorrow more than you will. That's why I've got to go."

She pulled away from him and ran down across the yard. Hank Bayard was saddling a horse for her at the corral. In a moment she was up, riding out with Hank and Pierre and the crew. Challon turned slowly back into the house. A couple of the boys had carried Halliard's body down by the corral and had tossed a hay cover over it, but his blood was still on the floor of the porch. Challon closed the door to shut this out. Tia Pozner went quietly into the kitchen. Challon sank down on the settee where he had been so short a time ago with 'Lena against him and a conviction of rightness pounding steadily with his pulse through him. Now 'Lena was gone and, with her, the conviction.

In a moment or two Tia returned with a cup of coffee from the pot always standing on the back of every grass-country stove when there was fire under the lids. She put the cup down beside him.

"It's hard for a man to know how much a woman loves him," she said softly in Spanish.

"He finds out sooner or later," Challon said harshly.

"Or thinks he does," Tia corrected. "A man can be a fool, but still his woman loves him. She can't help herself."

Challon glared accusingly at Jim Pozner's widow. She was Spanish. She was of the lava and the grass. Her people were in Range. Her husband had become a part of the gray-green sod. As much as one individual could, she represented this country which had been his life. She was an almost perfect example of the kind of people of which he had been thinking when he promised Marcy Bennett that the grass and those who lived on it would eventually defeat her and drive her from the XO. Yet Tia Pozner was not thinking of Marcy now; she was thinking of him. And she thought he was a fool.

He didn't answer her, and Tia went quietly back to the kitchen. Challon tried a cigarette and found it tasteless. He felt empty, tired, and he clutched at the thought he had possibly overdone, that weariness was preventing clear thought. Stretched out on the settee, he tried to rest, but the piece of furniture was too short for his frame. After a few minutes he rose and, kicking out of his boots, spilled down on the thick mattress in the bedroom. He failed to doze here, also, but a stubbornness kept him down.

It was darkening outside when he finally rose with an angry, churning restlessness, tugged on his boots, and went into the kitchen. The stove was cold. The lamp was not lit. All of the china and utensils were in place on the shelves. No preparations for an evening meal were in evidence. And Tia Pozner sat in a chair in one corner, her hands folded in her lap. He realized that she had been waiting for him — that she had waited through the long afternoon.

"You said I was a fool a while ago," he said roughly. "Why?"

Tia looked at him and smiled slowly.

"Because you don't know when you have what you want," she said.

" 'Lena?"

"Yes, 'Lena. But the other thing too. You've been waiting. What for? Until the woman who made your bed dirty had nothing. I have understood that. I think others have too. It was big thinking to demand so much in payment for an injury. We have expected big thinking from a Challon. We have expected this kind of a revenge. But not stupidity! Tell me, señor, what does that woman have now?"

She paused.

"The XO? There are papers filed in town which take it away from her. You heard that. She has a man, maybe? Anson Prentice is dead, and no woman can have the deadly little snake from Mora. She has hope? What can she hope for now? The waiting is done, but you don't see it. Isn't that being a fool, señor?"

Marc stared at her, realizing it had not been weariness obstructing his thinking which had kept him from sleep this afternoon. It had been the thinking itself. And he had refused to admit its inevitable conclusion. He thought he understood why now. He had beaten Marcy, if his original desire to see her one day stand barefoot and destitute on his grass was sufficient. But he had lost the larger stake for which he had been playing. He had lost the XO. Too much else had become involved in his quarrel with Marcy. Too much upon which he had not counted. So defeat was actually his. And it was this he could not face.

He could have gone into town as Pierre had gone, to walk a familiar street with the knowledge he would never again have his old place on it. But he could not meet the eyes of those who saw too clearly the colossal folly of having traded off two lifetimes of Challon effort for a brief instant of revenge.

He could see the resentment in Tia Pozner — in others who had lived long in the shadow of the Challons. No matter who held title to the XO, it would always in part be a public property, and Marc Challon had ignored the public interest. It was for this that he was not forgiven. He looked down at the small, slightly graying woman in the chair before him.

"Could you drive me to town, Tia?" he asked softly.

The woman smiled broadly and blindingly and stood up. Challon saw her coat and shawl were neatly folded on the back of the chair, ready and waiting. His lips tightened.

Then a man did not alter the mold and pattern of what he was. He didn't outwait the things to which he was bound. His shadow varied with the height of the sun, not with variance in his own nature. Tia Pozner had known this. She had known it when 'Lena and Pierre and the others had not. Otherwise she would not have waited as she had here. There was wisdom in her eyes. He hoped 'Lena would have the same wisdom in time — he hoped she would have her aunt's sureness as well as her beauty. There might be a day when Marc Challon would need sound counsel as he needed it now.

Turning, he strode rapidly back into his bedroom for his own gear.

18

With Tia Pozner at the reins beside him and again enthroned on the chair nailed to the buckboard platform, Challon considered his problems. With the evening air in his face and decision under his belt, they didn't seem complicated. The old feeling of directness was heartening. He understood the morass of indecision into which he had fallen — the refusal to face facts which had at first distressed and later infuriated Pierre. His plan had been so simple in the beginning. It had involved only Marcy and Anson Prentice and himself. He had foreseen corrosion in Anse toward Marcy and he had counted on it. But he had not counted on Van Cleave. He hadn't counted on a settlement between Anse and Marcy which would pass control and an avenue to regaining the XO out of his reach.

He had foreseen the day when Marcy would have had enough of the grass and the grass enough of her. On that day he had believed she would send for him, that she would beg him for help. And when she did, he had planned to use a portion of the Prentice money lying in the Challon account in Stuart's bank to buy Marcy and Anse off the ranch.

He would have bought close. He would have had profit left. Enough profit to complete his irrigation system without encumbrances. With relish for the irony, he had planned to call the new reservoir Lake Bennett — maybe Lake Prentice. New Mexico would have smiled at that and talked of Challon humor. New Mexico had known much irony and understood it.

But a shot in the back had intervened — a triple murder in a jail corridor and Tom Halliard's shattered face and a note in Jason Prentice's hands had intervened. And with his body broken it had been impossible to think as he might have thought on his feet. Van Cleave had become the barb, embedding himself deeper with each shift of events. Van Cleave's destruction at any time would have returned the others to the course he had planned, but a man half dead could not destroy Van Cleave, and in addition, the original plan had been passive. He had not wanted to abandon that. He had not wanted to destroy Marcy or her tools himself. He had wanted to wait while they destroyed themselves. Prentice had obliged, too handsomely. Van Cleave would not.

Now there was more to consider than Van Cleave, but it was still not complicated when a man moved toward it. Luck would finally decide who held the XO. Challon luck looked thin now. It didn't matter. Pierre could be saved, and Hank and the boys with there. Range could be saved a violence it hadn't earned. And perhaps he could save for himself the pride 'Lena Casamajor had once had in Marc Challon.

At a fork in the road Tia Pozner pulled up and looked questioningly at Challon. Both tracks led to Range. The southernmost and most direct did not pass by the home sections of the XO. Challon indicated the northern track with a tilt of his head.

"We'll see if he's there first," he said. "If he isn't, we'll go on into town."

Tia eased the shotgun slanted up along the seat beside her out of her way and shook out the reins. The buckboard rolled again in silence.

From three or four miles out bright lights were visible at the XO house. Challon wondered if Marcy needed this brilliance in which to grapple with her conscience. If it was not wholly dead, it must be giving her hell, at least as a small voice running endlessly over the totality and grossness of her mistakes. He wanted to see her. The question about Ed Bennett, for one thing. Others. But they had become trivial. Even Marcy had become so. He was short of time and he had not come to the ranch again to see her.

At the head of the lane, as they turned in

through the XO gate, Tia Pozner spoke of the lights.

"Twenty lamps," she said. "A lot of people."

Challon nodded. Among people frugal with oil, the size of a night gathering was appraised even at a distance by the number of wicks lighting it. A home dance could be four, five, or six lamps. One in a hall in town was at least a dozen, and two lamps would light a dinner for ten guests in any house on the grass. Marcy had every wick in the XO house alight.

Challon turned Tia down a service track branching from the lane. It crossed a dry ford and came into the bottom of the yard below the corrals. There was a dim light in the bunkhouse. All other buildings but the main house were dark. Challon touched the arm of the woman beside him, and she halted the buckboard, immediately snaking her husband's shotgun across her lap. Challon reached his own cartridge belt up from the floor, swung down, and stood beside the near wheel, buckling it on.

"Anybody here's in the bunkhouse," he said quietly. "I don't know how our luck will run. If there's shooting, wait till the first bunch breaks out the door, then use your shotgun and start your horses. That'll get you clear. Drive for town and find Pierre. Tell him exactly what happened and make sure he knows exactly why I stopped here on my way in. Understand?"

Tia Pozner nodded and cocked her weapon. Challon turned and started across the yard, knowing he could do so with his eyes closed. This was home ground. The knowledge steadied him.

A rectangle of faded yellow light was spilling out of the open bunkhouse door. He moved directly into it and swiftly across the threshold, knowing that if someone outside was watching his approach he would thus afford them no momentarily motionless target and little opportunity for identification. As he passed through the door he ducked aside and flattened his back against the thick dobe wall. The precaution was unnecessary. The bunkhouse had only one occupant. Dressed in a startlingly clean shirt and a neater pair of pants than his kind usually owned, the cook was sprawled on a bunk. Challon saw he was hopelessly drunk. An overturned bottle, evidently rummaged from the war bag of the man who usually occupied the next bunk, lay on the floor beside him. Van Cleave's crew was missing.

Challon ducked back outside and headed for the buckboard, then halted. The lights in the main house still puzzled him. A war parley could be going on there, Marcy and Van Cleave and the whole crew. Marcy would want a lot of light for that kind of meeting.

He angled up toward the ramada. Down the yard Tia Pozner saw him change course and shook her reins out a little. The buckboard began to move parallel to him and toward the drive curving in front of the lawn. The wheels rolled onto a stretch of gravel and made sound.

Challon had reached the lower end of the ramada and had stepped into its shadow, and Tia had pulled up again to wait, this time fully in front of the house, when the front door opened wide. Marcy came quickly up the two steps from the sunken threshold, paused an instant, then went lightly out the path toward the drive at a half run. Her voice reached ahead in the darkness toward Tia's figure on the seat of the buckboard. Her voice, all right, but curiously unsteady and forced and thinly veneered with an almost ludicrous hospitality.

"My dear!" she cried. "Light down and come in, please. You're a little early, I think, but the others will be arriving shortly, and anyway, we'll have a minute of talk to ourselves."

She halted at the buckboard wheel, face upturned.

"It's time I met my neighbors. I'm Marcy Challon."

A rush of understanding swept Challon. The lamps alight within the house were not for people already there but for guests Marcy was expecting. Enough of them to make a twenty-lamp party — every name she had ever heard mentioned in connection with a wide circle of grass. And her eager acceptance of Tia as the first arrival, although it was already nearing ten o'clock, accounted for her shaky welcome. Those she had expected had not come. Not one of them. Challon thought this accounted for the cook, also — his fancy receiving costume and his drunkenness when he realized the uncomfortable effort had been for nothing.

Marcy did not know Tia Pozner — had never met her — and so she could not understand Tia's wordless upright stiffness on the seat above her. Challon stepped into the ramada archway and quietly called out across the little lawn

"Watch your eyes, Marcy; she'll scratch them out. That's Jim Pozner's widow!"

Marcy pivoted with an almost complete loss of balance, such as she might have done had Challon's voice been a heavy bullet driving into her. She rocked a little for an instant, staring at his silhouette against the lamplight within the house. One hand rose distractedly to brush a strand of hair from her face. Then she swayed forward and walked slowly back along the path toward him, unwillingness to believe what her senses told her to be fact apparent in every lagging motion of her body.

Under the archway, a scant yard from him, she stopped. Her lips were a very long time forming the word:

"Marc!"

Then tension broke. She rushed against him, grasping the lapels of his jacket and tugging with a fierceness that sent a twinge of pain through the half-knit muscles of his back. Tears streaked her cheeks and choked her. She bit her lip for control, failed, and bit it again.

"Marc! Oh, Marc — Marc! Marc, I need you so desperately!"

"I'm in a hurry, Marcy," Challon said stonily. "Where's Van Cleave?"

She backed from him a little, hands outspread, her face tilted up.

"Gone!" she said. "I'm done with him, Marc. Done with his rottenness, his stealing, his — his savagery. I ordered him off of the ranch. Cy and every one of his men. Only Cookie is left. Marc, listen — Cy killed Anson. Right in the barn there, a week ago. Cy killed Anson and didn't tell me till tonight!"

"I know," Challon said. "Where did Van Cleave go — to town?"

"Marc, I've got to talk to you tonight — now! Not about me. About the ranch. Cy is going to try to take it. Anson's father got a judgment against me on a note I gave Anson. Treadwell sent me word this afternoon —"

"I know about that too."

"Cy is going to make a bid with money he's stolen, and his men are going to back him up. They'll kill men to do it. Sheriff Perigord — even Mr. Prentice himself!"

"They may try," Challon agreed. He glanced into the brilliantly lighted interior of the house which was still the center of his life. It seemed strange that Marcy's alien presence had never been able to alter the quiet security of the rooms. "You're expecting company?" he asked her.

Marcy was near hysteria. She clung again to his lapels, laughing unsteadily.

"My neighbors," she said. "An invitation to everybody in the county with a roof over their heads. The kind of a party you said your mother used to give on the XO in the old days. Proof for everyone that Marcy Bennett could sit her saddle on this ranch as well as any man! Then tonight, after Mr. Treadwell sent me word of that judgment and Cy told me what he was going to do, a hope that I could talk the county people into standing in his way — that they would put up the necessary money — on shares, maybe. I thought I could do it —"

She stopped, her laugh breaking like glass.

"I told you in the beginning —" Challon murmured.

"A hundred guests, and the only one to show up a dead man who wasn't even invited!"

Marcy checked herself then, and her old strength returned miraculously. She quieted between two deep breaths.

"You can stop Cy, Marc. Nobody but you could do it. The county would back up Marc Challon. And you've got the money — more than enough. You could make Anson's father be reasonable about the bid as easily as Cy could, and in the same way, if necessary. We'll go into town together, Marc. Not for me; for the ranch. We can settle the shares between us and any other differences later. I won't ask for much. Just enough to get started again —"

"We're not going anywhere together, Marcy," Challon said bluntly. "And you got all you're ever going to get from me a long time ago. We don't have any shares in the XO any more — either of us!"

Marcy drew back from him, accusation in her eyes.

"There's got to be something left! I was your wife for five years!"

"That's just it!" Challon murmured with a repression which shook him.

Marcy's face drained completely of color. It became a bleak, stony white mask Challon knew his memory would contain in infinite detail forever. A frigid white incarnation of hatred. This, then, was the thing for which he had played. This was his revenge.

He didn't like the taste in his mouth. He

felt a little sick and very empty. He turned away. Marcy caught his arm and pulled him sharply around.

"A buckboard with a Mexican woman driver, carrying a man still flinching from a wound that should have killed him, can't make very good time, Marc —"

Challon heard the icy softness and waited for the rest of it.

"There are saddle horses out there in the barn that could easily make Range half an hour ahead of you," she went on. "And I can ride the fastest of them. You know how I can ride."

"What you ride and where you ride to makes no difference to me, Marcy."

"Cy has what he intends to do pretty well worked out. He doesn't know you're alive and headed his way again. He's going to be shaken. That's your only chance, Marc. If he was warned before you reached town, you wouldn't live till morning!"

"I've done it before — quite a few mornings," Challon said. He disengaged her hand from his arm with a powerful grip. Her head came back and up. For an instant she looked like the headstrong girl he had met on the streets of Trinidad long ago. She looked as young and challenging — yes, and as desirable — except for the white mask of her rigidly immobile features.

"The old god and the young god and the

queen that's dead!" she spat. "The Challons! The Challons and the XO! I promise you, Marc, live or die tonight, you'll remember Marcy Bennett to your last breath!"

She wheeled and plunged into the house. Marc walked slowly out to the buckboard and swung up on the improvised seat. Tia wordlessly put the team in motion. They rolled out the lane and onto the road to Range.

There was a ford at the second section corner. Tia was slanting the buckboard down into this when Challon heard the hoofbeats behind them. He twisted around on his seat.

Behind them a great pillar of tumbling flame and ruddy smoke stood up against the deep blue night sky. Flame which fed upon the time-enriched timbers and furnishings of the XO house — Belle Challon's house — the heart of a dream two generations old. His own body in that heat could not have brought Challon a more sickening wave of agony.

This was Marcy's mark.

"I hoped you wouldn't look back, Señor Challon," Tia Pozner said. "I saw it only moments ago. There was nothing we could do then. She must have overturned every lamp!"

Above the roaring of the blood in his ears Challon again became aware of the horse coming up behind him. For an instant the animal and its rider were in full silhouette against the distant flame. A tall and powerful horse with a tremendous stride. The kind of animal strong men rode with the caution of a mutual admiration and respect. And Marcy up, hair flying, leaning loosely with the pistoning strides of the great beast, sitting her seat with the supremely careless confidence of a drunken Indian.

She splashed through the ford a rod downstream and scrambled up the farther bank without slackening her pace. She veered here and angled up along the side of a rising basalt and obsidian ridge, along the sheer flank of which ran a rugged but much shorter trail into Range than the road along the flats.

Sparks flew as iron shoes rang against volcanic stone and the horse thundered on the unbroken gait. Marcy could ride. Challon had seen some of the best, but he had known nothing which matched the superb recklessness of this.

"The old ones say that the devil rides across the mesas at night like that," Tia Pozner murmured.

Challon looked again at the towering flames behind them. There was a magnificence about the XO house, even in destruction. One thought was recurrent in him. The house had always meant even more to Pierre than it had to him. It was all that remained of the woman Pierre had brought into the Territory from Kansas City. This would kill Pierre; it would kill him more certainly than a bullet. Marcy had known this. She had certainly known the immense tragedy of it. Pierre had lived too long, his back had been too straight through the years, for him to die now of a broken heart.

Tia Pozner drove on across the ford and lifted the team into a reluctant lope on the far side. With a strong physical effort Challon turned his back on the XO.

"Might as well take it easier," he told the woman beside him. "We've got plenty of time now. Marcy will beat us into Range a long ways, the best we can do."

19

Tia halted the buckboard at the familiar willows on the edge of town. There was a curious air about a night approach to Range which seemed to force a pause in all who traveled this road. Not that so much of violence always impended here when the sun went down or that all who traveled the road were aware of it, but the street and the lights and the town slanting ahead up the broken knees of the mesa toward Goat Hill were a kind of barrier.

Challon thought this was it. As one came in from the flatland lying eastward, the slope of the town and the wall of the mesa were a sharp change, demanding a halt for orientation and adjustment before moving on into Range. At any rate, the clay was hard-packed over a considerable area where Tia halted, grass roots beaten from it by the hoofs of the horses and the tires of the wagons of others who had also paused. Tia touched Challon's arm.

"I can swing south and go up the hill from the back side to Uppertown — Chihuahuatown. 'Lena and I have cousins there. Food and a bed for you to rest awhile in. And we can send down the hill for news of the others — news of Van Cleave, if it isn't already known. This road will be watched, since that woman rode in ahead of us. It is not good —"

Challon gripped her shoulder gratefully.

"I want to get to the back side of the hotel without being seen," he said. "You do that, *hermanita,* then go to your cousins'. If you find 'Lena, keep her with you. I'll manage the rest."

"I hope so," Tia said. "I hope so. I will pray it, Señor Challon!"

Following an across-lots goat track below the main street Tia drove the buckboard surely through a patchwork of irregular garden plots, makeshift yards and fences, interspersed with the low, flat, one-room shacks of the *pelados* which fringed every community on the grass. When they were abreast of the rear of the hotel, she pulled up. Challon swung swiftly to the ground. So many lights were up and so strong a sense of subdued, restless movement hung over the town that it was apparent this was not a night of usual things. Challon was acutely aware of a sort of suspended silence over everything which reminded him of the pressured suspension which lay over the earth during the long, soundless seconds between the knifing of giant lightning in the sky and the ensuing roll of its thunder against the hills during the summer's savage storms in the high hills. Tia Pozner bent toward him.

"Morning," she said. "Wait until morning. You will be stronger then."

Challon stared at her without comprehension.

"It is a saying," she explained. "The good have no errands in the darkness — only in the sun. My people will be on the street in the morning — not tonight."

"You stay with your cousins!" Challon said sharply. And he swung away.

The buckboard creaked on up the hill. Challon moved toward the rear of the hotel. Solid purpose was in his mind. Pierre and Hank had brought the boys into town to back Hugh Perigord. They had been fundamentally right in this. Perigord was still the law tonight and had to be supported.

But Pierre knew only one way to handle these things: guts, sand, and guns. It was no detraction from the giant Pierre had once been to believe that in his most competent days he had not been the match of Cy Van Cleave in a thing of this kind. Certainly Hank and the XO crew were not the equals of the gun-hung hawks Van Cleave had brought up out of Lincoln County.

Challon knew the temptation of violence. It was pumping through his blood now, an almost uncontainable compulsion to sear out with the ruddy flames of his own anger the things which stood in his way. A towering desire to break with his hands, to use injury and death for his own purpose and to hell with the odds; a delusive conviction of invincibility. This was what he had from Pierre — the thunder of the gods. But a colder recess of his mind clamped a lid on it. His wound made it impossible for his body to meet even the first of the demands he would have to make of it in such a fury, and he was therefore obligated to a quieter channel.

Pierre would say this was not the Challon way, and Pierre would be right. It had not been the Challon way in the past to which Pierre belonged. But change was inevitable. The house at the XO was gone. The ranch no longer had enemies on the lava; enmity there had died with Jim Pozner and the Hyatts. Marc Challon was without a wife, without land. Challons had abandoned a fight for grass to fight for their lives tonight. And a railroad would be in Range before summer's end. All of these were changes. There was no returning to the days before any of them.

And there were some men to whom death by a gun was not defeat but a certain event of life, so that they died by a bullet and yet were not touched beyond their ruptured bodies. Cy Van Cleave was one of these. So there had to be a better way than Pierre's and it had to be used swiftly. It had to be used before Pierre uselessly poured the remnants of his life and his blood onto the thirsty sand which lay beneath this New Mexico sod. It had to be used before someone fired the bullet which bore Cy Van Cleave's name — before an accident of marksmanship let the man die defiantly on his feet, rooting the seed of a legend which might grow to conceal — even from those whose own memories could strip it way — the kind of man he had been.

Pierre had said the Challons were bound to the law they had created in Red River County. Pierre had been wrong in this. The law, in itself, was as unimportant as Hugh Perigord. But the law had been built to support justice, and it was of justice that Marc Challon was thinking.

The Palace Hotel was an old building. The exterior stairs climbing its rear wall creaked protestingly under Challon's weight. The door at their head, letting into the upper hall, stood open. Challon had no difficulty locating the door to Jason Prentice's room. Two men were lounging in chairs, one on either side of it. They looked alike. Cheap, wrinkled suits. White shirts with collar tabs too narrow and too high for either comfort or appearance. A curiously unattractive shape of bowler hat. And a professional brusque blandness of manner which must have taken considerable practice to acquire. It was curious that railroad detectives, each imitating the dress and manner of others of their profession, fancied they were achieving anonymity.

Red, white, and blue uniforms could not have been more distinctive. These Santa Fe men were no exceptions. But their presence here in this hall settled Challon's first question. Van Cleave had made no overt move in this direction yet. Jason Prentice was secure from him. Without being seen, Challon returned to the head of the outer stairs and descended quietly to the lot behind the hotel again.

At the front corner of the Palace, one foot up on the walk, he paused abruptly, checked by the simultaneous restraint of some mute sense and something he saw on the planking before him. Two empty brass shell cases lay on the walk. They had not been there long. Passing foot traffic would have dislodged them. Recent gunfire along the street was certain. A man had paused here at the hotel corner to reload a couple of chambers of his gun. And he was hurried or he would have retrieved the empty cases. Brass was expensive, and a man could reload fired cases at home at a quarter of the cost of boxed new factory loads.

The sensitory warning was something else. A sudden realization that the restlessness and

301

movement he had earlier sensed, coming into town with Tia Pozner, had not been street movement. It was behind shaded windows and closed doors and in men's minds. The street in front of him was ominously empty.

Challon drew back, circled again behind the hotel, and moved more than a hundred yards up the hill, well back from the street. Rank weed growth here gave him cover to the walk, and there were no intermediate lights. He crossed the street swiftly, going deep into the opposite lots, and turned back down, heading now for the rear of the court-house.

Near the service half door to the cellar, there at the end of a plain thirty-yard track dragged through the weeds, he stumbled on a slight body. A thin, dark face looked sightlessly up at him. Challon recognized the features. This was Hugh Perigord's prisoner, locked up only because he was the one available talking witness with information about Anson Prentice's death at Cy Van Cleave's hands. This was the Encelador kid, the yard hustler from the XO. A hard-swung gun barrel had crushed the crown of his head. He had been jerked from his protecting cell, killed, and dragged out here. Challon knew he would find the cellar door of the court-house open.

He pushed through this and started across the cellar toward lamplight falling dimly from above on a steep, slatted stair at the far end. Bent low under the beams overhead, he paused midway for a long moment, listening for sounds from above. He heard none.

There was blood on the stairs where the body out in the weeds had been dragged down them. At their head, in a little ell off the jail corridor, Challon paused again. He thought the street-level floor of the building was completely empty. He could not be sure of the floor above. Not yet. His shirt was wet with sweat under his arms. The reinforced cloth there was cold. The metal eyelets of the breather holes were cold against his skin. He was breathing harder than he liked, and the muscles in the backs of his thighs were too springy. Unsteadily so. He was moving too fast. That had to be it.

It had to be. He hadn't come to Range too late. He couldn't have come in too late. There were only so many tallies against a man. He already had suffered his share. His book was full. He knew damned well he wasn't too late.

Slowly, steadying himself, he moved past the gaping cell gates and turned into the corridor leading forward into Perigord's office. The corridor in which Cy Van Cleave had stood to put a bullet into his back. The office at its end was not lighted. This was good. He stepped into it. There was no disorder except for the lamp. Its wick was still turned high. There was a faint odor of warm oil still in the air. But the chimney and shade were gone. Their shards crunched like brittle gravel under the soles of his boots. And the street door stood wide open. A bullet from outside could have shattered chimney glass and snuffed flame like this.

Challon stepped carefully into the street doorway. The answer to his second question lay on the walk. Pierre and the boys who had quit the Pozner place with him had not been a sufficient defense. Starshine winked faintly from the silver badge pinned to Perigord's vest. The man was otherwise unrecognizable. He had taken a bullet quarteringly through his face. There was little of it left. He was dead.

Two more men lay farther out from the walk in the dust of the street. Challon saw with relief that he knew neither of them. Van Cleave's men. Hugh had always claimed his own handiness with a gun. This was possibly proof. Challon wondered if the man had taken his satisfaction with him. He was about to turn back from the doorway when he saw across the street, folded half limply over and against the rail before the Red River Saloon, a fourth lifeless figure. Even at this distance he recognized the man's piebald calfskin jacket. It had hung nights on an XO bunkhouse peg for half a dozen years. The man was Al Carlin, the best bronc handler who had ever drawn Challon pay.

This, then, was the source of the suspended feeling he had earlier sensed. The lightning had already struck. Range was waiting for the thunder. That it had not already come rolling in retaliation down this empty street meant only one thing to Marc now. He was much too late. There was no thunderer. Pierre was dead. This was the answer to his third question.

On a board over Perigord's desk hung a number of the implements of the law. Several handguns — some serviceable and some merely oddities, either in their own right or by virtue of prior owners. A pair of heavy rifles which had been shortened and bored out smooth to take the tremendous brass buckshot cartridges Texans had devised as the surest antidote to rail and stage-line violence. A notable collection of the knives which accompanied the Spanish language wherever it traveled in the world.

Challon's attention fell on this rack as he turned from the door. Curiously his attention was not drawn by any of the weapons but by three pairs of brightly nickeled handcuffs dangling with their keys from one row of hooks. He lifted one of these down, tossed it with grim thoughtfulness in his hand, and dropped it into his jacket pocket. At the same instant he heard voices and quick, light footfalls on the stairs leading from the upper floor of the building. He paused an instant in indecision, and one of the voices became intelligible:

"Damned right, I'm sure! Ducked in the cellar door. Just a flash of him. Don't know who —"

An interrupting query, then, undistinguishable, and an answer:

"Hell, no, he didn't come out. That's what I said —"

Two men, now in the jail section, moving rapidly toward the office. His presence discovered, Challon had no alternative. He stepped out the street door, crossing the walk past Perigord's body. One of those in the corridor behind him saw his movement and shouted. A gun fired. Challon doubled over and started to run at an angle across the street, silently cursing the unsteady stiffness of his body.

More guns fired, now from the second-story windows of the courthouse. Lead drove savagely into the dust beside him and he forgot his stiffness, running with longer strides. Across the street a familiar voice, under driving compulsion, startlingly sang out his name:

"Marc! Marc, here!"

He saw Hank Bayard's figure loping along the opposite walk. Hank cut into the street toward him, flipping up the gun in his hand to fire across at the face of the courthouse.

There was other shouting, angry and staccato, from this direction, and a rise in the cadence of the firing. Hank reached him, shouldering him hard toward the Red River Saloon, firing again toward the courthouse.

They hit the walk before the saloon, and Bayard went suddenly down in a flat, face-skinning dive, driving his head hard against the wall of the building. Challon thought he had stumbled. He pulled up, aware of the cannonading slam of lead into the weathered siding before him and the vicious whirring of splinters torn from it, waiting for Hank to regain his feet. Bayard moved, all right, his buttocks rising high as he pumped his knees under him, but his head stayed down like that of an axed steer.

He spilled over onto his side, his legs still pumping slowly, his boots making a dry, rasping sound on the walk planking which was clearly audible to Challon over the reverberations of the gun explosions across the street and the bullet strikes about him. With incredulous shock Challon saw a torrent of blood was spilling from Bayard's mouth.

The front door of the saloon was jerked open and his name sounded again:

"For God's sake, Mr. Challon!"

His instant of immobility shattered then. Bending, he hooked Bayard's uppermost arm. He could not lift the man with one shoulder still so bad. He dragged him, leaving a wide,

307

dark wet mark on the walk behind them. A man ducked out of the saloon door. Young Lou Fentrice, so scared every pimple on his face seemed raised to twice its normal height. Lou got Bayard up and across his shoulder. In another instant the saloon door was shut again and the angry night was on the outside. The old mustiness of the Red River was about Challon, and he knew he would find his father here. If there had been beds in this old saloon, Pierre would have slept here when he was overnight in Range.

Incomprehensibly 'Lena was here among the familiar faces of his old crew. Here and holding to Challon's arms, pressing her face hard against the buttons of his jacket, sobbing.

"Where is he?" Challon asked.

'Lena turned toward the game room at the back of the dimly lit saloon. Marc checked her, wiping one hand absently against the side seam of his pants. It had somehow got covered with blood. Bayard's blood.

"Hank," he said to the girl. "Look after him, 'Lena. He's hit badly."

'Lena backed away and knelt obediently down beside the man Lou Fentrice had unsteadily dumped on the floor. Outside the firing had broken off again. Challon pushed through his gathered crewmen, all of them gray-faced and silent, and moved on into the back room.

More XO boys were back here, not as many as Challon thought there should be, ranged beside the barred back door and along the wall. Silent, self-effacing, grim-featured men. Pierre lay blanketless and huge on a scarred pool table under the single hanging lamp. His shirt was off, but his boots were on. His hair was damply tousled in great ringed curls, as it often was when he removed his hat after riding long in the sun. Resting head in hands and elbows on knees beside the table was a young doctor, newly come to Range this season and known to Challon by face but not by name. He raised his head at Challon's approach, stiffening in his chair. And Pierre opened his eyes. The doctor made a quick, cautioning gesture toward Challon. Pierre saw it.

"Damn it, quit trying to mend a busted pick!" he said with thin peevishness.

The doctor shook his head with incredulity and weariness. Marc saw that Pierre had been giving the doctor a bad time. He saw also that Pierre was right with the blunt rightness of his kind. His pick was broken off short — too short for any mending. The great gray-matted expanse of his chest was marked with two geometrically neat surgical compresses which looked strangely at odds with the ruggedness of the huge body to which they were attached. And the doctor had a right to his incredulity. Challon thought either of the wounds would have killed outright any other man he had ever known.

"There's a man out front, just come in," Challon whispered to the doctor.

The medical man rose, nodding, lifted his kit from the floor beside his chair, and moved toward the front of the saloon. Challon bent above the head of the table. Pierre blinked at him.

"I did this, Pierre!" Challon said, self-accusation depressing his voice almost to inaudibility.

"The hell you did!" Pierre growled. "Don't cheat the devil of his due, boy! Van Cleave done it. Me and Hugh walking out front of Hugh's office there to hang a noose on Van Cleave's neck when he come loping into town an hour after sundown. A noose for busting Anse Prentice's belly and knocking over a Santa Fe pay roll and ventilating Stuart's safe at the bank. There's been worse things than that done in New Mexico, boy, and nobody hanged for 'em, either. But not in our county. That's the difference, Marc — not in our county!"

Pierre paused and coughed very slightly. His voice strengthened. There was relish in his tone.

"Hugh Perigord and Pierre Challon — we were good men in our day, both of us. But that little bastard cut us both down; one for Hugh and two for me. Sure as hell knew his odds. He can shoot like an angel!"

"I should have come in with you at noon!" Challon said bitterly.

"Damn your brass!" Pierre grunted. "You think you could wear my boots — or even Hugh's? Like hell! You wasn't born soon enough, boy. You timed it just right. Tia Pozner sent us word to the back door a little bit ago you was here. Hank went looking for you along the street. He find you?"

"Yes," Challon said. "Hank found me, all right."

Pierre closed his eyes for a moment.

"Good!" he said more quietly. "We always handled a tough chore in shifts, remember? Me first, then you. It's your turn now, Marc. And the odds are down for you. Me and Hugh and Hank and the boys raised our share of hell. Van Cleave ain't got over six-eight men left. Them that are ought to be as jumpy as jacks in a thunderstorm. And nobody's been hurt but them and us. You see to it nobody's hurt from here on out, boy. We've always kept our troubles off somebody else's grass. You see to it, hear?"

Marc made no answer. Pierre was silent for a long moment. He grimaced with a twinge of pain of which Challon realized he was no more than half conscious, then spoke again, very quietly:

"I'm glad you're here, boy; it's hell to be lonesome."

His eyes closed. The doctor returned. He touched Challon's arm.

"Too much talking!" he warned. "He's got to be quiet."

Challon backed incredulously from the table.

"You mean there's a chance?"

The doctor looked up at him with a strained, baffled expression.

"He should have been dead when he hit the ground out there," he said. "But he got up and walked in here on his own feet — slapped a man out of the way who tried to help him. What do I know of the chances of a man like that?" Then, more quietly: "No, not a chance in a million, Mr. Challon. Internal hemorrhage. Any time — any time."

The doctor scrubbed his hand dazedly across his eyes.

"Pour yourself a drink," Challon advised him bluntly. "You may have more customers."

And he turned back to the front of the saloon.

Hank Bayard was on his feet at the upper end of the bar, wryly sloshing his mouth out with whisky, dumping the red wash into a spittoon. Hank had lost half of the skin on his nose, lips, and forehead, and Challon thought he had lost some teeth, but he was still on his feet. He was otherwise unhurt. Like Challon himself, luck had carried him through the barrage flung at them from the courthouse. Challon stopped at his elbow.

"You clumsy damned fool, can't you keep your feet under you?"

"I'll learn," Hank said thickly, warping his puffed face into a grin.

Challon saw 'Lena waiting for him, apart from the others, and he moved on to her. She came against him, into his arms and close, with an eagerness divorced from affection. This was a need more elemental than the need of a woman for a man. This was fear, fear of something grown too terribly big to be longer understood.

"Pierre, Marc —" 'Lena said brokenly. "Pierre —"

"He wouldn't have it any different," Challon said. "Go back and ask him. He'll tell you."

"Marc, I can't —" 'Lena's body trembled. "I — oh, Marc, it was me that asked him to help the sheriff arrest those men!"

"That's what you wanted, then — Van Cleave arrested?" Challon asked softly.

The girl nodded.

"According to the law," she agreed. "I wanted Range to see it could be done that way — that the Challons could do it — that they wanted to. I wanted Mr. Prentice and Judge Farrady to see it. No guns, no broken windows, none hurt. Marc, I didn't understand. I didn't know. I thought —"

"I know," Challon said. "You knew Pierre was Pierre Challon. You thought he could do anything. It's all right, 'Lena. So did Pierre."

"But those men waiting across the street, waiting for morning or for somebody here to show themselves. Van Cleave has done just what he planned. He's emptied the street. He's killed anybody who might have put charges against him. He's frightened anybody else who still could into silence. What kind of an auction will it be in the morning with only his bid? Do you think Mr. Prentice will look for other offers or bid against Van Cleave himself?"

"No," Challon said. "Prentice is under a bed in the hotel. He'll stay there. Building a railroad is his business — not this."

"Next week the papers will start saying it was the Challons who came lawlessly to town tonight with Sheriff Perigord siding with them. The papers will say the Challons came to town to take by force what you sold that woman in good faith. And folks get to believing what the papers say in just a little while. They forget the papers have always been afraid of the XO; that they'll be more afraid of the ranch with Van Cleave on it."

"Where's Marcy?" Challon asked abruptly.

"She's here?"

"Yes. She's here."

"Marc, what can you do now?"

"Nothing, for a while. Pierre's lonesome. I should have stuck with him before. I have to now. Let's go out back."

As they passed Bayard, Hank fell in with them without a summons from either, accepting XO grief — Challon grief — as he had accepted all of the good and the bad on the ranch since the day he had gone to work as a boy for Pierre, without order and without question.

20

In the silent interior of the Red River Saloon, Challon men drank long and deeply, looking often at the high windows in the east wall of the back room, speculating in monosyllables as to the coming of the sun. But each knew it was not the sun for which they waited, but for an old man to die; and the knowledge brought to each his own grief, so that the virile whisky of the Red River warmed nothing within them. There was one exception. The young doctor had know Pierre only by hearsay, and his faith in his professional judgment had been shattered, and it was doubtful if he had ever tasted the likes of the six-foot brew in the Red River's casks. He became quietly and very thoroughly drunk and at last slept heavily in his chair, the deep rasping of his breathing often drowning out that of the dying man on the table beside him.

Challon and 'Lena and Hank Bayard stood motionlessly in a row along the table rim where Pierre could see them whenever he opened his eyes. It seemed to give him satisfaction.

He smiled once.

"It's a damned shame the governor couldn't have come too!" he said.

Much later, with almost no weight to his voice, he looked at 'Lena and spoke to her alone.

"My wife could bake biscuits," he said. "The damnedest biscuits! Can you?"

"Yes, Mr. Challon," 'Lena answered unsteadily.

"Pierre!" the old man growled faintly. "Biscuits, I said — not *tortillas!*"

"Yes. Biscuits — Pierre —"

A sigh of satisfaction gusted from Pierre. He rolled his eyes to his son.

"Only thing that worried me," he said. "Them Mexican pancakes ain't worth a damn for breakfast. Hard on the belly. You better marry the girl, Marc."

Challon nodded wordlessly. Pierre closed his eyes again. The windows in the east wall were bright. They grew brighter. The air within the closed saloon began to warm noticeably. Elena and Challon and Hank Bayard waited by the rim of the table.

"We'll put water on the three thousand acres east of the house first," Pierre murmured. "It's just a beginning —"

The words were not his. They belonged to his son. Challon and Hank and 'Lena looked at each other. The crewmen talked softly among themselves. The young doctor stirred in his chair, looked up with startled eyes, and rose stiffly beside the table. Challon was grateful he didn't touch Pierre's wrist, his eyes, with the curious, probing fingers of his trade.

"Somebody find a blanket or something," the doctor said hoarsely. He turned his head to Challon.

"He's dead."

They all gathered in the Red River's barroom. The waiting was over. Challon felt their quiet, intense regard, their speculation, their willingness. His hand in his jacket pocket was tightly clamped about a pair of chain-linked metal rings. Pierre had been entitled to his folly; Challon was entitled to his own. And this was what 'Lena wanted, what she had preached in her unobtrusive way from the day she had ridden out of this town with him. A day when his purpose had been vastly different from this.

Bayard was facing him. Challon pointed to the end of the bar, where his own gun and cartridge belt lay.

"No iron," he said to Hank. "No guns. Shed them."

Astonished, half angry, Bayard took a protesting step forward.

"Shed them!" Challon repeated harshly.

Bayard swung away, unbuckled his belt, and slammed it onto the bar. The others reluctantly followed.

"By God, I'm glad Pierre can't see this!"

Bayard murmured quite audibly.

Challon would have let it go, but 'Lena picked it up. She was looking at Marc with thoughtful speculation.

"Are you, Hank?" she asked without turning. "I don't think I am. I don't know —"

"Back me, Hank," Challon said. "Keep your mouths shut, but back me."

He freed the locking bar and opened the scarred front door. He saw Van Cleave. Perigord's body had been removed from the opposite walk. Van Cleave was leaning against the front of Perigord's office. One of his men was beside him. The others were still at the upper windows of the courthouse. Challon saw rifle barrels there. Van Cleave smiled as Challon and those with him came filing beltlessly out of the Red River.

"You had to see it sooner or later, Challon," he said across the street. "A man is only so big."

"Yes," Challon said.

He stepped down from the walk, starting unhurriedly across the street. He was thinking of Marcy. He couldn't see her. Van Cleave had shown no surprise at his appearance. He had known, then, that Marc Challon was not dead out on the grass. Marcy had told him last night. Or somebody else had told him. There were many who knew it by now. Marcy was not in sight. She could be somewhere in the courthouse. She could be somewhere else. Van Cleave had no need for her now, and he would keep nothing of no use to him. Marc wanted to know about Marcy. He wanted to know where she was. She had begun this. He wanted her to see its end. Pierre could not. He wanted Marcy to.

As he moved into the street he was aware of other movement. Art Treadwell and Stuart and three or four others in business dress had appeared on the veranda of the Palace Hotel three doors away. There was a common grimness among them. In their midst were four other men, plainly present by compulsion. One was unmistakably Anson Prentice's father. Two were the detectives Marc had seen in the upper hall of the hotel the night before. The fourth, Challon supposed, was the territorial judge from Santa Fe.

His own appearance on the street seemed to have been the signal for a general exodus. The street in both directions was filling, both groups moving in toward the center. Women among them. Challon saw Tia Pozner among the Spanish-Americans coming down from Goat Hill and Upper-town. He was puzzled. There was danger here, grave danger for every person on the street. Curiosity could not account for this advance. These people were not rallying to back him, certainly. 'Lena had told him Range believed him wrong and would not help him. And Range — the country about it — was 'Lena's more than it had ever been his; this despite the fact he had once owned a great square of it. 'Lena would know the mood of the people where he might not.

Van Cleave began to tense as Challon approached the center of the street. The man beside Van Cleave said something. Marcy's foreman looked sharply in both directions. Suddenly he snapped a command:

"That's far enough, Challon!"

Marc halted.

"You want something?" Van Cleave demanded.

Challon also glanced both ways along the street. He shook his head in denial.

"Me?" he asked. "This time, no. But you've got to talk to the county, Van Cleave."

The man shifted uneasily. Challon heard the metallic click of a rifle above him brought to cock.

"What is this?" Van Cleave demanded at a rising pitch. "What's wanted?"

"Your hide," Challon told him bluntly. "Give it up the easy way. You know the charges. Hugh Perigord tried to read a part of them to you last night."

Van Cleave flattened tightly against the building behind him. He grinned savagely.

"And what happened to Hugh?" he asked. "Leave it to a Challon to try an outsized bluff! I'll give this street just thirty seconds to empty. If it doesn't do it by itself, I'll empty it. It's too crowded for a man that's come in to do a legitimate piece of business!"

"This isn't a Challon play and it isn't a bluff!" Marc said steadily. "You and your boys better hoist your hands."

With this, Challon started forward again. Van Cleave slapped in the air, and his gun was in his hand.

"Challon, by God, I mean this!" he snapped thinly.

"You think they don't?" Challon asked with a slant of his head toward those coming along the street. "You and your boys got enough ammunition to cut down all of them? Ever see what a crowd could do to a man with its hands if it got stirred up? Any of your boys ever see anything like that?"

Challon brought his hand from his jacket pocket. The handcuffs he had taken from Perigord's rack glinted brightly in the sun. He stepped up onto the walk in front of Van Cleave. That he had been able to come this far was answer enough as to Van Cleave's men above — as to the pallid man beside Van Cleave on the walk. There was an inevitability to justice which made it terrible when it came like this. Van Cleave was alone. Alone with Marc Challon. The little man's gun, held far back against his body, steadied.

Van Cleave flung another glance up the street. He smiled thinly. And he fired his weapon.

A man's life did not often depend upon an ability to read motive and impending action in others, but there was bound to be some of such skill acquired in bossing the rags and tags of a big ranch crew from boyhood on. An instant before Van Cleave fired, Challon twisted sharply aside, striking outward and quarteringly downward with the chain-hung handcuff dangling from its mate in his hand.

Van Cleave's bullet passed close to Challon but did not touch him. A great welt of flesh parted along a red-flowing seam across Van Cleave's forehead, blinding the man with blood.

Challon kicked hard at the now extended gun hand, breaking bone in the arm with an audible snap and arching the weapon out into the dust of the street. Thrusting Van Cleave roughly against the building at the man's back, Challon brought his knee up savagely twice.

It was all a single, swift flow of motion, so that even those who had seen it would not remember clearly in an hour how it had been done. And it had cost no great effort. Challon's breath was still regular when he caught one of Van Cleave's wrists as the man sagged and snapped steel onto it.

A man could build a great ranch out of a

belief in his own rightness, ignoring all odds. He could shatter odds in another game with a similar belief. Challon jerked on the free cuff and passed it to Hank Bayard.

"Lock him up," he said. "He's got the others on lead strings. They'll come along."

It was afternoon before Challon and 'Lena had a room in the Palace to themselves, and then not wholly so. Pierre was still with them, and Marcy's shadow, and the brief instants of uncertainty scant hours ago in the bright sun of the street, and talk did not come readily between them. Challon thought 'Lena shared his gratitude when Art Treadwell came into the room. Art had a small paper parcel crushed in one hand. He was excited.

"Thank God the railroad is more important to Jason Prentice than anything he's got left," Treadwell said. "After watching that thing on the street, he's afraid the county might take a stand like that against the railroad if he sat on plain rights. He's refused to bid in on the XO."

"Somebody will," Challon said with conviction.

"You think anybody in the county would dare bid against a Challon in Range today?" Treadwell demanded. "Hell, man! I entered a minimum bid for you. Prentice just signed an acceptance and the judge approved it. Stuart is drawing up a draft for fifty thousand dollars for you to sign. You're going back onto the XO!"

'Lena's fingers were biting into Challon's arm.

"Marc!" she cried. "Marc!" Then, more quietly, "If only Pierre could have gone back with you!"

"With us," Challon corrected quietly. He was aware that the enthusiasm she had expected was not in him and that 'Lena was puzzled. She didn't know that this was best, that Pierre had been saved a hurt worse than his wounds. He would not have to see the ash overlaying the foundations of the home he had built on the grass for his wife. 'Lena didn't understand that this was not yet whole and complete. There was Marcy, who had vanished. Challon still wanted to know of Marcy.

'Lena's puzzlement didn't dampen her own enthusiasm. She had been grave and troubled so long that it was surprising to see the bright spirit in her now. She spun across the room to the door, then back to him.

"We can go back today — this afternoon!" she cried. "Back onto the grass. Hank and the boys and Tia with us. Marc, I've got to find Hank and tell him. I've got to send him for Tia. It's all right, isn't it?"

Challon grinned, slapping her affectionately across the round smallness of her hips as he might have an excitedly dancing youngster.

"Run all the way," he said.

"I will!" 'Lena cried. "I can't help it!"

The windows rattled with the bang of the door behind her, and her heels made a staccato clatter in the hall. Challon nodded at the closed door.

"I'm worried about that, Art," he said. "I never wanted anything more than I want to marry her. I should have lived with someone out of my own country in the first place. But Marcy still keeps on knifing me. This time it's her divorce. 'Lena's people go by the padres, and the padres have a law against divorce, against remarrying after divorce."

Treadwell nodded.

"Sit down, Marc," he said. "That's all right, too, though I'd say it was a hell of a small worry with that girl. I've got a notion her God's bigger than most rules. In the first place, Marcy's divorce hasn't cleared the courts yet, so it isn't on the record — and it won't be. Marc, look, a *pelado* who didn't want to disturb you today stopped me on the street this morning after the ruckus was over. He had a story. He'd come in over the ridge trail this morning. Well, I rode right out there, of course. That's why I was so late getting around to Prentice."

Treadwell drew a long breath.

"It was your wife, all right. She must have been riding like the wind, Marc. Missed a